Inheritance

Gift or Burden

For Pippa,
Hope you enjoy!

H.A. McHugh

authorHOUSE®

AuthorHouse™ UK
1663 Liberty Drive
Bloomington, IN 47403 USA
www.authorhouse.co.uk
Phone: 0800.197.4150

Published by AuthorHouse   02/10/2015

ISBN: 978-1-4969-9768-5 (sc)
ISBN: 978-1-5049-3580-7 (e)

CONTENTS

Part V

Part VI

PROLOGUE

From his position on his bed, Shay Corley had a view of everything he owned in the world. It wasn't much for a lifetime of sixty years. A few dog-eared and well-thumbed paperbacks, a battered valise, a small crystal ashtray, an ancient and inexpensive wristwatch, his one decent suit, a transistor radio, and his mother Florence's pearly white rosary beads. Aside from these items, his tiny London bedsit boasted a kettle, a toaster, two mugs, a few odd plates, along with a portable electric ring permanently playing support to a small blackened saucepan. The furniture too was starkly minimal, consisting of a small three-drawer chest and a sink in the corner, over which he had once fixed two shelves. Other than that, a short rail for hanging his clothes; an armchair; a small, round table with two mismatched kitchen chairs; and a pair of thin yellow curtains were all that the little bedsit contained. Shay was mesmerised by the sight of the raindrops running down the windowpane. He was used to this preoccupation, a habit of his developed over many years. His fascination had increased in recent days, as he was no longer able to leave his bed. He was wryly amused at the way the weather seemed to mirror his moods. No sooner was he confined to this tiny space than the lovely Indian summer gave way to day after day of constant rain and drizzle. He felt consoled, as he wouldn't have wanted to venture forth anyway. He had always loved nature, and the view of the park from his basement window was the one thing about this featureless room that had attracted him in the first place. The bright yellow curtains contrasted happily with the drabness of his surroundings. They always lifted his spirits, so he used them to frame his picture window and never, ever closed them. Even on dull grey days like these October ones, they drew his eye towards the wonderful variety of greens outside.

Over the past few weeks, he had found it strangely soothing to concentrate his gaze on the raindrops as they slid downwards, merging and splitting, separating and splicing. The constant movement, the ease of flow, matched his meanderings down memory's winding lanes of childhood. He was happy within himself at last. Knowing that the end was near, he had made his preparations carefully. Who was there who really cared anyway, he wondered. He could think of no one other than his mother and perhaps his sister Constance who would truly miss him. He'd grown used to eating very little over many years, especially when he had been drinking heavily. And now he found that his wasting body required very little to sustain it.

When he had first discovered the cancer, he'd hastily made plans for one last journey to the land of his birth. He planned it all in meticulous detail. He would visit his surviving siblings Nora, in Newmarket-on-Fergus, and Kitty, in Carralisheen, County Tipperary. Then he would head back to Knocknashee and the home place currently occupied by his beloved mother, Florence, and his older wheelchair-bound sister Constance, her husband, Brendan, and their family. But first he should visit his brother Michael, the eldest, from whom he had been estranged for the bones of forty years, in his posh Foxrock home in Dublin. Then he would visit his youngest brother, Ambrose, who had always loved and never judged him, and meet again with his sister-in-law May and their brood in Mountbrien, County Tipperary. While he was home he would visit the graveyard in Kiltyroe, to pray for the repose of the soul of his youngest sister, Hannah. Finally he would stop by the headstone of James Corley, national teacher, and try to make his peace with the ghost of his austere and demanding father. Shay had been named after his father, James, Séamus being the Irish equivalent of the name. He and his dad, who was a distant and severe figure, never really saw eye to eye. James was a perfectionist. He didn't suffer fools gladly and had little tolerance for flippancy. Despite his professional calling, he displayed neither much patience with nor understanding of small children. And so, from an early age, young Séamus had insisted on being called Shay.

In the heel of the hunt, it turned out that he didn't visit anyone at all. Towards the end he had decided not to travel. One reason was fear of reopening old sores and another was his wish not to burden his relatives with his troubles anymore. And so he handed in his notice at the biscuit factory, and having explained to his few acquaintances that he was retiring and moving back '*to the old sod*', he quietly disappeared.

While he was still able, he had made his peace with his Maker by going to confession in an anonymous inner-city church, where he revealed no details of his impending demise. He returned to his room happy in the knowledge that he had done all he could, according to the tenets of his faith, to ease his way across the eternal divide. Then he settled himself in his cocoon and patiently awaited the inevitable. As his body grew weaker, his days fell into an easy routine. When he awoke in the mornings, his mind now always turned towards the days of his early childhood. He loved to recall the day-to-day adventures of his youthful self, comfortable in the all-embracing love of his gentle mother. He recalls that he was very close to his brothers and sisters then. They all basked in their mother's love. They felt that, despite her tiny stature and sweet nature, she could always be depended on to stand between them and their rigid father. In the early days of his self-imposed incarceration, he loved to recall the stories his mother and his grandmother had told him. After a while their voices began to infiltrate his dreams, as well as his daytime wanderings down memory lane. To get some respite from their insistence, he had taken to jotting down what he could remember. On waking charged with happy memories, he would then steel himself to the task of preparing his spartan breakfast. Years ago he had got used to drinking his tea black with several spoons of sugar. Breakfast had long since become a mug of tea and a cigarette. He recalled that someone had told him once that this was called a 'prisoner's breakfast'. He'd put the kettle on, sit at the table while it boiled, and then he'd light his first fag of the day and, facing his window and enjoy his close-up of whatever was going on in the park. Breakfast over, he'd tidy up after himself and return to the bed for a little nap. Awaking somewhat refreshed, he'd then take out his latest copybook and write a bit more of his 'chronicle'. Some days he'd only manage a few lines, but on a good day, when things were going well, the words just seemed to flow, and he could cover page after page. At first he was scribbling away just to pass the time and to prevent boredom, but after a while it began to fill his days. The writing also had the advantage of preventing him from mulling over his life and regretting his decisions. Looking back now he found it hard to remember a time when he did not clash with his father, the self-important James Corley. He could not recall when he first ceased to be in awe of him and began to see beyond the façade of arrogance to the pompous and pathetic figure beneath. James fancied himself as a Victorian paterfamilias. He thought of himself as a cut above his neighbours and was determined to raise his family as strong and confident people who would not be tormented by feelings of inadequacy. He modelled himself on his heroes, a mishmash of local Anglo-Irish ascendancy characters and military types he'd read about. That's why he insisted that the children called him 'Papa' instead of 'Dad' or 'Father' at home. At school, of course, they called him 'sir', as all the other children did. Shay remembered well the very first time his resentment of his father came to the fore. He was in the kitchen, and the two older ones, Michael and Constance, were in trouble for some minor misdemeanour at school. Having physically punished them, their father was now insisting on a verbal apology from both of them. Constance had managed to repeat exactly the formula of words he had demanded. Michael, on the other hand, had omitted the mandatory *sir* in his version and had thereby merited further punishment. Even at three years of age, the young Shay had thought his father's behaviour excessive. He had butted in, asking, 'Why do we all have to call you sir, Papa? We don't have to call Mama Missus or ma'am or anything. She lets us call her Mama.'

This was Shay's earliest memory. Like it had happened only yesterday, he remembered it still. Papa was not impressed. In fact he was downright disapproving of the interruption. It was the first time that Shay had ever been on the receiving end of one of Papa's malevolent glares. But not the last, as he now recalled ruefully. He could see that glare still in his mind's eye. But what he has always found hardest to forgive was what he remembered as the incident with the violin. He was about eleven at the time and was quite proficient at the instrument. To tell the truth Shay loved music, particularly classical tunes for violin. He was blessed with a good ear and could often replicate a tune after a single hearing. Added to this, he was serious about his performance and, wishing to excel for the sake of the music, was happy to put in the necessary practice to play flawlessly. Shay was aware and quietly pleased to note that he had earned his father's grudging respect for his playing. What he didn't know was that Papa was already forming big plans for the future of his talented son. There was also a great love of traditional Irish music in the locality. Kiltyroe was a specially designated area where Gaelic was the spoken language of the people. The Corley schoolmasters over three generations had contributed significantly to the retention and protection of the Irish language, its music, and its poetry. A favoured pastime among the neighbours was set dancing. House dances were regularly enjoyed, at which musicians played traditional tunes on melodeons, concertinas, and 'fiddles'. Almost every household boasted a 'trad' musician or two. One afternoon after school Shay had gone to his bedroom to practise his music. He had been working on a difficult Brahms's concerto for well over an hour. Mama had just brought him up a cup of milk and a hot scone. While he was eating, the tune of 'The Minstrel Boy', which they had been singing in school earlier, kept running through his head. As soon as he had finished his scone, he took up the instrument and began to pick out the tune. Happy that he had got it right, he started to play it with verve and gusto. Suddenly the door was thrown open, and Papa appeared. His face was suffused with anger. Roughly, he grabbed the violin and bow from Shay, shouting, 'How dare you, you little whelp. There was I, thinking you might have the makings of a concert violinist, and what do I find? A buffoon scratching a mindless tune. You're no better than the local go-boys. If you have no respect for music or for an expensive and fine instrument, then you do not deserve to have the use of it. I'm damned if I'll raise a f-f-fiddler.' With that he stormed from the room bearing the violin with him. No matter how much Mama and Constance pleaded with him, he stuck to his guns, and Shay never got to play the violin again.

To save himself from the useless task of reliving the frustrations of his past, he had decided to record his own early years. He had long regretted the disappearance of the world of his youth and the vanishing art of letter writing so beloved of his parents' generation. It was only recently that he had discovered that his youngest brother, Ambrose, and his sister Hannah had been faithful letter writers as long as she lived. After her death, Ambrose had shown him some of her letters, and he was impressed with her style and surprised that her love and admiration for her favourite brother still rose from the paper like a well-remembered scent. Now he felt the need to leave some written evidence of those halcyon days, before things had begun to go wrong in his life. As yet he was unsure who might be interested in reading them, or whether he would just burn his efforts once he'd got it all down on paper. But for the moment, it offered him not just relief from his unhappy memories but also the challenge of filling his last days without self-pity.

Most days he continued doggedly with his writing until hunger eventually invaded his consciousness and he had to fix himself something to eat. If things were going well, he hurriedly ate enough to satisfy his hunger and then immediately returned to his task, often working away until the light faded. If, as occasionally happened, he was in severe pain or a rush of memories clamouring to be recorded flooded his brain, he would make his way back to bed and stare at the view beyond his window or close his eyes and try to get some rest. He would return to the task later if at all possible. He always set himself a target of two to three hundred words per day and was pleased if on a good one he clocked up a thousand or more. Once there was no longer sufficient natural light to continue, he would reward himself with a mug of tea and either a biscuit or a cigarette, depending on the contents of his meagre larder. He would then sit at the window, and with the aid of the street lights running along the park railings, he'd watch the birds as they retired for the night. He'd also spy on the local urban foxes as they emerged for their evening foraging. When he grew tired at last, he would make his way back to his waiting bed and hope for sleep. An avid reader since his earliest years Shay now found such absorption in his own jottings that he had no longer any desire to read the work of others.

Towards the end of October, Shay found himself sleeping rather better. The result was that he was now breakfasting much later, usually between nine o'clock and ten. He was still doing some writing, but now at a slower pace. The shortening days encouraged him to go to bed earlier too. On the evening of 26 October, he had retired for the night a little after nine o' clock and was sound asleep well before midnight. Just before dawn the following morning, he quietly breathed his last and, without waking, gently slipped away. His passing must have been peaceful and pain free, as his face retained an expression of serenity when his body was discovered three weeks later on 15 November 1966.

PART I

1

Ella

On 5 December 1975 Ambrose Corley passed away. He was only fifty-five. He had been complaining of stomach aches for some time and was being treated for ulcers. By the time the cancer had been diagnosed, it was too late. He died in his own bed, in the care of his beloved wife, May, and surrounded by his three sons, Ray, Eddie, and Jack, and two of his three daughters, Anna and Eva. His youngest daughter was missing. No one knew where I was, and so they had to proceed with arrangements in my absence. I was in the intensive care unit of a Dublin hospital. I had just lost my baby. I couldn't have visitors, because I had contracted a hospital bug and must be kept in isolation. The real reason I hadn't told anyone of my whereabouts was because I was a mess of battered flesh and broken bones. Richard Benton, my husband of less than two years, had beaten me to a pulp and killed our unborn child. Along with the hospital infection, I was also suffering from the effects of a sexually transmitted disease, an unwelcome parting gift from Richard. The night I confronted him, about this and the danger to our baby, he completely lost it and savagely attacked me. Without the intervention of Greg Mahon, the occupant of the upstairs flat who had called the police, it's highly likely that Richard would have killed me. When I awoke to the realisation that I had lost my baby, I welcomed the oblivion induced by the painkillers I was given. After several days in hospital, my battered body began to show some signs of recovery. My equally battered spirit tried to come to terms with the loss of my baby. And so it was only then that I remembered with a hammer blow of horror that my beloved dada was dying. Trapped as I was, I couldn't see him. Then I realised that I couldn't let Mom visit either, as Dada would spot on her face that there was something wrong, and neither of them needed the upset just then.

Then one day out of the blue, my neighbour, Greg Mahon, came to visit. He had noticed post accumulating and overflowing the post box. No one seemed to be coming or going from our flat in Rathmines. He had made enquiries and was told that Richard had moved out. He himself had been working away from Dublin for about three weeks, and so on the off chance that I might still be hospitalised, he decided to call and see how I was getting on. He arrived laden with flowers, chocolates, and a big bundle of letters retrieved from our post box. I was embarrassed at first, but Greg chatted away comfortably, as if visiting battered neighbours he barely knew was nothing unusual. After he left, I leafed through the post he had brought, sorting it into mine, Richard's, and ours. The bills I put to one side to deal with later. I hadn't heard a word from Richard since that horrendous night, and I wondered if I ever would again. Strangely, my immediate concern was what to do with his letters. Then the horrors of our last night together suddenly overwhelmed me, with the result that I couldn't face looking at my own letters just then.

It was the following day before I could face the task. There were quite a lot to go through, so it took a while before I realised that there were several with Mountbrien postmarks. There were at least five addressed in my mother's neat handwriting as well as at least one each from my siblings. There were a large number of what looked like cards with familiar handwriting on the envelopes, which I stacked neatly for later perusal. Then I opened all Mum's letters and, ordering them by date, began to read. Imagine my horror to learn of my beloved father's death in this way. I was swamped with grief. I couldn't get my head around the fact that his funeral had taken place before I had even been aware that he had died. For a long time afterwards I found it almost impossible to forgive myself, even though there was absolutely nothing I could have done about it. There were times when I felt that Dada's death was just a figment of my fevered imagination and that one day soon I would wake up from the nightmare. There were days when I was felt I was drowning in grief and loneliness. Hundreds of times in the course of each day I was overwhelmed with regrets that I hadn't had a chance to say goodbye to Dada. It tormented me that I could never explain my absence to him.

As if the loss of our baby, the scars, bruises, and infection were not enough of a legacy for Richard to have left me, his final gift was depression, exacerbated by this added blow. Unable to contemplate adding to the burden of the family grief, I kept my own trauma to myself. I remained in hospital almost a month. The doctors and nurses were reluctant to discharge me because of my depressed state. For several weeks, Greg was the only visitor I had. As we got to know each better, we became good friends. At that stage I had no romantic interest whatsoever in Greg, and, besides, he had a girlfriend at the time. It took me a long time to get over the loss of the baby. The added loss of my father was more than I could bear. My grief was tinged with guilt and disappointment, because I hadn't been physically there to lay him to rest. I was unwilling to meet with people, and so I kept to myself for a long time. I continued to avoid family too, because I was so ashamed of what had happened to me. In fact, I was still so raw that I couldn't even bring myself to contact home. In the end I took the coward's way out. I wrote a brief note to my mother explaining that I had just received the tragic news when her letters had finally caught up with me. I gave her to understand that we had moved to England for Richard's work and that I would write again with a forwarding address when we were more settled. Then I prevailed on Greg to ensure that the letter was posted in Manchester. I felt guilty about this deception but felt unable to cope with sympathy or pity, even from my mother. I grieved too for the loss of Richard. After I got over my anger, I actually missed him. Or maybe I just missed what might have been. After all, I had invested a lot of love and commitment as well as a good many years in this relationship.

After I had been discharged from hospital, I couldn't bear the thought of returning to the flat I had shared with Richard. I realised that Greg Mahon was becoming attached to me, and I couldn't bear the thought of his pitying me. All I wanted to do was hide away from all reminders of my past. I booked into an anonymous bed and breakfast close to the city centre while I recuperated. Later, as soon as I had established Richard's whereabouts, I sold the flat, complete with contents, and sent him half the proceeds through a solicitor. I wanted nothing further to do with him and felt that getting rid of the flat and all our mutual possessions would help me to distance myself from the trauma, and in time assist in the healing process. Not long afterwards I bought a little artisan dwelling in Killester and retired there to lick my wounds and try to face the future.

It was a full six weeks later before I felt strong enough to contact home again. I was still waking from troubled sleep, feeling bewildered and confused. My waking mind kept going over and over the hurt and the abandonment. Even as I struggled to get my head around Richard's unexpected cruelty and the savagery of his violence towards me, I blamed myself for the breakdown of my marriage. It would take several months and many prolonged bouts of crippling depression before I was able to return to work. Meanwhile it was time to re-establish contact with home. As I was still too fragile to go home to Mountbrien, I wrote, inviting my mother to visit me in my new home. It was with a mixture of excitement, apprehension, and guilt that I answered the door to May Corley the following Saturday afternoon. As soon as she saw me, Mom wrapped me in a warm embrace, and I felt the knot in my chest unravel. All the pent up emotions floated away in a torrent of tears. Neither of us was capable of speech for some time. I was a snotty mess of hiccups and hysteria. Mom tried to comfort me with muttered endearments and pats on the back. When I had recovered sufficiently, she kindly started to fill me on all that had transpired in the six months since last we'd met. It must have been hard for her, but instead of quizzing me, she proceeded to tell me all about Dada's death and the details of the removal and funeral. There was no hint of recrimination or criticism regarding my absence or, indeed, my subsequent lack of communication. Her maternal instinct was to await an explanation with patience and forbearance.

'There was a huge turnout at the removal and the funeral as you might expect, my love. Your dad was much loved and respected locally. What was particularly lovely was the number of people from the past who made their way from long distances to be with us in our grief. There was hardly a person who had ever worked with him who didn't show up to pay their respects to Ambrose's memory. I also received some heart-warming letters from former bosses and a really beautiful tribute from the widow of his very first employer in the bank in Birr. There are boxes full of Mass cards too, which I must sort through soon. Perhaps when you are feeling a little better, Ella, you might like to help me with that?'

'Oh, Mom, of course I will. In fact I have quite a bundle to add to the pile. People very kindly sent on Mass cards to the flat. A neighbour brought them to me in the hospital, but by then Dada was already dead and buried. In fact it was only then that I discovered I had missed his month's mind Mass as well.'

'Ella, my dear girl, don't you think it's time to tell me what happened? Both your Dada and I knew something was seriously wrong when we lost contact with you. Ambrose prayed constantly for you in his last days, knowing that there must be a very good reason why you were not visiting or even telephoning. Then when he died, we tried so hard to find you. Even as late as the morning of the funeral, your brothers Ray and Eddie drove to Dublin at the crack of dawn and called at your flat. There was no answer, and your neighbours on either side had no news of your whereabouts. All they could glean was that neither you nor Richard had been seen for at least a fortnight. Eddie had even peeped through the letter box and noted a lot of unopened post stacked on the hall table. He felt that there was an air of dusty abandonment about the quietness of the house. They were back home in time for the funeral Mass and didn't tell me where they had been for some days afterwards. Of course we were all worried about you. Your sisters and brothers tried to comfort me as best they could, and the extended Corley family and my own siblings also were a great support to us. You probably have no idea how worried we all were. When I received your letter at last, my first reaction was relief to know that you were alive. I have informed them all that you are now back in Dublin and that I am visiting with you this weekend. You cannot imagine the prayers of thanksgiving being said at this moment. But it will come as no surprise to you, my love, that some of your siblings will be cross with you for all the worry caused. Now, sweetheart, tell me your story. I have no doubt the missing Richard is at the heart of it all.'

With Mom's comforting arm about my shoulders, I at last unburdened myself of the whole sorry mess. Mom heard me out, her tears commingling with mine when she heard about the loss of the baby.

'How long into the pregnancy were you, love?' she probed gently.

'It was only nineteen weeks, Mom but I'd already felt the baby move. I was so excited and had been looking forward to sharing this magical experience with Richard.

He was supposed to meet me at the doctor's surgery after my appointment, but he didn't show up. I wonder if he suspected what Doctor Mangan might find and was too cowardly to face either of us, should the doctor share his findings with me. As it happened, the doctor merely said he'd like to see us both and soon. I was concerned at seeing how worried he looked, so I insisted he tell me what he had found. I told him that, as I'd already felt the baby move, his reaction had me seriously concerned. Reluctantly he explained that he would need to do tests on both myself and Richard, because he had identified some worrying symptoms of a sexually transmitted disease. He convinced me that there was "no immediate danger to the baby", but he would like to start me on a course of antibiotics as soon as possible. He then went through a series of intrusive questions, at the end of which it was clear that Richard must have had sexual congress with a partner or partners other than me. I was reeling with shock when I returned to the waiting room. Luckily the other women there were too bound up in their own worries to concern themselves with a tearful woman who might or might not be pregnant. When Richard still hadn't appeared some twenty minutes later, I slipped away and made my way home. It was very late that night when I finally heard Richard's key in the lock. I had been vacillating between anger and bouts of jagged crying for over five hours by then. On first seeing him, I was overwhelmed with relief that he had returned safely, but then I noticed that his contrite expression was merely a sham. He was drunk and trying to hide it. My anger rose to the surface, and I accused him of putting our baby in danger. That was when he completely lost his temper and attacked me. I did not recognise the monster that Richard had become. Such vile things he said while he systematically beat me with closed fists. When he had knocked me to the ground and I was folded into a foetal position to try to protect the baby, he continued to pummel and kick me savagely. The next thing I remember was coming to in the ambulance. A nurse was holding a cold compress to my forehead, and a man was sitting in the jump seat anxiously asking if I was all right. At first I thought it was Richard but then realised I didn't recognise the voice. Later I discovered that it was our neighbour, Greg Mahon, who on hearing my screams had come to offer help. When he arrived, the door of our flat was ajar. There was no sound from within. He had pushed open the door and found me unconscious on the floor of the living room. Greg had called an ambulance, and as there was no sign of Richard, he had agreed to accompany me to the hospital. I was in intensive care for some time to deal with the broken bones, the bruising, and the aftermath of the miscarriage.'

'My poor darling, I can't bear to think of you facing all that suffering alone and unsupported. If only we had known.'

'Oh, Mom, it is I who am sorry. I shouldn't have excluded you and the family, but honestly I was so ashamed, guilty, and miserable I just couldn't handle it. Can you understand that and forgive me?'

With her comforting arms around me, we wept together for a while. Then my ever-practical mom eased herself from my embrace and said, 'Look how the time has flown. It is almost dark. Let's get some food into us, replenish the fire, and continue talking later.'

With that she produced some of her lovely brown bread and home-baked scones, and we managed a companionable supper. Once the ice had been broken, the floodgates opened, and we talked long into the night. With my mother's loving support, I felt that I might finally turn the corner and begin the slow road to recovery. Over the next several weeks, she kept in touch with letters and insisted that I install a phone, the price of which she claimed was an overdue birthday present from herself and Dada's estate. Eventually, with her encouragement, I made myself go home to Mountbrien on the first weekend of June. Typical of my mother's sensitivity, she had ensured that I wouldn't have to face the family en masse. Quietly and without fuss, she persuaded the others to make arrangements for the weekend. Eva alone would be coming home. Only then did she ring me to suggest that perhaps it was time I made the journey home.

I arrived home a little after eight o'clock on a Friday evening. It had been a glorious day. The sun had shone from early morning, and the air in Mountbrien was heavy with the scent of new-mown grass and the heady perfume of my mother's wonderful roses. Knowing that Dada wouldn't be in his usual spot in the kitchen and the realisation that I'd never see him again struck me very forcefully on arrival, but before I could get out of the car, Mom appeared and opened the door for me. She led me around the corner of the house to where she had put a cloth on the rustic garden table and set out covered dishes of salad and freshly baked breads. In the shade of an overhanging tree, she had a bottle of chardonnay chilling in a bucket of ice. When we sat down, Mom, referring to the third place setting, said, 'I'm expecting Eva to join us if you don't mind. She's already on her way, but if you're feeling uncomfortable, she'll be happy to have her supper indoors. None of the others will be around for the weekend.'

By the time Eva joined us almost an hour later, I had recovered my equilibrium, and Mom and I were engrossed in conversation. She was busy explaining to me that while going through Dada's papers she had found a large package of notebooks with a letter addressed to me. She remembered that the notebooks had come into Dada's possession after his brother Shay's death.

'When Shay died, your dada and Uncle Michael had to travel to London to identify the body. You were quite young at the time, and knowing how fond of your Uncle Shay you were, your Dada wanted to spare you the shock of what he had experienced. In accordance with his wishes, we never told you youngsters that Shay had been dead for at least three weeks when his body was found. Ambrose never really got over the horror of it. He was haunted by guilt that poor Shay had died alone. He and Michael had found the notebooks in the flat. They were really old-fashioned children's copybooks in which Shay had been writing a kind of memoir in the final weeks of his life. He had started out with his very early days and the stories he remembered from then. But pretty soon he had gone on to write about his parents and his grandparents as well as his siblings. All of the portraits were accurate. Some were sensitively drawn, but others were cruelly true. Your dad felt that Shay would have liked to share his memories with the family, if not a wider audience, but Michael was adamant that 'washing of dirty linen in public' was not the Corley way. It was my own opinion that the decision should be left up to Florrie, but Michael had insisted that his mother be spared reading Shay's drivel. In the end the bundle ended up in your father's care. Many years later Ambrose decided that you should have them. In fact I thought he had given them to you long since. I know he intended on sharing them with you when you turned twenty-one.'

Having finished our meal and the bottle of wine, Mom and Eva and I sat as the balmy evening cooled into sunset. Mom filled Eva in on the bones of my story. Within minutes of our meeting, Eva had forgiven me, and we had enjoyed the rest of the lovely evening reminiscing. She told me how worried she and the others had been when I had disappeared without trace. They had argued among themselves as to the reasons for my absence. There were those who were concerned for my safety and those who wondered what in hell's bells I was playing at. Eva referred to the two factions as the 'Ella fans' and the 'Ambrosia brigade', referring to Eddie's old nickname for me when he and the brothers wanted to tease me about being 'Dada's girl'. Mom began to laugh when she heard this.

'You have no idea how much Ambrose enjoyed that little sally, even though he knew the boys were at pains to keep their devilment from him.'

Much later, tucked up in bed in my old childhood bedroom, I opened Dada's letter.

'Kiltyroe'
Mountbrien
Co. Tipperary
27/02/1970

My dear Ella,

You will remember your Uncle Shay and how fond of you he was. He also had great respect for your intelligence and often said that you thought like he did. When you showed an interest in creative writing, he was absolutely thrilled. I confess that I often sent him your short stories and samples of your work. He was particularly proud of the fact that you won that short story competition. Anyway, when your Uncle Michael and I had to go over to London to identify his body, we went to his flat, and he had the local newspaper cutting of your prize-giving pinned to his wall. We also found some copybooks filled with his own writings. Michael and I read through some of what he had written. It appears to be some kind of memoir, but as his brothers, we felt it was all too raw. We also felt that at times his characterisations, though accurate, were too close to the bone and sometimes indeed unnecessarily cruel. Michael wanted to destroy them, but I didn't agree. In the end the bundle was left in my care. Over the years I've taken them down and re-read them from time to time, always with a sense of closeness to Shay. But I'm no writer, so wouldn't dare venture an opinion on the quality of the work. As you have an interest in writing, I felt that maybe you might know more about their value. Anyway, I thought you might like to have them. Who knows—if nothing else, they may prove inspirational for you sometime.

Your loving Dada.

For a moment I wondered why Dada hadn't given me the copybooks back then, until I remembered that it was around this time I had announced my intention to marry Richard. With the benefit of hindsight and recent heart-to-heart conversations with Mom, I now knew that Richard Benton had rubbed my father the wrong way from the very beginning. Dada felt that he was overfamiliar, as well as overbearing. Mom, in her gentle way, had tried to like Richard. She had done her best to make him feel welcome in our home. She had ignored his rudeness and tried to smooth over the awkwardness and tension he inevitably created when he visited. Richard's disrespect for my mother was what aggravated Ambrose most. He was prepared to put up with Richard's churlishness and his condescending attitude for my sake, but he couldn't bear that this young upstart felt he could treat May so badly. Worse still, he found it hard to shake off his conviction that any man who treated his girlfriend's mother with such casual cruelty couldn't possibly love her. He hated that his beloved daughter couldn't see beyond the façade of good looks and seeming charm to the callous and selfish character beneath. It pained him to see how besotted I was and prayed daily that I would soon see the light and make good my escape from this malign influence, sooner rather than later. But, as is the way with youthful infatuation, I had gone ahead and insisted on marrying Richard. Blind to my parents' reservations and bedazzled by my dashing boyfriend, I couldn't wait to marry. Thinking back on it all now, over seven years later, I barely recognised the carefree, star-struck young girl who had so happily waltzed down the aisle with hope in my heart and a foolish grin on my face. When I went to put the letter back in its envelope with the long out-of-date stamp affixed, I noticed for the first time some writing on the back of the envelope. It was in my father's unmistakable handwriting and was dated 10 October 1979, just a few days before he died.

Ella a stór, sorry I didn't post this when I wrote it first. Better late than never maybe? Whatever life brings, remember you will always have your family, who love you. Don't isolate yourself as poor Shay did. In case I do not see you before I go, enjoy his legacy and mine. The silk scarf was wrapped around the notebooks when I found them in Shay's bedsit.

I opened the packet and, carefully putting aside the delicate scarf in various shades of pink, I started to read what Uncle Shay had written. I became instantly absorbed. It was an enthralling saga. The story was fascinating in itself, but the fact that it was about people I knew and loved gave it that extra edge that made it impossible to put down. The more I read it, the more curious I became about these flesh-and-blood characters seen through the eyes of a beloved uncle. I was torn between what I considered a beautifully written and believable account and my own dada's reservations about making public family history. By the time I fell asleep in the early hours of the following morning, I was looking forward excitedly to reading on and learning more about my family and their history. On my return to Killester, I immediately set about reading the notebooks in sequence. Over the next few weeks, I was drawn to them over and over. Uncle Shay had begun his journal with his memories of childhood in Kiltyroe.

PART II

Shay's Memoir

2

The Early Years

We Corleys of Kiltyroe were a very close-knit family. Even though we did not always agree with each other, we had an unbreakable habit of closing ranks if an outsider dared to upset or even contradict one of our number. Even the younger members of the family who had grown up very much in the shadow of us, their older and usually more vociferous siblings, shared this sense of familial pride and strong self-belief. We had been brought up to believe in ourselves and each other. From a very young age we had all been encouraged to become involved in Irish cultural activities. Our lovely mother, Florence, was a national champion Irish dancer. She had taught us and our cousins, as well as most of our neighbours and friends, a wide variety of jigs, reels, hornpipes as well as sets and polkas. Our papa was a top-class musician who played several instruments expertly in different musical genres. He was passionately interested in the Irish language and in traditional Irish music. From an early age, all seven of his children were encouraged to sing and to perform individually and as a family group. We entered local and national music and dance festivals and competitions. We were almost invariably worthy winners of trophies and cups, not to talk of gold and silver medals. The result of this kind of exposure was that, as a group, we Corleys gave the impression that we were self-assured people who exuded confidence and high self-esteem.

As far as performance went, this impression was probably even true. Individually some family members turned out to be very confident; some were shyer by nature, and others became positively arrogant.

What helped save our father, James, from complete unpopularity among his peers and the general community was his obvious devotion to our gentle mother, Florence. Her family, the Mulveys, and close friends called her by her given name. But James had called her Florrie from the beginning, and it had never even crossed his mind to seek her opinion on the matter. Everyone loved Florence. She was such a sweet-natured person, gentle and self-effacing but with a strong core. She always saw things from both sides, was utterly unselfish and at all times willing to compromise. She was not a pushover either, and because he loved her so much, over the years James learned to trust her judgement, to accept her opinion and respect her non-confrontational solutions. If and when James's arrogance or bullying got up the noses of his friends and neighbours, they consoled themselves with the thought that anyone who was lucky enough to be loved by Florence couldn't possibly be all bad. If truth be told, most people who knew them were puzzled that James had won her heart in the first place, and probably not a little surprised that they had continued to be happily married all the long years down since. It was a tribute to Florence's character that my parents had such a lasting and happy marriage. Born as she was in an era when a woman's place in the home was very clearly defined, she had accepted it as part of her wifely duties to play a subservient role to her husband. But being a strong woman and independent by nature, she believed that this did not necessarily mean she would have no power in the relationship. She knew that there was no book of rules as far as marriage was concerned. It was up to people to figure out for themselves how their relationship would work. So if James needed to separate her from her own family by calling her Florrie, then Florrie she would become. She knew instinctively that her new husband's sense of self was very much bound up in how he was perceived in the community. James had come from a long line of teachers. His father and grandfather had been principal teachers in Kiltyroe. His great-grandfather had been a hedge schoolmaster, whose father before him had been a private tutor to the sons of the local landlord. Despite the fact that Florrie herself had qualified as a national schoolteacher, she knew that, on her marriage, she would not continue to teach. James would see it as a poor reflection on himself if his wife had to go out to work. As it transpired, by the time James returned to school after their summer wedding, Florence was already expecting their first child. She didn't mind staying at home in these early days of marriage. In fact '*home*' was James's paternal home, Ashdene House, Kiltyroe, Knocknashee, County Clare. They would share Ashdene with her parents-in-law. James Corley Senior had suffered a stroke a few years previously. He was now housebound and pretty much bedridden. James's mother, Maud, was very tied to looking after her ill husband and her two remaining children. She welcomed the presence of another woman in the house and did her best to make Florrie feel at home. For her part, Florence accepted this arrangement, as the only practical solution under the circumstances. In her heart she would probably have preferred her own space, but being pragmatic as well as being in love, she never allowed herself to think about what wasn't going to happen. She came into Maud's home, clear in the knowledge that, as the outsider, it was up to her to make the situation work. She made it her priority to ensure things ran smoothly in her marital home. From the very beginning, if ever any tensions arose between James and his parents, she would immediately apologise for herself and on behalf of James. It didn't take long for Maud to recognise that Florrie was no threat but rather an ally in her home. And so from Florrie's arrival, the Corleys' intergenerational home was a happy place for all who lived there. Quite soon it became in a very real sense neither Maud's kitchen nor Florrie's kitchen but a workspace owned by neither and shared by both.

My mother told me that from the moment their first baby was born on 15 April 1904, he was doted on by his loving parents, an ecstatic young aunt and uncle, and two besotted grandparents. Never was a child more welcomed. Florrie wished to call the boy Michael after her beloved father, who had died the previous May, but was fully prepared to go along with what she suspected would be the Corley family choice. Her James was the fourth James Corley, so it was a foregone conclusion that their firstborn son would be the fifth to bear the name and no doubt be destined to become a primary teacher too. Florrie was confident that James loved her as she loved him, but she also felt that this was not worth fighting over. In rural Ireland there was no point in fighting against tradition. As the christening was to take place within a few days of the baby's birth, there wasn't much time for discussion on the matter of naming the child. As was customary, the father of the child brought him to the church, accompanied by the godparents, while the mother remained at home until she was well enough to be 'churched'. James's youngest brother, P.J., was to be the godfather, and a cousin of Florrie's was to be godmother. James left for the church with three names for the baby: James, Michael, and Patrick. Florrie understood that her son would have all three names and in that order. But when James arrived home, he announced that the boy had been named Michael James Patrick and would be called Michael. Florrie was inwardly delighted that James had taken her wishes into account, but her immediate concern was for how her parents-in-law might be feeling. Maud immediately took her grandson in her arms and, cuddling him close, said, 'Welcome home, my precious little Christian. Michael, my darling, I'm so glad you have your own name. There are enough Jameses in this house already, God knows.'

Later in the privacy of their bedroom, Florrie said, 'Thank you, James, for naming the baby Michael. I understood that he'd be James Michael Patrick, and honestly I was okay with that. What made you change your mind?'

'What makes you think I changed my mind, love? I knew that you'd want our baby named for your late father. I also knew that, being the kindly soul you are, you wouldn't make a fuss about it. And as it is not just my duty but also my intention to make my beautiful wife as happy as can be, what else would I do? Anyway before you start fretting about my parents' opinion on the matter, you saw Mama's reaction already, and as you know Papa James always agrees with her. Now let's see if we can get this little fellow to go to sleep, so you, my dear, can get some well-earned rest.'

—⁓—

The question of whether or not Florrie would return to teaching was further deferred when she realised, early in the summer that she was pregnant again. Constance arrived into the world in a hurry, only eleven months after her brother. And twelve months later, on 24 December 1906, I was born. This time there was no question that I would be named for my father. It was Grandma Maud who suggested that, to avoid confusion, perhaps they should use the Irish version of the name, and so I was christened Séamus Dermot. By their third wedding anniversary, Florrie and James were the proud parents of three babies under three years of age. Taking on a full-time teaching position was now completely out of the question, as Florrie was far too busy with her young family and her other household responsibilities. However, she hadn't given up on her dream of someday returning to her chosen profession. It would be five years after her marriage that Florrie would eventually manage to persuade James to allow her to become involved in teaching Irish dancing to local youngsters, along with her own three. Reluctant though he was to have his wife work, James had to agree with Florrie that she was going stir crazy being confined to the house now that the youngest of her children had gone to school. His one condition was that she not accept a monetary fee for her services. Florrie happily agreed. But James was no match for his neighbours. They could not accept that their teacher's interest in, commitment to, and encouragement of their children's talents should go unrewarded. Almost immediately after the lessons started, gifts large and small, valuable and less so began to mysteriously appear on our doorstep. On any given day it might be a handful of hen or duck eggs, a bag of potatoes, freshly caught lake fish, an apple cake, or perhaps a rabbit, a farl of griddle bread, a pork steak, or a black pudding from a recently slaughtered pig. In season, cabbage, lettuce, scallions, beetroot, rhubarb, and apples appeared, and sometimes even jams and preserves. Mama received all these gifts graciously and considered herself very well paid indeed. She thanked the donors heartily and discreetly when she ran in to them after Mass in the village or at the market in Ennis. Sometimes she had to make a note to herself to remind her to acknowledge those who lived far away when she'd meet them at the next performance at Feis or concert.

Over the next few years, the youngsters from Kiltyroe built on their reputation as worthy winners of Irish dancing and set dancing competitions at district, county, and national levels. Florrie enjoyed travelling with them and was proud of their success. What most of them were too young to understand at the time was that they learned a lot more from their dance teacher than just the techniques of poise, rhythm, and movement. They also learned timing, stage presence, and discipline and team cooperation. These were valuable life lessons that many of us only appreciated more fully as we got older. Michael, Constance, and I were fully participant in all this activity as well as becoming accomplished musicians in our own right under the demanding tutelage of our Papa. Evenings, after school, were extremely busy for us with homework, dance practice, music lessons, and performances. These were happy times too. The physicality of the dancing offered a pleasing contrast to the sedentary nature of homework and the exacting standards of our father's musical demands. In the autumn of 1914, almost four years after I had started school and as Mama was thoroughly enjoying the success of her dance school, she found herself pregnant again. She didn't allow her pregnancy to interfere with the routine of her lessons. The latter weeks of late June, just before the baby was due, coincided with final polishing of the dances just prior to competition, so the necessity for demonstration was much reduced. Besides, Mama could now call on quite a number of her senior pupils, including Constance and myself, who were now champions in our own right. The lessons always took place in the spacious wood-floored downstairs living room at Ashdene. And once our new sister Nora arrived, the lessons continued without interruption. The high, old-fashioned baby carriage was wheeled in, and little Nora, and a year later her sister Kitty, spent her earliest days listening to the sound of music and dancing feet. In the fullness of time, not surprisingly, of all the Corleys these two were the most talented dancers. It became a bit of a family joke about them, that they couldn't but have great rhythm, since if what they must have imbibed with their mother's milk was not enough, their unbroken attendance at dance practice couldn't fail to give them excellent rhythm and timing.

3

Constance

When Nora was barely two years old and baby Kitty had just celebrated her first birthday, Constance became ill. She returned from school one afternoon complaining of a headache. She was only twelve years old at the time. Florrie tucked her into bed with a hot water bottle and went downstairs to prepare a tasty tidbit to tempt her to eat something. On her return to the bedroom a short time later, with some scrambled egg and toast, Florrie found Constance feverish and fractious. Florrie attempted to feed her a little, but Constance turned her mouth away, explaining that her throat hurt and that she was unable to swallow. She also had a pain in her back and a stiff neck. When her mother tried to comfort her by placing a hand on her forehead, Constance immediately complained that the hand hurt her and was too heavy. Feeling quite frightened by now, Florrie decided to send for the doctor. Luckily James was home and as it happened was about to take his prized Model T Ford for a spin when Florrie caught him. It didn't take him long to drive over to Doctor Frawley's house, and fortunately he found him at home. Once James had described the symptoms, the good doctor wasted no time in rushing to the little girl's bedside. Once he had examined Constance, he stated gravely, 'Florrie and James, I fear that I have very bad news for you. Her symptoms suggest to me that Constance may have contracted a rather serious viral disease. I'm afraid it could be poliomyelitis. Let me explain. There are three types of poliomyelitis: subclinical, non-paralytic, and paralytic. Unfortunately there is no known cure for this disease. The good news is the child is in good health and strong. She may very well win the battle against the virus. There's not a moment to be lost. We need to get her to the hospital straightaway.

'Once there, a clinical diagnosis can be made which will confirm which type she has.

Patients with paralytic poliomyelitis need to be carefully monitored for signs of respiratory failure. All I can hope for is that I'm wrong or that she will have one of the less virulent forms of the disease. I'll take her with me in my car. Florrie, come with me. James, you can follow later when you can.'

Grandma Maud took over straightaway, so within twenty minutes of the doctor's dash to the hospital in Ennis, James had arrived to comfort Florrie. All through the late evening and long into night, they sat in the waiting room or paced the corridor, wondering what was happening and worrying about their precious daughter. The doctor and nursing sister were busy monitoring the child's struggle to catch her breath. The other nurses on duty were busy with their patients and their chores. No one thought to update the parents on what was going on. About five o'clock in the morning, the fever broke, and Constance was able to breathe more easily. Having observed his patient for a further half an hour, a much-relieved Dr. Frawley came in search of the child's parents. He told them that, in his opinion, the worst was over, and he was hopeful of recovery. It was much too soon to say whether or not it would be a full recovery, and of course there was no way of knowing just how incapacitated Constance would be in the end. What he didn't reveal at this point was his firm contention that she was suffering from the paralytic form of the disease. After all, it was only his opinion, and it would be several days before the hospital's laboratory staff would be in a position to confirm the diagnosis, when the results of the blood and cultures tests would become available. For now all he could do was reassure the Corleys that Constance was in safe hands and that they should return home to their other children and try and catch a few hours' sleep before morning.

Meanwhile, back in Ashdene House all was now quiet. The little ones had been put to bed quickly and efficiently, at their usual bedtime, by Grandma Maud. Michael and I worried and waited by the fireside until her return. Maud was impatient with us and cross at finding us idle.

'Speculating about your sister's condition will do no one any favours,' she said. 'It would be more in your line to get on your knees and pray for her speedy recovery.'

With that she knelt down and started the rosary. Michael and I followed suit. We took our turns at giving out the Hail Marys and responding with the Holy Marys for the Glorious Mysteries. This was followed by Grandma's endless trimmings in accordance with the nightly ritual of our home. But when she proceeded after all this, with the five Sorrowful Mysteries, we became less enthusiastic in our participation. But because we were worried and scared for Constance and knew how serious it must be when both our parents had still not come home from the hospital, we were careful to make no objection. But then Grandma

Maud launched into the five Joyful Mysteries without any indication that she might stop anytime soon. By now my impatience began to manifest itself, first in sniffling and shuffling. Soon Michael also began to display signs of restlessness, flexing his fingers, cracking his knuckles, and shifting from one knee to the other in an effort to ease his discomfort. By the time Grandma Maud had finished praying, we were not only exhausted but stiff and sore. We had been kneeling for well over an hour. As our elderly grandmother had been kneeling for just as long and was stoically showing no signs of discomfort, we didn't dare complain. Maud made no secret that she was disappointed with our behaviour. She told us so, in no uncertain terms, and as a result she sent us to bed without any supper. Her parting shot was to suggest that if Constance's recovery were to be contingent on our behaviour, then God help us all. Glad to be released, we made our way quietly to our bedroom. Michael settled down to sleep, cold and miserable though he was. I couldn't settle. I burned with resentment at Grandma's cruelty. If ever I wondered where Papa got his unfeeling streak from, now I know. He and Grandma are as bad as each other,' I complained to Michael. 'I'm sick and tired of the pair of them. It's not fair that they can bully us like they do. Do you think that Mama would have sent us off to bed hungry? Do you think she'd have made us say all those endless prayers?'

I sat up in bed and looked across at Michael, waiting for an answer. But Michael said nothing. He was either asleep or pretending to be. But the real reason I couldn't get to sleep was guilt. I couldn't get it out of my head that if Constance died or didn't make a full recovery, it would be all my fault for not praying properly. I wanted above all else for Constance to get better but found I couldn't bring myself to pray. In the end I sobbed myself to sleep, feeling deeply ashamed, abandoned, and alone.'

'Over the next several weeks, we suffered the highs and lows of hope and despair. Doctor Frawley's diagnosis proved to be correct. For the forty-eight hours following her admission to hospital, Constance's condition appeared to have stabilised. Then her fever flared up again, and there was a thirty-six-hour period when everyone feared for her life. Then things improved again, and within a few days she was sitting up and beginning to recover her appetite. Soon she was in a position to have short visits from our parents. The bad news slowly emerged. This vivacious girl with the beautiful smile and the sunny disposition would never walk again. A lassie who loved activity, skipping, playing camogie and rounders competitively and enthusiastically, cycling and walking, not to talk of being an award-winning dancer, would spend the rest of her life wheelchair-bound. The eight-year gap between us older three children and the younger two meant that, for all practical purposes, Mama now found herself rearing two families as well as looking after her recently crippled daughter. Times were not easy for her, but never prone to self-pity, she faced forward with positivity and determination to assist Constance in overcoming her handicap and developing her intellectual capacities and her personality to her full potential. That summer Michael went away to boarding school. Not only was he missed for himself but also for his role as eldest and big brother to the rest of us. On his departure the family dynamic changed of course. Now suddenly the oldest boy in the house, I began to flex my muscles, and Constance became painfully aware that, at least as far as I was concerned, she had become almost invisible. This was the final straw that broke the camel's back. She was both hurt and annoyed, and then she vowed that she just wasn't having it. She realised that if she didn't assert her position now, she would be side-lined forever more, just because she could no longer walk. She recognised immediately and completely that only she herself could shape her future. The first thing she did was to accept Mama's support. They had always been close, but the bond between them strengthened during Constance's illness. She began to appreciate Mama's strength of character as well as her positive attitude and her pragmatic outlook on life and its difficulties. Ever since her return to the family home, Papa had shown a softer side of his nature. He was inclined to smother her with love and pity. She was secure in the unconditional love of both her parents, but Constance needed her mother to preserve her from her father's compassionately stultifying overprotectiveness. He saw her inability to walk as a complete catastrophe. As far as he was concerned, her life was permanently blighted. His lovely daughter was damaged. He feared she would never attract a husband of her own. She was doomed not just to her wheelchair but to a dull and dependent spinster's existence in the chimney corner. His wonderful little girl, with the soul of an angel and not a mean bone in her body, would never experience the joy of motherhood. Knowing that she needed a buffer between herself and her grief-stricken papa's negativity, Constance sought my help. I became her ally in this unequal struggle, initially because of guilt but increasingly because I wanted to help her to adjust. She was such a determined little fighter. Almost as soon as she was discharged from hospital, she had tried to do as much as she could for herself. She hated the way we all fussed over her and tried to outdo each other in being first to do things for her. No matter how she tried, she couldn't dissuade either Papa or Michael from babying her. So she had set about making Mama, Grandma Maud and me understand that doing things for her wasn't a helpful long-term plan either for her or for us. Then she explained that she intended to live a full life, and therefore ignoring her, or side-lining her, was not an option. She told us that she wanted to participate fully in all family activities. From now on we would help her only when she asked for help, not when we thought she needed it. But most of all she was still the eldest girl and expected to be treated in exactly the same way as she had always been when she was able to chase around with and after the rest of us. She would take her turn in helping out with the babies and handle her share of the babysitting, but so too would the boys when we were home, she warned. I had noticed that Constance had summoned all her determination and spirit to push herself to the limit. She was frustrated that five months after coming home she was still inclined to tire easily. Mama wanted her to take an afternoon nap, but Constance resisted this on the grounds that it was more, not less, activity that she needed. I had been helping her develop her upper body strength with some gentle exercises. Now I decided to up the ante. I insisted on taking her outside for some more robust and fun exercises. We'd start with racing challenges around the yard, me in my homemade go-cart and she in her wheelchair. Then as Constance showed signs of improvement in speed and accuracy, I introduced obstacles and increasingly challenging routes. We'd finish up by playing a modified version of handball in the local ball alley before racing each other home, Constance whizzing along in her chariot while I ran at my best to keep up with her. Michael disapproved of all this exercise and carped about it continually. She was due to return to school after the summer holidays, and she was looking forward to it.

That was the turning point for Constance I think. Within days of returning to school, everyone had forgotten that she was no longer able-bodied; such was the enthusiasm with which she participated in all activities to the best of her ability. As the months passed she discussed with our parents her hope to go away to boarding school the following September as planned. Mama was on her side on this one, ably supported by Grandma Maud, but it took most of the next three months for all three of us to persuade Papa. Eventually it was I who broke the deadlock when I threatened that if Constance didn't have to go away to boarding school, then neither would I be forced to. After that, arrangements had to be made to find a school that would be able to accommodate and welcome a disabled student, not just tolerate one. So Constance had got her way. In September she happily faced the challenge of her new surroundings in a privately run secondary school for young ladies in Derryarramore, County Galway.

Constance took to the new school like a duck to water, and by Christmas she had settled in well and made friends with some of the girls in her class. By the time I was ready for boarding school the following year, the household routines had at last returned to normal. Constance, by sheer determination and exuberance, had kick-started the process of acceptance of her condition. The rest of us had no option but to follow suit.

4

Boarding School

I will never forget the evening of my arrival at St. Cosmas's College. It was the first day of September 1919, and I was twelve years old. Until now I had never spent a night away from home. Oh many a night I had slept in hay sheds and under the stars, unbeknownst to my parents, but always within striking distance of Ashdene. On first arrival, with the hustle and bustle of over two hundred uniformed boys of all shapes and sizes, varying in age from twelve to eighteen years, making an unholy clamour, I was initially caught up in the excitement and newness of it all. Michael, who knew the ropes, had immediately abandoned me. His attitude was it would be best for me to find my own way about. After all, when he had come here three years earlier, there was no big brother to mollycoddle him. I pretended not to mind and swaggered off like I knew where I was going and hadn't a care in the world. Inwardly I was terrified. Everything was on a vast scale. The ceilings were enormously high, windows were huge, and the clatter was deafening. Every sound reverberated in the cavernous rooms. Nothing had prepared me for this weird experience of being alone amidst such bedlam of constant movement and noise. Supper consisted of tea and a hunk of baker's bread miserably spread with a scraping of margarine. The tea was dispensed from large teapots, with milk and sugar already added. It looked grey and watery and tasted vile.

If you weren't quick enough to grab your bread, someone else would have already snatched it. I had never witnessed such savagery in my life. Boys who seconds before had appeared to be perfectly normal had turned into monsters on entering the refectory. After supper we were all herded into the college chapel for night prayers. Here the rosary was recited, and then the dean gave us a 'welcome to the new school year' homily of the fire and brimstone variety. After that we had to make our way quickly and in silence to the dormitories. The dormitory for us first-year students was an enormous space with a highly polished wooden floor. There were twenty cubicles on each side running the width of the room. Two tall, narrow windows pierced the stone wall to the front of the building, with sills so high that not even the tallest adult could catch a glimpse of the outside world. The wooden walls of the cubicles reached about eight feet high but were still considerably short of the lofty ceiling. These walls enclosed a space of no wider than four feet, just enough room to accommodate a three-foot-wide iron-framed single bed pushed against one wall, with barely adequate space for a slight boy to stand. Fortunately for me, I had gleaned from Michael that time was now of the essence, so as quickly as I could I undressed; got into my pyjamas; and, toilet bag in hand, headed for the communal bathroom. I was lucky enough to get to the last vacant stall in the line of ten. I had barely managed to put my toothbrush in my mouth when the bell rang. I knew I didn't have enough time to rinse before the lights would go out. Anyone not in their beds when the monitor did his round would warrant immediate punishment. Heart in mouth, I reached my cubicle as the dormitory was plunged into impenetrable darkness. I had managed to get into the bed in time by the skin of my teeth. Various bumps and thuds could be heard as well as grunts and exhalations as the latecomers tried to make their way to their beds in the dark. Immediately the heavy footsteps of the monitor could be heard from the doorway. He shouted, 'Halt, stand where you are,' as he shone a torch into the room. Nine unfortunate boys of the forty of us had failed to make it to their beds on time. Torn between sympathy for the others and relief that I was not among them, I shivered in my bed under the thin blanket and listened to see what punishment would be meted out.

'Your names please. Tomorrow you will report to the dean of discipline for six of the best. That means, you lazy little snot-nosed brats, you'll get three slaps of the leather on each hand. That'll teach you to get a move on. My only surprise is that there weren't more of you caught. I'll be quicker off the mark in future. Goodnight all.'

It was only then that I recognised the voice. Our monitor was my brother Michael. That first night of misery, with its aching loneliness and smothered snivelling from other cubicles, was just the predecessor to many more. Amazingly, given that we were all in the same boat and roughly of the same age, the bullying began that night. Unwilling to incur punishment by being caught out of their beds, the bullies confined themselves to whispered taunting of the homesick creatures who had been reduced to tears. At this stage 'crybaby, Mammy's boy' followed by sucking sounds was as bad as it got. Instinctively I knew that this was just the beginning and that the level and intensity of the bullying would escalate as time went on. Lying rolled into a foetal position in my lumpy bed, I swore I'd keep my homesickness to myself. I determined there and then that no sound would ever emerge from my cubicle that would make me vulnerable to such hateful taunting. The fact that others nearby were suffering too was of no consolation to me. In fact it was not a question of 'a sorrow shared is a sorrow halved', rather even those of us who initially empathised with 'the weepers' very soon began to lose patience with them. The sound of sobbing, sniffling, and suppressed hiccupping tended not only to keep us awake but also to weaken the resolve of those of us who, though equally lonesome, were trying to be more stoical about it. Sleep eluded me that first night and indeed for many subsequent nights. But eventually I began to get acclimatised to the sounds of crying, sobbing, snoring, and farting, and so I managed a few consecutive hours. Some of the boys could sleep through any amount of noise. Some were too miserable to sleep, and others like me managed snatches of oblivion before being awakened by the ever-increasing torturing of the weaker ones by the bullies. By mid-term the leading bully, George Rudge, and his sidekick, Festus Murphy, and their coterie of faithful, gutless followers had worked out that their chances of being caught were much reduced between 4 a.m. and 5 a.m. And so they had their sport. Those unfortunate youngsters who were suffering most became their first victims. As is the way with bullies, they seemed to have a zoning instinct for the weakest and most vulnerable. So first they picked on those they termed the 'crybabies'. Initially the bullying took the form of teasing and name calling, but it soon developed into taunting, before escalating to unacceptable levels of physical violence. There was usually a period of quietness after the lights went out and the monitor had departed. If you were lucky you might get to sleep in this interval before the baleful whisper identifying that night's victim came from Rudge's cubicle. Rudge was the ringleader, a hulking great lump of a fellow who used his not inconsiderable intellect to find novel and interesting ways of tormenting his victims. But Murphy was a different proposition. Though not as intellectually gifted as Rudge, he was clever as well as devious. He took pleasure in carrying out Rudge's schemes with added twists of cruelty and sadism. In my opinion Festus Murphy was pure evil. The whispered announcement had the effect of terrifying the named boy, who of course wouldn't sleep a wink in anticipation of what was to come. But of course neither did many others, as Rudge was quite capable of changing his mind at the last minute and picking on someone else entirely. The tension among victims built, and soon the usual night-time noises could be heard while the bullies took their rest. At a signal from the appointed 'caller' around 4.30, the bullies would slip from their beds to carry out their depredations. Some poor boy would be dragged from his bed and ducked in a toilet bowl or have water poured over him as he slept. Someone might wake in the morning to find his ankles firmly bound together with leather thongs or bootlaces, causing him to fall flat on his face as he responded to the morning bell. Or some unsuspecting lad might stretch in his sleep only to be rudely and painfully awakened by a well-placed mousetrap snapping shut on a finger or a toe. Variations on French beds, various items placed in their beds, thorns, thistles, pebbles, briars, brushes, crumbs, toast buttered or dry—these were pranks bearing the stamp of Rudge, but of course Murphy added his own nastier variations. Frogspawn, jam, treacle, honey mixed with sand or salt for maximum mess and discomfort were more Murphy's style. But when Murphy decided to replace the water in the leaky hot water bottle trick with urine even Rudge was outraged. His solution was to distance himself from the 'sport'. This happened about two weeks before the Christmas holidays. With Rudge's withdrawal, things got completely out of hand. The gutless wonders continued to follow Murphy's lead. The pranks entered a new phase, and 'a reign of terror' began. Murphy suggested that the 'crybabies' weren't just weaklings but were homos in the making and therefore needed to be punished. Elaborate kangaroo courts were set up, and boys were stripped, lashed, and beaten, forced to confess to unspeakable crimes against persons. The punishments meted out as a result of these confessions were to perform the acts confessed to. Refusal to do so resulted in further beatings, being immersed in cold baths for hours at a time, catching of fingers in slammed doors, and even ripping off of fingernails.

Being the younger brother of the hated dormitory monitor, I knew it was only a matter of time before I would be singled out for punishment by Murphy and his gang. So it was with a heavy heart and a good deal of dread that I left Ashdene and the family in January 1920 to return to St. Cosmas's College. The first few nights passed without incident. But on the Friday night, or rather the early hours of Saturday morning, I was dragged from my bed. My pyjamas were torn from my body, and I was forced to stand naked on a chair surrounded by ten or eleven jeering boys. The 'court' got under way. Murphy was doing the cross-examination while Bill Brown was poking me in the genital area with the hook end of a long window pole, to the sniggering amusement of the ring of gutless wonders.

'I suppose you think you're immune just because you have a big brother who's a big shot monitor. Well guess what, Corley. You are in for it now, you little queer. But first you'd better answer the questions I put to you. In case you haven't noticed, Big Brother isn't here now to protect you.'

'The hell he's not, Murphy,' came Michael's voice from the doorway. 'Come with me, now. You too, Brown'.

Then, turning to the onlookers, he growled, 'you lot will be dealt with tomorrow.'

Casting a withering glance in my direction, he indicated with a curt nod of his head that I should return to my bed. The look of contempt on his face still haunts me all these years later. It was as if he thought the bullying was somehow all my fault. Or, heaven forbid, did he suspect that perhaps Murphy's allegation was true? If he did think I was a 'nancy boy', then it was patently obvious he was disgusted by the idea. The antics in the dormitory ceased abruptly that night. The following day all forty of us first years were subjected to a long lecture about bullying from the dean of discipline. He berated us all, bullies, victims, and onlookers alike, for the disgraceful behaviour which had gone unchecked for the bulk of the previous term. The guilty parties would be duly punished, he promised. As for the victims, it was high time they learned to cope with the minor discomforts of life in boarding school. The group he had greatest contempt for were the cowardly onlookers who didn't have the gumption to report what was going on. I got the distinct impression that he had a certain grudging respect for the ingenuity of bullies. Interestingly it was not

Murphy who took the brunt of the punishment. It was George Rudge, who was expelled, and Billy Brown, who had a series of menial tasks to perform until end of term. It was several months later that I found out why. The sneaky Festus Murphy had implicated Rudge, pleading that he was merely filling in for George, who was the instigator, and had been bullied into carrying out Rudge's instructions. He further consolidated his position by pointing out that any suggestion of impropriety on his record would jeopardise his chances of being accepted in the seminary on finishing his schooling in St. Cosmas's. Whether the powers that be were merely venal or he had some sinister hold over someone, the consequences were that Murphy got off scot-free. Poor old Rudge accepted the punishment without demur. Perhaps he felt guilty for initiating the pranks and thus facilitating Murphy's evil behaviour. The last I heard of him was that, to the great disappointment of his parents, who had great expectations for him, he returned to his native village in Kilkenny. Here he attended the local secondary top for the next two years. After that he emigrated to England at the age of fifteen. He worked hard in construction until in his twenties he put himself through college and qualified as an engineer. He had set up his own company subsequently and became a benevolent employer of many Irish young men over the years. His sons and grandsons still run the very successful Rudge Construction Company in southeast London.

I settled down to school routines and as time moved on learned to cope better with my homesickness. I found refuge in the library and read voraciously every chance I got. But I still couldn't sleep at night. I knew that I had made a deadly enemy in Murphy, and that sooner or later I would pay dearly for the thwarting of his bullying of me. He had to be careful at first, knowing that he was being watched, but he still managed to intimidate me with snide comments masquerading as humour in public and petty acts of vandalism in private. I would find my textbooks defaced with lewd scribblings, sections would mysteriously disappear from homework or essay assignments, and library books I was the last person to check out began to either disappear or have pages roughly torn from them. He had to have engaged the services of others to help, such was the level of tormenting behaviours I was subjected to over the next three years. A wide variety of evil-smelling liquids found their way into my locker, my bed, even my trunk. Never in the history of St. Cosmas's had a boy's uniform been known to have the variety and amount of staining as mine. Mama had long since lost patience with my excuses, as she had yet again to replace items of clothing. Hurling and football practice were nightmares. If I wasn't missing a boot or a sock, I'd be unable to get into my shorts or my jersey, as they'd be glued together with some obnoxious, evil-smelling substance or other. Soon I had earned a reputation for being the grottiest boy the school had ever had. I had acquired an impressively long list of nicknames. I was variously known among the boys of all ages as

Stinky, Smelly, Absent-minded Professor, Clumso, Shitpants, Dribbler, Oddser, Freako, and Vomitface. These were only some of them; others were too coarse to be recorded and others still mercifully forgotten. Murphy was convinced that Michael's sudden appearance in the dorm on that fateful night was no accident that somehow I had managed to summon him to my aid. He was determined to get back at me. The devious and conniving often have the virtue of great patience. I continued to be on the lookout for when the axe would fall, while Murphy gloried in the enjoyment of playing cat to my terrified mouse. He bided his time well and had made plans to strike where he knew it would hurt most. He knew that Michael, a prodigiously gifted student, had finished in St. Cosmas's the previous summer with a magnificent academic record. Gold medals were awarded to the student or students who had earned the highest marks awarded in Ireland for each subject area. Our Michael had won gold medals in three subjects in the leaving certificate examinations. The school was enormously proud of his achievement, not to talk of the immense satisfaction enjoyed by our father, James, and the entire Corley clan. As the end of year approached and we were about to sit the intermediate certificate exams, Murphy's plan was to destroy my papers and so scupper my chances of returning to the school to complete the leaving certificate programme. He knew that the disgrace of failure would not be mine alone but would reflect badly on Michael and the Corley name. Years later the then sleek and suave Father Festy Murphy regaled a group of our classmates at a reunion with the tale of how he had engineered to be seated directly behind me in the exam hall for maximum disruption and ease of access to my papers.

'But typical of Corley, the sneaky bastard, he managed to thwart me yet again. But not to worry, Corley old boy. I'll sort you yet. It's a long road that doesn't have a turning, and remember that an elephant never forgets,' he sneered.

But way back then we were only boys, and Murphy had managed to inveigle his way into becoming head boy of our third-year class. He had succeeded in fooling quite a number of the priests and most of the seniors with displays of leadership, good behaviour, and toadying, as appropriate, and of course he had long since learned how to cover his tracks and deputise his dirty work. The designated invigilator was taken ill on the day before we started the exams. So on the first morning we were all surprised to see Father Brendan Hanrahan, the dean of studies himself, seat himself at the front of the hall on the raised dais. 'Hawkeye' Hanrahan was reputed to miss nothing. It was rumoured that his hearing was so keen he could hear grass grow. Certainly there was nothing amiss with his eyesight. He paced the aisles as silently as a wraith, instilling terror into those who might have harboured thoughts of cheating and managing to be invisible to those engaged with their work. Looking back now I wonder if he had an instinct about Festus Murphy. He seemed to hover at his shoulder an inordinately long time in his perambulations. Anyway, his vigilance prevented Murphy from carrying out his plan. On my return to school in September, with a decent inter certificate result, which pleased me and Mama and seemed to satisfy Papa, I discovered to my relief that for the vast bulk of my classes I was not in the same group as Festus Murphy. Better yet I had been elevated to the position of dormitory monitor for the first years. As a result of the bullying we had been subjected to three years earlier, each monitor now slept in an enclosed cubicle within the dormitory. This meant that for the coming year my contact with Murphy would be extremely limited. For the first time I began to relax and enjoy the experience of boarding school.

To give Mr James Corley his due, he prepared all his pupils very well for transfer to second-level schooling or indeed for entering the world of work, whether at home or abroad. On arrival at St. Cosmas's College, I began to appreciate for the first time just how good a teacher Papa was. Despite being a very harsh disciplinarian, he managed to instil in us all a love of learning, a thirst for knowledge, a passion for reading, and most significantly a critical sense of appreciation of prose and poetry. Because he loved mathematics so much himself, he carried us forward on a wave of enthusiasm for the joy of calculation, numeracy, and problem solving. He made it all appear so straightforward and down to earth with his environment-based challenges that we took it for granted that we'd excel at maths. But it is my mother I must credit with honing whatever writing skills I may have had when I transferred to secondary school. She too loved to read and was a prolific letter writer. From the time the first of her children went to boarding school, Florrie had insisted on responding immediately and at length to their compulsory Sunday letters. She would not tolerate any mistakes of grammar or spelling or indeed any carelessness of usage. If we erred, we knew that the letter would be returned to us with Florrie's cryptic comments in her next missive. Then we would have to use the offending word in its proper form and context at least five times in the next letter home. We soon learned to write not just correctly but also carefully and with impeccable handwriting. When I asked her about it as an adult, Florrie explained that it was James's idea in the first place but that she had absolutely supported him in it. She further contended that she had never regretted the practice, as she felt that we had all benefitted from it. Michael and Constance never had a problem with it, so she was surprised to hear that I resented it. She and our papa were very ambitious for all their children. They saw this intervention as a supportive and practical way to keep us on our toes. Because the younger members of the family had grown up with the tradition, no one else complained about it. Mama explained that Papa was also extremely proud of us and loved us dearly, even if sometimes it was hard for him to express that love. By her own admission, she herself had used her weekly letters to keep close to her precious children. Many years later she told me that she felt the need to offer me support. She was aware that, despite my tough exterior, I needed to draw on her strength for comfort, recognising better than I did at the time just how like my father I was in so many ways. According to her, of all the Corleys I was the one who needed her most and would be the last to ever admit it. Without my ever mentioning it, she understood that I was lonely and homesick at school. She also had a strong suspicion that someone was making life difficult for me in those early years. She encouraged me to read often, sharing her own insights on what she was currently reading. And so her letters were interesting, full of enthusiastic recommendations of biographies, autobiographies, and novels both classic and modern. She elicited my views and prompted me towards more analytic comment, especially after I had done rather well in English in the inter cert. As a result of Florrie's praise and encouragement, I had gained in confidence and literary prowess, so that by the time I was in my third year of secondary school, I had begun to win prizes for my prose as well as my poetry. My English teacher, Mr Williams, took note and persuaded me to enter some of my essays and short stories for competitions in magazines and for radio. By the time I sat the leaving certificate examinations, I had already accrued a sizable income from my writings.

5

Florrie

Michael, Constance, and I were home for the summer holidays in 1920. Nora and Kitty were ready to start at primary school in September, and, best of all, Mama was expecting again. Years later she confided in me that for a fraction of a second, when first she suspected that she might be pregnant again, the thought had flashed across her mind, *Just as I was looking forward to a bit of free time.* Immediately this thought was followed by the realisation that this was not the first time she had thought a change of lifestyle was beginning. She had been here before, and so she apologised to the new life within her and with a little thrill of excitement went to share her secret with her mother-in-law, Grandma Maud. The two of them got busy preparing a special teatime meal as a fitting backdrop to letting James and the rest of the family in on the good news. James was thrilled that he was to be a father again. He was immensely proud of his growing brood. At the time Michael and I were a little embarrassed at the announcement, but on the whole we were happy, because our parents were so obviously pleased. The younger ones were delighted that they would have a new baby to fuss over and play with. Kitty especially was looking forward to no longer being the youngest. But perhaps Constance was the one who was most excited at the news. She was thrilled to share in Mama's excitement and happiness. She hoped that this new arrival would bring joy back into the house. And she firmly believed that preparing for and looking after the new baby would provide plenty of opportunity to demonstrate to everyone just how well she could cope. She wanted the whole family to know that not being able to walk had not diminished her capacities in any way, and if she were to move on and eventually live a full and independent life, she needed to be treated like everyone else. While the rest of Europe was embroiled in the Great War, life continued at its pastoral pace in Kiltyroe. With all five children at school, Mama found that she had time to enjoy this pregnancy. That summer was one of the happiest the Corleys had experienced in quite a while. Mama continued with her classes of course, but as these did not begin until after school, she had all morning and the early afternoon pretty much to herself. She and Grandma Maud had always got on extremely well, and with the passage of time, their relationship had deepened into friendship. Our grandfather, James Senior, had battled long and hard but in late August had finally passed away. He had been housebound for sixteen years and bed-bound for the last nine of them. After his funeral and burial in the local graveyard, life in Ashdene House resumed its even tenor. Mama and Grandma Maud, sitting companionably by the fire at night, chatted about the details of the day and the antics of the children as well as what was going on in the village and the locality. Grandma liked to talk about the early days of her own marriage and seemed to draw some comfort from sharing her memories with Mama. She recalled with obvious pride when James Junior had taken over the principalship of the village school, following in his father's footsteps. She confided in Mama that when she and James had got married earlier that summer, James Senior was delighted. He used to say that it was a happy day in paradise the day his son had met and fallen in love with Florence Mulvey. Within hours of being introduced to Florence, he was convinced that James and she were meant for each other. In his opinion she was, without a shadow of a doubt, one of the easiest people to talk to whom he had ever met. Later on as he became ill, he appreciated hugely that she was able and willing to treat an older, sick, and incapacitated man with compassion and interest, without any trace of pity or awkwardness. He loved that she had a gift of being able to put people at their ease immediately on meeting them. By the time Florence had moved into the family home, both James and Maud saw her as an ally and a friend rather than as an intruder.

6

Shay's Last Schooldays

Those final two years in St. Cosmas's College were the happiest of my schooldays. I enjoyed the academic challenges and proved myself on the playing fields. I had earned a bit of a reputation among my peers for my writings. I was also enjoying being something of a hero to the two groups of juniors for whom I had been dormitory monitor. And so time passed swiftly. While home on holidays in the summer of 1922, I had spent many happy hours hunting and fowling. Mama and Constance were delighted when I returned with a variety of game birds and rabbits for the table. They both loved to cook and often vied with each other in the making of pies and stews, each swearing by her own favourite recipes. I was often put in the impossible position of not only having to guess which of them had cooked the various dishes but also having to rate their offerings. I was never happier than when trudging uphill and down-dale communing with nature. I remember how I would disappear for hours on end, bird watching and hill walking. That was the summer I bought myself the pellet gun. I was about fifteen at the time, and I had used some of my prize money for the purchase. I had great fun practising, and soon I had become a crack shot and was bringing home game birds for supper. I have good reason to remember that wonderful summer not just because it was my first taste of freedom and independence but because for the first time I realised that I actually enjoyed my own company. Being alone in the great outdoors was wonderfully exciting, and the silence and solitude were comforting rather than threatening, and I was no longer lonely. There was far too much of interest going on in nature all around me. Also that summer an elderly neighbour called to Ashdene House. His name was Fowler Lynch. He had always been a keen fowler, but now in his seventies, he reckoned his shooting days were over. He knew I was interested in the sport and was already a skilled huntsman. Indeed it was he who had introduced me to fowling in the first place. Fowler Lynch had no sons or nephews of his own but was fond of me and had told me several times that he would leave me his prized possession when he died. Fowler had called to the house to make sure that it was okay with James and Florrie for me to have the gun. Having got their blessing, Fowler duly handed over the shotgun with great pomp and ceremony. I was delighted with the gift and couldn't wait to try it out. However, when I did get the chance, I discovered that the famous Fowler's shotgun was not in the best of condition. Worse, it had been dropped at some point, and the sights had become bent and distorted. Try as I might, I couldn't manage to shoot straight with Fowler Lynch's famed fowling piece. In the end, I gave it up as a bad job and reverted to using my own pellet gun again. In the fullness of time, I acquired a double-barrelled shotgun, and the much-loved pellet gun was soon forgotten like all outgrown toys.

Looking back now, that was the happiest period of my life. Nobody bothered me, I escaped my father's notice almost completely. He and Michael spent hours together in erudite discussion or sharing a passion for classical music, which they listened to for hours on end on the wet-battery wireless when they weren't accompanying each other on violin and silver flute. My only duty that entire summer was the command performance of all of us at Papa's musical soirées. These events were organised at least twice a week over the summer months, when school teachers from the neighbouring parishes and various friends of Papa's were invited round. Mama, increasingly with Constance's willing assistance, spent hours in the kitchen cooking and baking wonderful concoctions for the guests. We, from eldest to youngest, provided the entertainment. We all played instruments. Since the debacle with the violin, I had been assigned to play tin whistle. I assume this was Papa's idea of punishment, and I felt it a cruel demotion. The only bright side was he excused me from practising with the others in return for my promise to be note perfect for the performances.

Our soirée programme varied from week to week, drawing from the vast range of material in our musical repertoire. We were all encouraged to sing, and of course dancing was also an integral part of these evening entertainments. We all enjoyed the opportunity to perform, the more extrovert of us taking greatest pleasure in being in the limelight. I'm sure I wasn't the only one who found the required rehearsal time tiresome. It's only now that I wonder how the others felt about the fact that from that summer I was the only one who was ever excused from mandatory attendance at these daily practice sessions. Papa took the rehearsals himself with very few exceptions. If he were unavoidably absent, Mama, and later on Michael, would substitute for him. If Michael were in charge, things were run to the same exacting standards and time schedule as if Papa were there. Mama was equally exacting as far as standard of play and behaviour were concerned but much more flexible with regard to time, especially if the weather was fine. Another reason to remember that special summer was the fact that baby Ambrose had tried to get in on the act. When Kitty was singing her party piece, 'Red Is the Rose', the little mite joined in the chorus to the surprise and delight of the assembled guests and family. He had a sweet treble voice, which Papa declared augured well for later life. At the time he wasn't quite two years old, but already James was dreaming of a glittering career as a singer for his youngest son. Such was the excitement and praise heaped upon him that little Ambrose soon consolidated his place on the programme. It is a wonder that all this adulation didn't spoil the child completely and forever. That was the summer when my school pal Brendan Walsh began to show more interest in Constance's company than in mine. Brendan was a lovely lad, and it dawned on me that he was falling in love with Constance. She hadn't a clue and thought his constant butting in on our time a bit tedious. After the initial shock, I was pleased for them both. Brendan saw beyond her disability, if indeed he saw it at all. They had lots in common, and I felt that when she got to know him better, Constance would come to love Brendan.

I returned to St. Cosmas's that September rested and well and ready to face the challenges of my final two years in school. Time flew by on wings of speed, and soon the summer of 1923 was upon us. Because the previous summer was so significant, this one somehow failed to be memorable. I fished and hunted as usual, but I must have spent the bulk of my time reading, in preparation for the gruelling year ahead, my last before the leaving cert. I studied hard and worked conscientiously all the hours that God sent, determined to prove myself to the rest of the Corleys, especially Papa and Michael. I was competing not only against every other candidate in the country but also against my elder brother's impossibly high record of three years earlier. Realistically I didn't expect to equal his achievement, but I was hell bent on doing the very best that I could so as not to be accused of rubbing the gilt off the golden boy. The effort was well worth it in the end.

The exam results were out on August 16, and Papa had decided to make a day out of the occasion. He wanted to bring the whole family to town for the day, but Mama, bless her, dissuaded him. She decided that Papa and I should go and get the results in the early afternoon, and she and the others would have a celebratory meal ready on our return. In the end Papa had disappeared after lunch in his prized Model T Ford. By the time he returned it was after four o'clock. I was fit to be tied. The long wait hadn't improved the state of my nerves. Mama understood my impatience and at the last minute decided she would accompany us, leaving Constance in charge of putting the finishing touches to the party food. It was almost six o'clock by the time we arrived at St. Cosmas's College, and inevitably the school was closed. We had to go to the monastery to see if we could find the dean of studies. We were left kicking our heels in the parlour for three quarters of an hour while

Father Henderson was having his supper. He arrived like a whirlwind, apologising for the delay and obviously upset that we had been kept waiting for so long.

'Congratulations, young man. You did very well. Mind you, you took your sweet time getting here. You must have been comfortable that you'd done well.' Turning to my parents then, he congratulated them both, saying, 'Mrs and Mr Corley, you must be very proud of this young man. Shay has done us all proud, his family, his college and, most of all, himself. Well done, Shay. Enjoy your achievement. You deserve it. This is your day. Now open your envelope and see just how well you have done. Take a moment to savour the moment while I offer your parents some refreshments after their journey.'

With hope coloured by trepidation, I opened the envelope to see if I had indeed done well enough to please Papa. I stared in disbelief at the list of results but most especially at the accompanying note, which appeared to suggest that I had managed to win a gold medal of my own. Unsurprisingly it was for English. I was thrilled of course and almost equally well pleased to discover that I had scored 98 per cent in mathematics. I had gained marks in the nineties in all my subjects, with the exception of Geography, where I had scored 87 per cent. I thought the parents would never finish the tea and dainty sandwiches, which had mysteriously appeared some minutes after Father Brendan had pressed a push bell on the wall beside the fireplace. I was dying to share my news with Mama, and to tell the truth I was looking forward to seeing the surprise on Papa's dial when he heard about the medal.

At long last the goodbyes were over, and I was able to hand Mama the precious bits of paper on the way back to the car. She quickly scanned the two sheets before excitedly handing them over to Papa as we climbed into the car. Perusing the results quickly, he said, 'A gold medal in English, Shay. Good lad. But what happened that you missed the one for maths?'

Why in God's name did he have to be like this? Why was he so hard on me? Why did no one else I knew have a parent like him? Why for once could he not be normal like everyone else's fathers? Could he not for just this once not spoil everything? After that the celebratory dinner was a washout as far as I was concerned. But it gave Papa an excuse to have yet another go at me. He berated me roundly for not appreciating Constance and Mama's culinary efforts and casting a pall over the evening with 'a face that would trip a tinker', as he described my lugubrious expression. He seemed to have no clue as to why I might be unhappy. With Mama's encouragement and at the advice of Father Hanrahan, I had set my career expectations high in anticipation of decent exam results. I'd hoped for a university place to study English and history. Michael would graduate that autumn with a double first. He had won a scholarship to University College Dublin and had taken an arts and a commerce degree simultaneously. I prayed that I might do well enough to gain a scholarship too, or failing that my parents might somehow manage the fees. I had also applied to St. Patrick's Training College in Drumcondra for the two-year course to qualify as a primary teacher. And of course like most of my classmates, I'd applied for the civil service, the post office, accountancy firms, and various banks and insurance companies. Unlike many of them, I had no interest in becoming a seminarian. In the intervening years I have often thought that I would have made a reasonably good teacher. The lifestyle appealed to me, and I know that I would have loved imparting knowledge to the young. I suspect too that temperamentally the job would have suited me. In the sense that skills and trades are often passed on from generation to generation within families, I fancy that teaching was probably in my genetic makeup. There were teachers in my background on both the Mulvey and the Corley sides. But with the rashness of youth and in immature retaliation for the hurt he had caused, I turned my back on teaching as a calling to spite my father. When I was offered a place in St. Patrick's College, I refused it. Papa's revenge was swift and unequivocal. I had made my bed and could lie on it. I was free to continue to make my own decisions, but there would be no university course for me.

7

Dublin and the Public service

When I was offered a posting in the civil service, I grabbed it with both hands. I couldn't wait to get away from Kiltyroe and start my new life in Dublin. There I could be independent. I could be my own man away from the stultifying influence and baleful eye of my overbearing father. I'd be free to do as I wished. So I turned my back on my home and with hardly a backward glance shook the dust of the place from my shoes. I was so cheesed off with Papa's treatment of me that I fully intended never to spend another night in Ashdene House. Of course I knew that I'd miss Mama and Constance and that they in turn would miss me. But it would be a complete waste of time trying to explain to Mama how I felt. She would never understand that the James she loved and respected could cause such resentment and frustration in me. As for Constance, she was heartbroken at my decision. On the night before my departure she wept and pleaded with me not to cut myself off completely. In the end I had to promise her that I'd write to her and to Mama, but my mind was made up. Papa and I did not part on good terms. He felt that I was selfish and ungrateful and too big for my boots. He swore that if I wanted independence I was welcome to it, but as far as he was concerned I was no longer welcome in his home, where my name was not to be mentioned ever again in his presence. True to his vow, the morning I left Kiltyroe he refused to appear to bid me farewell. I said my goodbyes hurriedly to Mama, Grandma Maud, Constance, my two younger sisters and Ambrose. Papa's spitefulness actually eased the pain of my departure, as it served to keep my anger aflame. My father's attitude freed me to concentrate on my new life.

Mama had insisted that I would spend my first few nights in Dublin with Michael until I got settled. I was ambivalent about the notion, as over the years we had grown apart. Somehow after Constance's illness we never really connected in the same comfortable brotherly way we had before. After that Michael deliberately distanced himself from both Constance and me. He saw himself as on the side of the adults. He treated Constance like some wounded bird rather than the feisty equal she had been to him. As far as his treatment of me was concerned, he became ever more patronising. In his view he was wiser elder brother to an immature youngster, though there was less than three years between us in age. When he went away to school the gap widened further. The fact that he was dormitory monitor in my first year and therefore in a position of authority over me and my classmates didn't improve matters. At this stage Michael had joined the civil service too. With his two degrees and his excellent results, he had joined as an executive officer, already two steps up the promotional ladder. I, on the other hand, was coming in as a mere clerical officer. Michael was in the Department of Finance which had added cachet in the civil service. In accordance with civil service policy, I would not be working in the same section or even department as my brother. So I had been assigned to the Department of Education. My brother, in accordance with Mama's request, had come to meet me off the bus. It was a little after half past five, and he was on his way home from work. On this beautiful, sunny Autumn evening I was waiting for my brother with my suitcase at my feet, my shirt sleeves rolled up, and my suit jacket across my arm. A tall, slender man in a dark suit, white shirt, and sober tie, wearing a homburg hat and carrying of all things a furled black umbrella was striding towards me. It took me a few seconds to recognise that this was Michael. He looked so like Papa it was eerie and frighteningly pompous and old to me. He greeted me warmly enough before suggesting that I put my jacket on so I might appear less of a ragamuffin on the streets of Dublin. We walked together for more than half an hour, by which time I was well and truly footsore and sweaty. Despite the heat, Michael appeared to be comfortably cool in his executive uniform. We had finally reached Michael's flat in Rathgar. When we arrived I realised that it wasn't a flat as such. Michael and two of his college friends, Don Scott and Fred Ahern, were renting an imposing three-storey house in Kenilworth Square, a leafy suburb in Dublin's south side. Don worked alongside Michael, and Fred had qualified as an architect the previous year. Their landlady lived in a separate flat in the basement. The rooms were beautifully proportioned, and these serious, young, professional men were pleased with their comfortable and roomy accommodation. So that first evening I was warned by all three that the house was to be kept in pristine condition at all times. House rules must be obeyed to the letter and in timely fashion. There was to be absolutely no noise after 10 p.m., and no one could invite guests without first clearing it with the others. They were all very kind about my intrusion, but I already felt in the way. I couldn't wait to find a place of my own and get out of there and let them get on with their lives.

My first day at work flew by in a whirl of introductions to new people and new tasks. The usual mild teasing of new recruits went on in mutually good-natured fashion. I was sent to despatch for purple ink and encouraged to address Miss Curtin by her Christian name, which they assured me she insisted upon. Of course when I called her Annette she looked at me as if I were something unpleasant attached to her shoe. It was only then that I noticed the sniggering and smirking of my fellows. As far as the work went, I was busy and interested in learning, so I was content. Within two weeks of arriving, I had escaped my brother's clutches and was happily sharing a basement flat on the North Circular Road with a happy-go-lucky workmate from Cork called Seán O'Brien. Seán was a caricature of an Irishman in appearance, complete with dancing mischief-filled blue eyes and roaring red corkscrew-curled hair, freckles that pooled in clumps across his cheeks and forehead, and, as he himself described it, a roman nose that roamed all over his face. He was witty, fun, and intelligent, and his madcap good humour was infectious. Within weeks of living with this firework personality I was sleeping the sleep of the just and had almost forgotten what depression felt like. Our days fell into a pattern of work, play, exercise, entertainment, social events, and fun. Arriving back at the flat only when the need for sleep eventually caught up with us, we burned the candle at both ends before falling into exhausted slumber. Then up again next day to repeat the process with variations on the theme of living life to the full and enjoying every second of it. Our only focus outside of work hours was in having as much fun as possible. Over the next two years we went to the cinema, to the theatre, to the pub, and to parties all over the city. We hosted some hilarious parties of our own, and soon we were at the centre of a group of likeminded young men and women filled with the exuberance of youth. When Christmas came I refused to go home to Kiltyroe and was pleasantly surprised when Seán opted to stay in Dublin with me. He laughingly said, 'Home was never like this,' and there was no more discussion about it. With a full week off work, we partied long and slept late. We had a great time, though perhaps we overindulged a little in terms of alcohol consumption and more than a little in terms of food. The mothers of our Dublin friends felt it was their Christian duty not to let these country lads die of hunger. It wasn't long before Michael heard of some of our more hair-raising pranks, and of course he came calling. I was subjected to the usual dressing down so typical of my father that for a second or two I felt that if I closed my eyes Michael would vanish and Papa would appear in his place. Michael droned on about bringing the civil service into disrepute and bringing shame on the Corley name. But when he started on about how ashamed of me Mama would be when he told her what I was up to, I lost my temper and threw him out. I admit my language was intemperate. I remember calling him a sanctimonious bastard, a smug hypocrite and suck-up with a poker up his ass who wouldn't recognise fun if it bit him. Warming to my theme, I roared that he was a pompous prat and a bombastic bully. My final shouted insult was that he was old before his time. It didn't bother me in the slightest that I didn't hear from him again over the next few years. With the selfishness of youth, I was glad to be free of his interference. Looking back now I'm shocked to note that I only ever met him again twice over the next thirty-five years. On both of these occasions we were attending family funerals. The first was Grandma Maud's in 1925. But twelve years later when Papa died, I had refused to go home for his funeral. The second and last time we met coincided with Papa's twenty-fifth anniversary Mass and our sister Hannah's untimely death in 1962.

When our youngest brother, Ambrose, was born, Michael was sixteen years old, Constance was fifteen, and I thought I was fully grown at fourteen. As older boys, Michael and I pretty much ignored the new arrival, who was the centre of attention of all the girls and especially loved by Constance. Over the next several years I was very self-absorbed. School and dreaming about my future occupied all my waking thoughts. Even when on holidays at home I selfishly busied myself with hunting and shooting and other outdoor activities. I continued to spend time with Constance, and we planned and carried out variations on our exercise regime. Little Ambrose was no more than a minor irritant in my busy life. Papa still insisted that we play music together as a family. To tell the truth the whole command performance thing was beginning to get on my nerves. The practising was tedious enough without having to supervise the squawking of Nora and Kitty on their instruments. The last straw as far as I was concerned was the summer I was twenty and I had returned home for Grandma Maud's funeral. When Michael broke the news of

Grandma's death to me by telephone at work, I immediately stated that I had no intention of returning to Kiltyroe, her funeral, or anyone else's. Michael's response was terse.

'Shay, you'll do as you see fit. Going on recent past experience that will be to opt for the easiest and most selfish course of action. I expect nothing more of you, and neither does Papa. I am merely passing on the news. I was about to offer you a lift. But you do whatever the hell you like.'

That same evening Constance rang me on the payphone at the flat. We had a good chat, and she appealed to my better self by reminding me that Papa had lost his beloved mother, so the least I should do was suspend hostilities, if not for his sake, for my own. She also pointed out that our mother, now in the latter stages of her seventh pregnancy, had not only lost her mother-in-law but her closest friend and ally for nearly forty years. She also offered a solution as to where I might stay if and when I returned to Kiltyroe. She and Brendan Walsh had been seeing a lot of each other recently, and he had sensibly suggested that I stay with him while I was home. In the end I had allowed myself to be persuaded. I arranged to travel down with Michael in his brand new Baby Austin on the clear understanding that he would drop me off at Walsh's before proceeding home to Ashdene. Being in Papa's presence was going to be hugely problematic for me, I knew. So I planned to attend the removal that evening and the funeral the following morning. After that it was my intention to head straight back to Dublin and the two whole weeks of holidays stretching out before me. But back in my native place with all the extended family gathered, lots of good food, and plenty to drink, suddenly my need to get away from Kiltyroe wasn't quite as urgent as I had thought. Against my better judgement I had somehow given the impression that I intended to stay on for the remainder of my holidays. Constance told me she was worried about little Ambrose and his violin lessons. She had overheard Papa saying 'I'm thinking of taking over Ambrose's tuition myself. Constance has enough to be doing as it is, and anyway she's making a right Molly of that youngster, spoiling him the way she does.'

'I worry that he'll forbid music in the house for at least a month out of respect for Grandma Maud's memory. By then Ambrose will have lost interest, or worse, he'll be so rusty that Papa won't have the patience to teach him. And really, Shay, the little fellow is quite talented and showing great promise. Please, will you just take over for a few days while I try and work something out. I can get Brendan to bring him over there for an hour or so each day. Please, Shay, if not for my sake, do it for Ambrose. Playing the violin is the only bright spot in an otherwise boring day for the lad. Please.'

I said I'd think about it and later discussed the idea with Mama, who persuaded me to at least give it a try. Over the next several days Brendan brought his young charge over home on one pretext or another. To my surprise Ambrose proved to be a willing pupil. He was also quite adept. He loved to play, didn't mind at all having to practise, and in my view had the makings of a talented musician. Over these days inevitably Ambrose and I became close. The devotion of this lonely little boy was appealing and his wide-eyed admiration touching, but I had to admit I learned as much from him as he did from me. He hadn't a mean bone in his body. He contended stoically with his frequent bouts of ill health. He rarely if ever took offence and was always quick to offer an excuse if Papa was cross or if Mama was distracted or his beloved Constance too preoccupied to pay him the attention he had come to expect. Little did I know then, but after that summer I wouldn't see him again for almost two decades.

8

Dublin and London

On my return to Dublin, Seán and I resumed our hell-raising lifestyle. We partied, danced, drank our fill, went to every event on offer, and loved the traditional music scene. We could be found in the trad pubs and gatherings until the wee small hours, whether impromptu or planned, irrespective of what night of the week they happened. I suppose it was around that time that alcohol began to get its hold on me. Always the life and soul of the party, Seán could enjoy himself with or without alcohol. He would enjoy a pint or two, but then he could happily sip a mineral or drink tea or water for the rest of the long night. I kept pace pint for pint with the best of them and wasn't averse to drinking tots of whiskey when offered it. Things were going fine at work too. The work itself was routine and undemanding, and I managed to keep out of trouble without too much effort. There were times when I was bored, but keeping the show on the road at junior levels in the civil service was easy. There were so many of us drones it would have been almost impossible to draw attention to yourself. This could be achieved in only two ways. Either one was spectacularly ill behaved or outstandingly brilliant. It was common knowledge that the former would bring a much quicker response. As always in large organisations, 'honour among thieves' pertained in the lower echelons. We would all rally round and protect each other as best we could if someone got into a spot of bother. So it was not unknown for people to get away with minor infringements such as tardiness, appearing a little under the weather the morning after the night before. For the most part our bosses turned a blind eye to what they must have known were patent lies, amazing lacks of observation, marvellous feats of communal amnesia, and contradictory versions of cover-up stories. I had become an expert at keeping my nose clean and actually got promoted to staff officer within my first eighteen months in the department. This gave me some added responsibility and a raise in salary but not much else. The work was still unchallenging, the workplace still the same, but now I had a desk at the back of the room beside a window and near a radiator in the huge room where thirty of us bent to our daily Sisyphean tasks. Eventually my luck inevitably ran out. It wasn't that I had slipped up personally, but I could have. I was caught out in a blatant lie, covering up for a colleague who had shown up mid-afternoon too drunk to be hidden from even the most cursory observation. I had taken Jim into the gents' toilet and splashed cold water over his face and neck. Then I had called a taxi, escorted him into it, and sent him home to sleep it off. When about 3.30 I was asked where he was, I had lied and said that he had gone for a very late lunch, as we were busy, knowing full well that he had left the office at 12.30 on the dot.

'Where is Mr. Kelly now, Mr. Corley? I want to see him right away.'

Instead of coming clean of course, I compounded the error by adding more lies to the ever-lengthening list, digging myself into a deeper and deeper hole. My punishment was demotion, effective immediately. The humiliation was public and brutal. By end of day I had to clear my desk and seat myself at the lowliest spot among the recently recruited. Two years after joining the service, I was back exactly where I had started. The final irony was that Jim Kelly was promoted in my stead. On waking the following morning with an horrendous hangover, he had decided to ring in sick. He had told the duty officer that he had got food poisoning from a dodgy sandwich at lunch on the previous day and had gone straight home to bed. His lie had benefitted Kelly, while mine on his behalf had landed me in deep trouble.

My first reaction was one of anger. My second was to press my self-destruct button. I started drinking, I mean serious drinking; actually that was when I started drinking to excess. After a couple of weeks of complete stupidity and pretty continuous intoxication, Seán had had enough. He came to the rescue all guns blazing. He would brook no more nonsense.

'Mr. Corley,' he began, 'this is the day you grow up and learn to be worthy of that title. Somewhere in the last fortnight I've lost my friend Shay. You are just a pathetic imitation of the man I was proud to call my friend. I cannot call you Shay. I cannot bear the sight of you. If you do not cop on and pull yourself together, I am out of here. You do not deserve my friendship. You do not even deserve my sympathy. I've put up with your carry-on for far too long. You now have exactly one week to straighten yourself out. No booze, no belly aching, no smashing up the place. I won't stick around to see the mayhem, but I will check in on you from time to time. This time next Sunday you'll either be clean and sober, in which case we'll talk, or rotting in your own filth and self-pity, in which case I'll leave for good. Best of luck.'

After Seán had gone, I wallowed in misery for a while, alternating between blaming him and feeling sorry for myself, all the while drinking whiskey from a mug. I woke up stretched on the kitchen floor with the empty bottle for company. It was cold and quiet and somewhere in the middle of the night. I crawled into bed. When I woke next it was after ten o'clock on Monday morning. I washed my face and headed upstairs to use the payphone. I cleared my throat and asked to be put through to Mr. Jim Kelly. I had just started to speak when he interrupted me

'Shay, there's no need for you to explain. Seán was on to me first thing. He tells me you have a serious dose of flu and not to expect you at work for at least a week. You'll need a doctor's cert of course. Now get back to bed like a good man.'

I stood staring for several long moments at the earpiece in my hand still emitting the lonesome sound of disconnected bleeps. Returning to the flat, I made myself a pot of tea and sat at the table smoking and sipping tea while reviewing the last few weeks. I thought about what Seán had said and concluded that he was absolutely right. I vowed to turn my life around. I started straight away. I cleaned and scrubbed the flat from top to bottom. I dumped an obscene amount of booze bottles of various shapes and sizes. The vast majority of them were empties, but a surprising amount were either full, as in out-of-date beer bottles, or contained different levels of dregs of all kinds of alcohol in an assortment of spirit bottles. By the time the place was clean enough to meet the standards of the most exacting of inspections,

I was exhausted. I made a sandwich with what remained in the larder, boiled milk on the electric ring, and made myself a cup of cocoa before retiring for the night. When I got up the following morning, it was late. I'd fallen into a deep sleep early on but had wakened about 3 a.m. feeling horrible. I was cold to the marrow of my bones. My entire body shook and shivered, my teeth chattering in my head, and all I wanted was a drink. When I realised there was not a drop of booze in the house, I was not best pleased. I had to make do with drinking copious amounts of water to deal with the delirium tremens, or the DTs as it was commonly known. When eventually I fell into an exhausted slumber, I was disturbed by nightmares as well as itching and scratching. I was still dehydrated on waking, and by then I was hungry too. I went in search of food and drink and managed to resist the temptation to head for the nearest early house. Returning home with my shopping, I made myself something to eat and drank lots of tea. I read the paper and did the crossword and wondered how I'd put down the rest of the day without going mad. I was afraid to venture outdoors for two reasons: one, I might be spotted when I was on sick leave and reported on, but even more worrying, my resolve to keep away from the pub might weaken. I really do not know how I survived the rest of that week, but the first few days were the hardest. In desperation and to relieve the boredom, I got in touch with the landlord and asked if I could undertake the rewallpapering of the living room that he had proposed. He was pleased with the offer of free labour, and later that Tuesday evening he brought over seven rolls of wallpaper and paste along with a bucket and brushes. I set to straight away. I went to bed in the early hours of the morning, slept like a log, and got up the following morning eager to get on with the project. I was still hard at it when Seán appeared to check on me on Wednesday evening. He stayed a while, and together we put up the border. I thanked him for his help, but he left soon after. Neither of us made any reference to the reason for his visit. I didn't want to raise the subject, and I imagine that Seán was equally reluctant to talk about it for fear of jinxing my efforts. When he returned on Sunday I had made the newly decorated room shipshape and the rest of the flat equally clean and tidy. I had dressed myself neatly and looked rested, if a little grey in the face. I'd fallen off the wagon on Friday night and had a skinful in a grotty pub in Smithfield. Saturday morning was a memory I was trying hard to erase. But I'd spent the rest of the day putting the flat to rights, and with the help of what felt like several gallons of black tea, I was hoping to pass Seán's scrutiny undetected. Things went well at first. Seán seemed pleased to see me. He commended me on how the place was looking and joked that I didn't look so bad myself. He agreed to move back in with me on condition that I stayed off the booze. He explained that in his view, social drinking was no longer an option for me.

'Shay, you have to accept that you are a drunk. You are well on the way to becoming an alcoholic. See it this way: booze is a poison for you. If you drink, you do not know how to stop. Your only option is not to touch the stuff. You can have a good time without it. I'll tell you what we'll do. We'll both give it up. Why don't we join the musicians rather than just watch them? I know you can play loads of instruments, and though I'm not up to much I have a good sense of rhythm and can play the bodhrán and the spoons if they'll have me. But I'm warning you now: one slip, and I'm out of your life for good. I mean it, Shay. This is your last chance.'

I was grateful to Seán though peeved that he had turned on me, maybe a little ashamed too that he had assumed the role of adult to me as child. The upshot was that I took on board his offer and his conditions and got myself back on track. Soon after, Seán got transferred to the Department of External Affairs on promotion. His new and exciting job brought him extra money, extra responsibility, and extra status. It also meant that a good deal of his work involved late meetings, and he was away from Dublin a lot. Meanwhile I was working hard to recover lost ground in the Department of Education and feeling that I wasn't getting anywhere. Over a late breakfast one Saturday morning, I mentioned my frustration to Seán, who immediately suggested that I should apply for a transfer to another department. I took his advice and within a few weeks found myself moving to the Department of Lands as an executive officer (EO). It was now almost a year since I had given up alcohol. I was very pleased with myself having beaten the demon drink and recovered my place on the promotional ladder.

Over the following months I was more that contented with my life, both socially and professionally. Seán and I had joined a group of trad musicians as planned. Soon we were regulars on the circuit, especially at weekends, and thoroughly enjoying ourselves. Our favourite haunt was a pub called The Dog and Duck not far from The Five Lamps, where we could be found whenever we didn't have a gig elsewhere. I soon got used to staying in the company of the tea and mineral drinkers. Playing an instrument made it easier of course. Having both hands occupied for the bulk of the evening put drinking anything in its proper subordinate place. Seán continued to play with us, his enthusiasm more than compensating for any perceived lack of skill. About this time Kieran Halligan, the guitar player, started to bring his twenty-year-old daughter, Helen, along to the sessions. Helen was a beauty. She had a little heart-shaped, elfin face; the palest of alabaster skin; and long, wavy tresses of blue-black hair. She was shy and retiring, but it didn't take Seán long to bring her out of herself and encourage her to join in the talk. Inevitably she fell under his spell. But Seán had already lost his heart to someone else and didn't see the effect he was having on Helen. He often referred to his beloved Alice, but Helen clung to her mistaken notion that he was referring to his sister. Kieran was pleased that Helen was having some attention from young men of her own age. At a celebratory evening for her father's birthday, we heard her play the mandolin for the first time. She was an accomplished player who could draw tears from a stone with the sensitivity with which she played her hauntingly beautiful slow tunes. Soon afterwards we were able to persuade her that she should join the group. With Kieran's encouragement, she did, and we all felt that her contribution to the group enhanced our appeal. Seán's increased workload, especially his need to attend meetings late in the evenings and other new duties, made his attendance at sessions less dependable, and over time I found myself heading out on my own more and more. If I was ever tempted to have a drink, fear of Seán's disapproval was still sufficient even in his absence. The music and the company of musicians continued to be my lifeline. As well as that, I had begun to harbour feelings of more than affection for Helen. But poor Helen was broken-hearted at the loss of Seán's company. My work in the new department was more challenging, and on the whole I found my workmates more congenial. The atmosphere was less formal than in education, and our work spaces less regimented and less crowded. My transition from one government department to another was further eased when I found myself working side by side with Niall Finn. Niall and I had joined the service on the same day and had worked together during the first six months of our probationary period. During those early days we had become friends but had lost touch in the interim. Now we were both EOs in the same section.

When Seán O'Brien got a posting abroad, leaving me without a flatmate, it seemed only natural to ask Niall if he'd like to share with me on the North Circular Road. We got on very well together, and shortly after he had moved in, Niall got into the habit of coming with me to the music sessions. He loved the trad scene but didn't play any instrument. He had a good tenor voice and was happy to sing a song at the drop of a hat. Niall also loved his pint, or more accurately his pints of porter. We came to the sessions together and went home in each other's company, but Niall sat with the pint and whiskey drinkers, while I tried to make myself of some interest to Helen.

She had become increasingly withdrawn after Seán left, and I knew her dad was very worried about her. One evening he arrived at The Dog and Duck alone, and when I enquired after her, Kieran broke down and confided in me. His lovely Helen suffered from depression. She had lost her mother when she was only twelve years old, and since then he had done his best at parenting her alone. She had been hospitalised for several months in her leaving cert year. He had taken to bringing her to the sessions quite simply because he was afraid to leave her at home alone. She seemed to enjoy being in his company and shared his love of music. Since Seán and I had joined the group she had become much more interested in accompanying him to the sessions. At first Kieran was delighted, especially when she had agreed to play with us. During this period, she was at her happiest since her mother's death, he said. But sadly she was taking her disappointment at Seán's departure very hard indeed. Earlier that day he had had the unenviable task of committing his beloved daughter to the psychiatric ward of St. Anselm's Hospital. I volunteered to visit her, and over the next several weeks I did so religiously. Helen's moods swung alarmingly from euphoric to catatonic. I never knew which Helen I would find. When she was in good form, I dared to hope that she thought kindly of me, at least as a friend. But when she was down, it was impossible to get a word out of her. As the lazy days of summer began to cool towards autumn, it was decided that Helen should be discharged. I accompanied Kieran to the hospital to help him bring home Helen's possessions, which had been accumulating in her locker for over three months. She appeared in good spirits, and as her dad and I packed her stuff into various bags she seemed chatty enough. We walked to their home in the cool of evening. I stayed a while and then returned to my own place. Two evenings later I got a phone call from a distraught Kieran. He'd only nipped to the shop for milk, and on his return he had found his lovely Helen had hanged herself from the banisters. I rushed around to the hospital where they had taken her. Kieran had aged by ten years since I'd last seen him. He was traumatised. Of course he blamed himself. He was inconsolable. I will never forget his grief. It was like watching someone physically disintegrate before your very eyes. On that first awful evening I sought out the company of Niall, having failed to get hold of Seán O'Brien. Niall was upset by the news of Helen's death but unprepared for how badly it was affecting me. His solution to the problem of my devastation was to drag me to the pub and try to soften the pain with alcohol. I was too overcome to protest and grateful for the anaesthetic effect of the whiskey.

The next few days until the funeral was over were a living hell. I went through the motions of getting up going to work, surviving the day, and drinking myself into near stupor at night. Despite my best efforts, I couldn't make contact with Seán. I wanted to share my grief with him. After all, my best memories of Helen were linked with him. Knowing him as a compassionate and warm-hearted friend, I was convinced he'd be as shattered by the news as I was. At first I thought he must be out of the country and not getting my messages. I heard nothing from him in those early days. He failed to appear at the removal. I craned my neck looking for him in the church and later in the graveyard afterwards, but there was no sign of him. Later as I returned home on the bus I thought I caught a glimpse of him sheltering in the doorway of a pub in Phibsboro but dismissed the notion as a figment of my fevered imagination. Later Niall and I went to The Dog and Duck to be with the group and offer some support to Kieran. Sitting with a large group of his friends in the corner furthest from the musicians was Seán. I approached the noisy group with an outstretched hand, pleased to see my friend even at this late hour, assuming he was here to sympathise with Kieran. He remained seated, and when I asked him if he'd got my messages he denied it. I hurriedly explained that Helen Halligan had been buried earlier that day. He looked shifty and dismissing me with a wave of his hand said 'Okay, okay, Shay, I'll be over later to sympathise with Mr. Halligan.' Almost everyone in the pub was there as a mark of respect for Helen and to help her grieving father by sharing their tributes to her with him. The noisy group in the corner lent a jarring note to the otherwise muted atmosphere. As they got more and more drunk and raucous, I glanced over and noticed that Seán O'Brien had slipped away from their company. He had also left the pub without talking to Kieran or me for that matter. I was flabbergasted. How could it be that he was so unfeeling? I have no memory whatever of how I got home that night. All I can say is it was a good thing that when I finally came to the following day, I was relieved to discover it was Sunday and not Monday.

Over the next weeks I did my best to ease Kieran's indescribable pain by visiting, but in the end I think I was not particularly helpful. Perhaps my youth was too much of a reminder for him of what he had lost. For me this was yet another failure to add to my already long list of failures. Seán's inexplicable behaviour, my increasing dependence on alcohol, and grieving for the loss of Helen and what might have been pushed me towards the edge of the precipice. By now I had reached the point of no return and was well down the slippery slope to depression. Shortly afterwards things became seriously problematic for me at work. It was only matter of time until I'd be fired, and deservedly. I really didn't care, and so I resigned abruptly from the civil service. I knew I couldn't survive very long in Dublin without drawing shame on all who knew me, and so I fled to the anonymity of London.

Within weeks I had drunk all my savings and had become a derelict, sleeping rough and cadging the price of a drink wherever I could. At my lowest ebb I was rescued by the Salvation Army and brought to a shelter. There I was dried out and was lucky enough to be given a second chance. A benefactor who chose to remain anonymous kept an eye on my recovery, and when I was well enough he sent around a friend of his to interview me. This friend, Mr Brian Greene, turned out to be a very successful businessman with huge experience in recruiting, promoting, and developing personnel in a wide variety of working environments. It didn't take him long to extract the whole sorry story from me. He was a skilled listener, and slowly but surely he not only elicited from me all the details of my former employment but also shrewdly interpreted the underlying causes of my angst and my breakdown. He quizzed me about my skills, forcing me to concentrate on what went well at work and how I had handled a series of challenging situations. Having satisfied himself on these matters, he asked me who in the civil service would be most likely to give me an unbiased and usable reference. He visited every day, and we went on long walks together. Over these sessions he had quietly built up my confidence. Within a few weeks he had secured a decent reference for me and set up an interview in the British civil service. Appreciative of the efforts of Brian and my unknown benefactor, I welcomed the opportunity offered and determined not to let them down. I missed my mother's wisdom and her unflinching faith in me and wished that I could talk to her. For the first time in ages I prayed for a good outcome. The interview went very well, and I was offered a post at executive officer level in the Department of Justice. When I shared the good news with Brian he insisted on taking me out for a celebratory dinner to his gentleman's club. In the course of the meal he congratulated me on my success on his own part and on behalf of his friend. He and his friend would continue to support me, he said, but on one condition. I must seek professional help for my drinking problem. It was not an insurmountable problem, and in his experience many people lived healthy and fulfilling lives as 'recovering alcoholics'.

Then he took me by surprise, saying, 'Shay, don't doubt me. I know what I'm talking about. I'm one. Now back to you. We do not want to interfere in your life, so how you proceed from here is up to yourself. If, on the other hand, you'd like some help, I can recommend a sponsor for you.'

I will never forget the kindness of these two strangers, who continued to be part of my life for almost twenty years. It was a good life. With their support and encouragement, I prospered. By dint of good advice and example, I rose steadily within the ranks of the civil service. I enjoyed my work. It was stimulating and satisfying. Above all it was regimented, and I now fully appreciated the value of an orderly existence. I avoided pubs. I even gave up going to music sessions, for fear of being led into temptation. Instead I focused on my career, and in my spare time I went to the theatre, the opera, and the philharmonic. I could laugh at myself for becoming what the locals at home would consider a 'toff'. In an effort to repay my benefactor, I joined Brian Greene in offering my time and expertise to a long list of people in need. I never got to the bottom of how our mysterious benefactor continued to find his endless supply of 'lame ducks', waifs, strays, down-and-outs, alcoholics, homeless kids, bums, and unfortunates. They came in all shapes and sizes, from all backgrounds and nations. The only thing they had in common was that they were down on their luck. Some just needed a cash injection, others a listening ear, others still medical attention. They all needed someone to care about them. Unfortunately it was too late for some. I speak of the suicides. Others couldn't help themselves and bit the hand that fed them, stealing and vandalising. Our benefactor turned no one away. He died penniless. After his death, Brian and I and many others tried to continue his work, but eventually without his guiding influence the organisation such as it was fell apart. I continued providing support and assistance to my junior colleagues at work, and this filled the gap for a time. Because I had been lucky enough to be welcomed into the civil service, I was always encouraging of applicants from Ireland and indeed from other nationalities who wished to avail of the opportunities the service offered. This is how I met Robert Fitzmaurice.

PART III

9

Robert's Story

Robert Fitzmaurice would always remember in the most precise detail the day he left Kiltyroe. Every second and nuance of that long-ago day was imprinted on his memory as a tattoo penetrates deep under the skin. He seldom allowed these painful memories to intrude nowadays, though occasionally they leaked through in his dreams. In the thirty-two years since that horrible day, he had never been back to Ireland, nor had he ever considered setting foot there again. But this morning's post had delivered a sucker punch from which he doubted he'd ever recover. Robert, or Fizz as he was known to his friends, had awakened as usual at 6.29 in his fashionable Knightsbridge apartment. As always, he waited for the seconds to tick down until his electronic alarm began to buzz sonorously. Then he reached across, pressed the off button, and in one smooth movement swung his feet onto the floor and headed for his state-of-the-art bathroom. After his shower, he dressed in the suit, shirt, and tie he had carefully laid out the night before. Then, after selecting a pair of black socks from the plethora of identical pairs nestling together in his neat sock drawer, he slipped his feet into his highly polished neat black loafers and made his way to the kitchen.

Once in his galley kitchen, he squeezed a couple of large oranges with the aid of his electric juicer. He switched on his espresso machine, which he knew would produce a perfect demitasse in the short interval it would take for him to drink his glass of orange juice. As was his wont, he had kept an ear out for the arrival of his post, which varied by only seconds from day to day. He always got a small kick out of timing it just right so that he could open the door as the postman was about to stoop to the floor-level letter box. Thus he would spare the poor man the uncomfortable crouch and greet him with a smile and set a happy tone for both his own and the postman's day. He had timed it just perfectly this morning too.

'Good Morning, sir, lovely day by the look of it. Letter for you from the Emerald Isle today it seems. Hope all is well over there. Imagine in all the years I've known you, I never realised you had Irish connections. Here you go, sir.'

Glancing at the bundle of post in his hand, Robert backed hurriedly into the still-open doorway of his apartment.

'Thank you, er … Postie,' he stammered, a livid blush staining his cheeks as the postman walked away. He knew the day was ruined as soon as he saw the postage stamp on the letter, even before the postman's comment had had time to register. He gazed for the longest time at the Irish stamp, his mind lost in the past. Eventually shaking himself out of his stupor, he focused on the postmark. Noting how his hand trembled and his knees threatened to buckle under his weight, he staggered to the nearest armchair and sank gratefully into it. His eyes were not deceiving him; the postmark was definitely from Kiltyroe. But since his departure, he had never received any post from the village of his birth. He had learned of the deaths of his estranged parents from his friend Shay Corley, also domiciled in

London. He racked his brains to help him figure out who could possibly be writing to him from Kiltyroe. Since the death of his mother, ten years earlier, he didn't have a living relative in Kiltyroe, as he was the only child of parents who had no siblings. He was amazed at how distressed the arrival of this unexpected letter had made him. All thoughts of going out were now banished. He didn't even think to cancel appointments or let his secretary or colleagues know he wouldn't be coming to work today. He looked at the letter with dread. He couldn't help feeling that it would bring grief in its wake. He stared at it with trepidation, convinced that he could sense malevolence emanating from it. He just couldn't bring himself to open it. He put it aside and paced the floor for some time. He tried to distract himself by making tea. He sat staring out at his panoramic view and sipping the scalding tea in an effort to postpone the inevitable. Then suddenly he jumped to his feet, grabbed his overcoat, and fled from the comfort of his home and the letter which was threatening his composure. Once outside, he realised how cold the morning was and immediately regretted rushing out without a scarf or gloves. He noted also that the sky was overcast and knew that it wouldn't be long before the glowering clouds would begin to discharge their load of miserable sleety rain. He continued to walk onwards, oblivious of his surroundings. When the rain began in earnest he glanced about and discovered that he was only a few blocks from where he worked. He turned up his collar and hurried onwards towards his office.

On arrival Robert was greeted by anxious workmates and a very relieved Clara Tilsley, the firm's ultra-efficient legal secretary. They had all been surprised that he hadn't arrived as usual a little after 7.30. By the time the 8.00 meeting was over and he still hadn't shown up, they were getting concerned. By 8.45, before the offices opened to the public, Clara could stand it no longer. She rang his apartment, but the call went straight to answering service. She broke the connection, and by now she was seriously worried. Over the next several minutes she had tried his number over and over to no avail. Eventually she left a message.

'Robert, Clara here. It's a little after nine o'clock. Will you please let me know where you are and why you are not answering your phone, as soon as you get this message?'

When she had heard nothing by ten o' clock, she made her way reluctantly to the managing director's office. She knocked gingerly, and when requested to enter, she poked her head around the door.

'I'm so sorry to disturb you, Mr Morton. Robert hasn't arrived this morning, and he is not answering his phone either. I'm very worried about him. You know how reliable he is.

He has never been late for work a day in his life. If he were ill he would surely have let us know. I'm concerned that something untoward has happened to him.'

'Clara, this panic is most unlike you. Perhaps his alarm failed to go off. Robert is not getting any younger. Maybe he just fancied a lie in for a change. Don't worry. He'll show up. Meanwhile there isn't much else we can do, is there? Now stop fussing. You'll see Robert will be as right as rain.'

Clara hurried back to her desk. She had a bad feeling about this, so she dialled Robert's home once more and waited. The phone continued to ring out. She tried it again and again, but each time it just rang out. Just then she heard a commotion outside her office and, rushing outside, was delighted to see Robert surrounded by his colleagues. He was wearing a heavy wool overcoat, which was soaking wet. His bare head was drenched, and his damp face was grey and sweating. He looked not at all well and most unlike his usual dapper self. Clara rushed forward to relieve him of his sopping coat and to offer coffee or tea. Mr Morton suddenly appeared rubbing his hands together and saying, 'There you are, Robert. You've given us all quite a fright this morning. Clara, two coffees to my office now, please. The rest of you, please return to your work. Robert, I've just the thing to put in our coffees to warm us up on this miserable morning.'

A half hour later Robert reappeared and, making his way to his desk, got on with his work as if nothing had happened. Later as they were leaving, Robert surprised his younger colleagues by joining them for a few Friday night drinks before heading home. They were all curious about his late arrival that morning, but Robert now appeared in good form, and as he volunteered no explanation, no one dared ask for one. One by one their colleagues drifted away until only Robert and Clara remained in the bar.

'Robert, it's time for me to go too. Can I give you a lift home?'

'No thanks, Clara. I'll just have one more, and then I'll go. Goodnight, my dear, and thanks for the company. See you Monday.'

'I don't like leaving you here like this, Robert. You've had rather more than enough wine already. I'll only worry about how you'll get home if I go now. Please, it's no bother. Please let me drop you off on my way home?'

'I'm so sorry to have delayed you, Clara. I shouldn't have presumed on your good nature. You've been a good friend to me as well as an excellent work colleague. You have a life of your own and shouldn't be stuck here with an old fellow like me. If the truth be told I've been putting off going home. I'll be all right now. I promise you I'll get a taxi home later. There's no reason for you to delay any longer or to bother your pretty head about me. I may be old and cowardly, but I'm neither foolish nor foolhardy. Off with you now, my dear and thank you for your concern. I'll see you at work on Monday as usual. Goodnight, Clara. Have a safe journey home.'

Next morning Robert woke with a splitting headache. He knew it was late by the quality of light from the window. It took a while for him to realise where he was. Then, moving his head as gently as possible so as not to reactivate the little demons that were busily cracking open his skull with their jackhammers, he noticed that he had failed to close his bedroom curtains the night before. He crawled carefully out of bed and made his way gingerly to the bathroom. After spending twenty minutes under the shower, he was beginning to feel a little more human; so he got dressed and headed for the kitchen. The letter stared accusingly at him from the kitchen counter, where he had abandoned it more than twenty-four hours earlier. He backed away, filled the kettle, and while waiting for it to boil, decided that he should ring Clara. He thought he should let her know that he had arrived home safely. There was no answer, so he assumed she was happily engaged in her Saturday morning tasks and not bothering about him. Then he heard his doorbell and, as if he had conjured her up, heard Clara's voice.

'Good morning, Robert. I'm heavily laden. Will you open your door please? Your doorman kindly let me in when I explained I was on a mission of mercy.'

Robert did as suggested and found a smiling Clara on his doorstep carrying two takeaway cappuccinos and a bag of what smelt suspiciously like freshly baked croissants. He welcomed her inside and ushered her into the kitchen, where she proceeded to unpack what were indeed croissants, and a nice variety of them at that. He handed her a large plate and then, setting two places at the counter, he decanted the cappuccinos into tall, fine bone china beakers, and invited her to sit down. Settling happily in front of the impromptu breakfast, Clara apologised for the intrusion. In some confusion, Robert realised that in all the years he had known Clara, he had never invited her to his apartment. He felt uncomfortably churlish at the realisation. Blushing, he made an apology of his own. As they ate and drank, the letter on the counter kept drawing Robert's eye, until he finally felt obliged to remove its malevolent presence from his sight. But Clara had noticed his sideways glances, and when he bent to remove the letter, she stayed his hand.

'I suspect this letter is what has upset you, Robert. I couldn't help seeing the postmark; it's from home, isn't it? Don't you think it's high time you shared your burden with someone? I'm not suggesting that it should be me. What about confiding in a friend, maybe that chap you're so fond of, Shay Corley isn't it, could help? Or I can recommend a good counsellor if you'd prefer. I just hate to see you like this.'

She helped him to an armchair, and patting his shoulder, she seated herself opposite on the sofa. Robert carefully placed the letter on the coffee table between them. Then, shrugging his shudders away, he started to talk. He continued in a slow, low monotone for the next hour or more.

'Clara, this is hard for me. You and I have known each other now for nearly twenty years. When you came to work at Mortons, you were only a teenager, and I was already a settled old geezer in my forties. Even then you were a kindly soul; but you were young, and I didn't expect you to give the likes of me the time of day, never mind offer the hand of friendship. From the beginning I've always considered you my friend, but it is only now that I realise that I've not been as good a friend to you. Cripes! I've never even invited you to my home before. I've deliberately kept you at a distance. Heck, I've pushed you away time after time! But only because I couldn't bear the thought of you turning your back on me once you'd realised what I am. I'm just a miserable coward, you see. I've been blind and selfish too. I didn't give you credit for the kind of person you are. I've become so used to being rejected that I've forgotten how to trust people. I'm now as bad as the homophobes and the racists in that I've turned my self-hatred into rejection of others. I am truly sorry, Clara. By the way, when did you discover I was gay?'

'Oh! Fizz, Fizz, you silly, darling man, what a crazy question. I always knew. From the very first time I set eyes on you. Why are you so defensive, Robert? What has happened to you to make you so fearful and full of self-loathing? Sure you can no more control being gay than I can help being straight. It's as mad to blame yourself for that as it is to hate yourself for being short rather than tall. Come here and give me a hug, you daft happ'orth.'

After a very awkward attempt at an embrace, they both sat down again with some relief, and Robert resumed his story.

'Clara, my dear you can have no idea what life was like in rural Ireland in the 1940s. The Catholic Church held the Irish people in thrall. Being gay was not just considered an aberration; it was also a mortal sin. It was not just the behaviour of gays that was condemned but their very being. A suspicion of being gay was enough to have one 'read from the altar'. I was an only child of older and indulgent parents. I know I was considered a bit of a mammy's boy by the local lads. This idea no doubt stemmed from the fact that I did not attend the local school. Instead I travelled away from the village to where my parents, Frank and Eliza Fitzmaurice, taught in a little rural two-teacher school some three miles' distance from our home. Despite that my childhood and primary schooldays were very happy ones. I must have been about twelve years old when I first heard the term 'nancy boy'. If I had any doubts that this was anything other than a pejorative term, the pelting of stones which accompanied the name-calling quickly dispelled them. The next few years were no picnic, believe me. As soon as I enrolled in secondary school, the tormenting began in earnest. Not a day went by when I wasn't bullied, ridiculed, or worse. There was no one to turn to. Some of the teachers were as homophobic as the boys. After several beatings, I learned to defend myself. I became quite handy with my fists. I was reasonably safe while the attacks remained one on one. But when boys find a victim who fights back, they rarely play by the rules. I tried to vary my homeward routes and times, but still I got waylaid and beaten up by pairs and groups on a fairly regular basis. All this time my parents chose to ignore the fact that I frequently returned from school bloodied and dishevelled. The only comment ever made was a terse comment from my mother, threatening that if I didn't stop scrapping, she would "cease to replace items of uniform, and I could go to school in the rags I appeared to prefer". As time passed, I noticed that both my parents grew colder and more distant towards me, as if they saw me only as a trial to their Christian patience. Eventually I joined the local boxing club, not because I had any interest in pugilism as such but as a means of self-preservation. Anyway, one way or another I survived secondary school. I was a good student, and I loved learning. Being a loner probably helped me to focus better and so I excelled at exams. At seventeen I left school with an excellent academic record and no social skills whatsoever. Neither had I any clue what I wanted to do with the rest of my life. The day the leaving certificate results came out, I went to the school for the last time. I picked up my envelope and went outside to open it. I had achieved over 90 per cent in all seven subjects I had studied. No one spoke to me, nor did I talk to anyone. I went home to share my good news with my mam and dad. On approaching the family home, I noticed both my parents watching me from the front window. When they saw me turn in at the gateway, they came to the front door and ushered me into the sitting room. Here they stood with their backs to the fireplace and without preamble mother said,

"Robert, I see you've collected your leaving cert results and no doubt they are as good as you expected. Your father and I feel that the best thing all around would be for you to leave home immediately. You must know that Kiltyroe is no place for the likes of you. I've packed your bag for you and your father has put some money in an envelope to get you started wherever you end up. Your dad and I will get on with our lives here as best we can. We wish you well and hope you will be successful in your future, but we cannot condone or forgive you for what you are. We've decided not to say another word about it, on the basis that least said soonest mended. We do not expect to see you ever again. We hope you will respect our feelings by not entering into any correspondence with us. The time is now 11 o'clock; you'll make the 11.30 bus to Dublin if you leave now. God bless and keep you safe, son."

'She then pointed to my bag and, turning on her heel, headed back to the kitchen and her household chores. My father then handed me the envelope, awkwardly hugged me, and with the glitter of unshed tears in his eyes bade me goodbye. I found myself retracing my steps to the gate within minutes of my return home. In my left hand I was clutching two envelopes, one containing my unshared exam results and the other an unknown sum of money. In my right hand I had a bag, the contents of which were as yet a mystery to me. My heart was bursting with misery and rejection and my head was throbbing with shock and bewilderment. I have no idea how I got there and no memory whatever of buying a ticket, but somehow I found myself on the bus to Dublin. Later the same day I made my way to the North Wall and onto the mail boat, and by the following morning I had arrived here in London.'

Clara looked sympathetically at him and, taking his hands in hers, said, 'Oh! Robert, you poor thing! You must have been devastated. Did you ever reconcile with your parents? Oh my God, is that letter from them? I'm sorry for interrupting; please go on with your story.'

'Okay! At first I didn't know which end of me was up. But I knew that two hundred pounds wouldn't last very long in London in 1942, even though it was a sizeable amount for my parents to have saved in Kiltyroe. So I buried the hurt as deeply as I could, pretended to myself that I didn't care about my parents' rejection, and swore I'd never set foot in Ireland again. More than that, I promised myself that I would lose the accent, the language nuances and any identifiable marks of Irishness as quickly as possible. I had enough problems in this alien place without inviting anti-Irish prejudice. But first I must get a job. I presented myself for interview for recruitment to His Majesty's civil service. The chairman of my interview board set me at ease straightaway by welcoming me in an accent so similar to my own that for a second it crossed my mind that he might be mimicking me. The interview proceeded and I had no problem answering any of the questions put to me. Just before ushering me out, the chairman thanked me for coming and explained that I'd hear from the board within a few days, before adding, "Well, Mr Fitzmaurice, I bet you didn't expect that anyone here would know where you hail from. Believe it or not I'm from Kiltyroe only a stone's throw from where your family lives in Knocknashee. My name is James Corley, though I prefer to be called Shay. You must know my family. My mother, Florrie, and my sister Constance and her husband, Brendan Walsh, all live in Ashdene House."

'Within two weeks I was employed as an executive officer in the British Department of Justice. I had landed a fine, pensionable position in a venerable institution. I was on a good salary, with prospects of further education and promotion to look forward to. As soon as autumn came, I attended language classes and even took acting lessons in an effort to reinvent myself. I wanted to leave all vestiges of my past behind me as thoroughly as possible. In that at least I appear to have been successful. I managed to fool a smart girl like you, now didn't I?'

'I'll grant you that, Robert. I didn't even know you'd worked in the public sector. Shows how much I know. But please go on; I'm fascinated,' said Clara.

'I believe that I owe a lot to Shay Corley' continued Robert. 'He was an excellent and motivating boss and in time proved to be a good friend. He was the fairest person I ever met. He couldn't bear injustice of any kind. He was also incredibly intelligent, a fact that he tried hard to hide behind a façade of banter and devilment. Aside from all that he was brilliant company, full of wit and wisdom. If he had a fault it was that he had no patience with what he considered to be unnecessary red tape and had a tendency to let his heart rule his head. After I started working with him I felt I had to fill him in on the circumstances of my departure from Kiltyroe in order to prevent him asking me for home news. He was warmly understanding and very discreet. It was he who first suggested that I study law and he supported me in my self-improvement efforts, even though it saddened him that I could take no pride in being Irish. He was always in my corner and ensured that the workplace at least was a safe environment for a young, gay loner with issues. Even after he had left the department he kept a look out for me. When I told him that I had been passed over again and again for promotion, he encouraged me to move into the private sector. When I did eventually do that, I found, as he had predicted, that in the main people were less prejudiced. I wish I knew what became of him. I only met up with him a few times since I joined Morton's thirty years ago. On two of these occasions we met at his request, in order for him to break the news to me of the deaths of my parents. The last time we met was a chance meeting at Euston Station almost eight years ago. I was on my way back from a conference in Scotland, and he was rushing to catch a train to Holyhead. Shay was on his way home to Ireland for a family reunion. He was ill- dressed and in a hurry, and despite his promise to contact me on his return, I haven't heard from him since. The last I heard, he had fallen on hard times, and no one seems to know where he disappeared to. How selfish have I been? I've made no effort to find him.'

Here Robert paused, lost in thought. Clara was unwilling to break the spell and equally reluctant to intrude on his privacy. She crept quietly to the kitchen, where she put on the kettle for a welcome cup of tea. Glancing at the clock, she was surprised to see that well over three hours had elapsed since her arrival with the coffee. It was now almost two o'clock, and Robert had been talking all that time. Returning with the tea, she found Robert still in a brown study but looking a little less fraught. She handed him a cup and, seating herself again, sipped her own tea.

'You must be exhausted after all the talking, Fizz. Are you feeling any better? I wondered if we should have a bite to eat. I could rustle up something from your larder if you'd like, or maybe we could order something in. Or how about a breath of fresh air? We could walk to the café on the corner.'

'No, no, my dear, you have wasted quite enough of your Saturday on a pathetic old man. I cannot hold you any longer. Clara, my dear, I am more than grateful for your kindness and especially for your sympathetic listening to my ramblings. But most of all let me thank you so sincerely for your lovely company. Bless you for the pick-me-up; I'll be all right now.'

'Whatever you say, Fizz. I'll just finish my tea, and I'll leave you in peace. I hope it's been a help to talk it out, and thank you for trusting me with your story. You know that you can depend on me not to breach a confidence. But before I go, are you sure you don't want to open this letter you've been avoiding?'

'Oh God, I'd actually forgotten it for a moment. Okay, you're right again, my dear. There's no time like the present. Let's do it right now.'

Robert grabbed the letter and ripped it open. He unfolded the single sheet of paper, searching for clues as to who it might be from. He was surprised to find that the letter was handwritten, in an elegant if somewhat old-fashioned style. On closer perusal he saw that the top right-hand corner bore the address Ashdene House, Kiltyroe, Knocknashee, County Clare. He recognised it as the Corley's address, and examining the signature, he was able to decipher the name Constance Walsh. It took him a couple of seconds to register that Constance was Shay Corley's sister. He read.

H.A. McHugh

Ashdene House,
Kiltyroe,
Knocknashee,
County Clare.
25/10/1966

Dear Mr Fitzmaurice,

Forgive me for me for taking the liberty of writing to you. Believe me when I say I would not have dared intrude if I weren't absolutely desperate. I have not heard from Shay in over two months. He has not always been the most reliable of correspondents, but since our beloved Hannah's untimely death eight years ago, he hasn't been late with his fortnightly missive home, not even once.

I was concerned about his health, as I felt he wasn't himself when he was home last summer, but thought it might just be a recurrence of his 'old trouble'. I've written three times to the last address he gave me, and I haven't heard from him. I am now frantic with worry.

You, Robert, are the only friend from his London life he has ever mentioned to me or to our mother as far as I know. You were so thoughtful as to send a Mass card on Hannah's death, and that's how I had your address. At the time I wanted to write to thank you, but Shay advised against it, as you had broken all ties with Kiltyroe. I wondered if, for his sake if not mine, you would be so kind as to call around to Apartment 1, 47 Whetstone Square South, Holborn, WC2A and check on him please.

I will be forever in your debt.

Yours sincerely,
Constance Walsh

Robert passed the letter over to Clara and sat down with a sigh. On the one hand he was relieved and on the other amazed at the turn of events. He couldn't explain why exactly he had been so fearful of the letter, but now that he knew what it contained he could relax. Constance's request was after all a reasonable one and of course he would comply with it as quickly as possible. Meanwhile both he and Clara were struck by the coincidence of having his query regarding Shay Corley's whereabouts answered so swiftly and so serendipitously. Of course it also supplied him with the perfect excuse to legitimately postpone another agonising round of trying to understand what caused his ordinarily level-headed parents to so suddenly, completely, and permanently cast him out of their lives. His soul shrivelled within him every time he was reminded that both of them had died without either forgiving him or reconciling with him.

10

Shay's Return Home to Kiltyroe

But in September of 1943, after a particularly bad bout of depression and a spell 'away' as we euphemistically called it in those days, I headed home to Kiltyroe for a bit of pampering by Mama and Constance. Ashdene House was the only place on earth where I could be myself and really feel safe when my demons came visiting. It was always my refuge when recuperating. A few days after my arrival home I opened the kitchen door one evening and bustled in. I had been out all day fowling and hunting. I was carrying a brace of rabbits and a breech action shotgun broken open across the crook of my arm. In my other hand I had a heavy canvas leather strapped bag, which I was about to drop near the sink. Mama and Constance were sitting at the table talking to a young man. As I was leaning the gun against the kitchen dresser, he jumped up and rushed towards me, throwing his arms about me. It was only then that I recognised him. It was my youngest brother, Ambrose. Soon we were all sitting around the kitchen table drinking tea and talking nineteen to the dozen. We were delighted to be in each other's company after all these years. But first I had to unpack the bag, revealing several snipe and a few wood pigeon, the fruits of my early morning fowling expedition. Later Mama and Constance would convert these offerings into a tasty and nourishing game pie for dinner. From past experience we knew that we would find it both delicious and satisfying.

That first night Ambrose and I were delighted that we had a whole week to spend together at home. He was happy to spend a lot of time in my company. We barely knew each other, but now thanks to the coincidence of this free time at home, we were able to make up for lost time. Last time I had spent time with him Ambrose was a wee sickly boy and I a self absorbed teenager taking pride in my recently acquired shooting skills. Now so many years later, twenty-three-year old Ambrose was learning how to shoot with the self-same gun I had used then. I had long since acquired a shotgun of my own, with which I had learned to shoot extremely accurately. Ambrose watched in awe as I demonstrated my superior skill by taking down practically every bird I got in my sights. Despite all my rhetoric, coaching and cajoling, poor Ambrose came home empty-handed for the first few evenings. Needless to mention, I didn't bother to tell him about the damage to the fowling piece. I couldn't have him stealing my thunder. It was many years later before I got to the bottom of how a few evenings later Ambrose had brought home as good a bag as my own. The previous night when I was otherwise occupied, he had sneaked outside with my prized gun and the old fowling piece. He had set off to the high wall between the large hayshed and the lower meadow, some distance from the house. There he lined up a series of empty tin cans along the wall. Then carefully focusing through the sights of my weapon, he managed to knock all twelve of them off and into the adjoining field. Then he collected them and lined them up again. This time he aimed the Fowler's old gun, and in spite of focusing carefully, he missed the first three. Now he examined both shotguns and both sets of sights. At first he couldn't see what the problem was. On closer examination, he noticed that the sights on the old gun were skewed about a centimetre and a half to the right. He figured if he lined up the can in the sights, and then moved the muzzle a centimetre and a half to the left while holding steady, he just might hit his target. Nothing daunted, he started again. Bearing in mind his plan, he lined up and shot at the first can. Wham! Over it went. He repeated the process through cans 2, 3, 4, 5, and 6, meeting success every time. He missed can 7 and just rattled can 8 before he settled himself and succeeded again with cans 9 through 12. He reset the cans three times more and shot them off the wall successfully each time before hugging his delight to himself. Then he headed back to the house. Here he carefully cleaned both guns and put them away. On my return I found him seated in the quiet kitchen chatting with Mama. Everyone else was out, so Florrie had taken the opportunity to get to the bottom of what seemed to be bothering Ambrose. She began by quizzing him about the job, about Birr, and in particular about whether he had made friends. In the end she had to prompt him to tell her about his friendship with Father Dan Conneran. He summarised the bones of the story as best he could, trying to make light of his hurt. Florrie was not to be fooled, but she kept her counsel. Then she flabbergasted him by asking was the real reason for the curate's transfer, that the narrow-minded Father Murphy distrusted the appropriateness of their friendship? Ambrose had had his own suspicions in this regard, but as Father Dan had made no reference to it, Ambrose hadn't mentioned it either.

'I would have thought Bishop Ryan would have had more sense; but I suppose he had to react to Father Murphy's concerns, even if he was as wrong as could be about poor Father Dan,' said Florrie.

The week flew by on wings of speed. On leaving Ashdene on that September Sunday in 1943, Ambrose and I were to share a hackney car to Limerick, where we would part company. I'd get the train to Dublin, and Ambrose would catch a bus to Birr. The driver was a neighbour famously taciturn and extremely hard of hearing. So cocooned comfortably in the back of the car allowed us the privacy for intimate conversation. I quizzed Ambrose about his feelings about returning to Birr. Over the previous few days he had told me about his life there, leading up to the need for this recuperative break. Little by little I had elicited from him just how unhappy he had been. I listened carefully to what he had to say and more importantly to what was being left unsaid. Ambrose appeared to draw great comfort from unburdening himself and seemed to appreciate my empathic response. A peaceful silence ensued, broken eventually by me as we approached Limerick.

'Ambrose, I apologise for not being a better model of behaviour and also for neglecting my brotherly duty to you. I've been very selfish. No one of your tender years should have had to shoulder the burdens of responsibility laid on your shoulders. At seventeen to have to become sole support to your mother and carer-in-chief to our Hannah was a hugely onerous task. But you should not have had to battle alone.'

'Shay, don't be so hard on yourself. What could you realistically have done to ease the pain? And don't forget

I wasn't completely alone; I know I never will be while Constance has breath in her body.'

'Nonetheless I blame myself for being too wrapped up in my own problems to have cared enough to support you. No wonder you were so stressed. By the way, where the hell was Michael in all this? And what about the bold Kitty and Nora? From what I hear all three of them were so busy looking after themselves to even pay much more than the odd cursory visit home, and then I bet they'd arrive together and be more trouble than they were worth to Mama and Constance. Am I right? Oh! Sorry, Ambrose, you don't need to hear me raving. You are much stronger than you know and much more like Mama than you give yourself credit for. Promise me you'll get help straight away if and when you are feeling down. Don't let depression take over your life as it has mine. Try not to be as cussedly independent and stubborn as this fool of a brother of yours. And thank God daily that you haven't inherited the Corley pride and arrogance. In turn I promise you that, insofar as I can, I will keep in touch. Will you write to me? I'll give you my work address, which as you know I've not even given to Mama. Use bank stationery so I'll be able to recognise it immediately, and always sign off with a reminder of my promise to reply. If I fail to respond, forgive me, as it will mean I am not myself. Okay? Now we're nearly at the station, so let's put on our happy faces.' When we got out and paid the driver, I patted Ambrose on the shoulder, saying, 'Chin up, lad. Chest out, and until we meet again may the good lord hold you in the palm of his hand.'

Then, hoisting my bag, I set off jauntily for the station without waiting for a reply. I could feel Ambrose's gaze on my back before he turned and headed for the bus to Birr. I was delighted to have had the chance to get to know the grown-up Ambrose over the few days we had spent at home. I was proud of the young man he had turned out to be. It was only on my way back to London that I realised I had failed to tell him so.

I vowed to keep in touch. Over the next several months we corresponded regularly and arranged that we'd spend some time together at Christmas time, perhaps in Dublin or maybe he would visit me in London. He told me that on his arrival back in his digs that Sunday night he had found his landlady was out, so he went to bed feeling lonely and without any supper. He was debating writing to Hannah but couldn't work up the energy. He sat for a time with his head in his hands, deep in thought, recalling the ups and downs of the previous week. After a while he realised that he had two choices. He could wallow in misery, or he could face forward and make the most of his job and the new responsibilities he was about to be offered. He vowed to take the second course and fell asleep happy in the knowledge that he had made the right choice. Next morning he decided to start the way he meant to go on, so he greeted the landlady with a smile and a cheery 'good morning' before setting off for work. He presented himself at Mr Rutland's office first thing rather than waiting to be sent for. He was welcomed warmly by the bank manager, who immediately commented on how well he was looking.

'Well, well, young man, did you enjoy your break? You certainly look the better for it. You have all the signs of having been well fed and looked after at home, and indeed you look well rested too. Now, Ambrose, tell me all about your week away from us'.

In his first long, news-packed letter to me, Ambrose told of how he had first thanked his boss for the time off and then given him a full account of his holiday in Kiltyroe. Mr Rutland was so taken with the account he wanted to know where exactly this 'Shangri La' was situated. Without giving it much thought, Ambrose realised that he had just invited his boss to visit Ashdene House, where he assured him he would find the best of food and entertainment and the most hospitable of Clare welcomes. Mr Rutland thanked him kindly and said that he would be pleased to call if ever he found himself in the vicinity of Kiltyroe. Then, reminding him of his new duties as junior cashier, he accompanied Ambrose to the front desk, leaving him under the watchful eye of Mr Hogan, the senior clerk.

Refreshed after his holiday and determined to look forward positively, Ambrose soon found that he was beginning to enjoy the work. His allotted tasks were neither hugely challenging nor very interesting, but he had begun to find fulfilment in providing the best service he was capable of. From these early days and for the rest of his life, he lived out the belief that he was duty bound to provide an honest day's work for an honest day's pay. It wasn't long before he noticed that instead of waking with a knot of dread in stomach, he was actually looking forward to getting up and heading out to work. Of course he still missed Father Dan and often thought about him, wondering how he was faring in his new parish. He also missed his mother and siblings, and Hannah in particular. But now he was able to see the necessity of making the break with home and childhood. He was still prone to bouts of loneliness and introspection, but his depression seemed to have eased for the moment at least. He loved keeping in touch with Hannah and home by weekly letter, and now he had Father Dan's and my not-so-frequent but equally welcome letters to look forward to as well. He was very pleased that I was keeping my promise to write to him. And so weeks turned into months and months into years and Ambrose found that he was enjoying his life at work. The turning point was of course when he had the good fortune to be introduced to May Phelan, who instantly became the love of his life and in time his beloved wife and the mother of his children.

When Ambrose was transferred to Roscrea, after spending four years in Birr, he was amazed that his co-workers told him that they would miss him. These expressions of goodwill came in a variety of ways. Mr Rutland presented him with a beautiful pen, and his colleagues invited him to join them for drinks in Dooley's Hotel on the night before he left. Despite the fact that he didn't drink alcohol, Ambrose was prevailed upon to attend. They sat around the fire in the bar chatting and drinking for a while, and then Mr Hogan appeared. He made a farewell speech complimenting Ambrose on his four-year service to the people of Birr. In the course of his oration, he made reference to the quiet and shy Mr Corley, who in those early days was known among a certain set as 'Brose the Morose'. He then went on to tell the assembly how conscientious and hardworking Ambrose was and how much he would be missed, not just as a good example to his colleagues but as a person. His unfailing courtesy, his wry wit, his willingness to help others and his unswerving loyalty to the bank and his colleagues made him a very valued member of staff. As a token of their respect for him, his colleagues had had a whip around and wanted to present him with a very special gift to remember them by. They were sure they had chosen well and expected that he would love and treasure it. Then with a flourish, Mr Hogan called for those hiding in the snug to please come forward. From behind the heavy curtain marched five musicians: a flute player, an accordion player, a concertina player, a fiddler and a young man with a mandolin. They proceeded immediately to play a medley of Irish tunes. After a few minutes Mr Hogan called for silence and, reaching behind his chair, produced a beautiful violin. It was obvious from the patina that this was not a new instrument but rather a well-loved musician's pride and joy. He presented the magnificent instrument to Ambrose, saying, 'Your colleagues have done their research well and we can all see that you are itching to join in; so, on their behalf, I want you to have this violin as a token of our appreciation. Its previous owner, Rory O'Carroll, was a wonderful musician who died only last year. Having no children of his own to pass it on to, Rory had left his precious instrument to his spinster sister Nellie. As it was of considerable value, Nellie was free to sell it. She could sell it, however, only if she was satisfied that it would go to an accomplished player who would value and treasure it and lovingly care for it as he had. We were happy to reassure Miss O'Carroll that it couldn't go to a better home. Now, young man, please join the others and show us what you can do with our gift.'

Ambrose expressed his thanks most eloquently by playing with the group for the next several hours. In the course of the evening he also played hauntingly beautiful solos on his new violin. He was thrilled to discover that it had a lovely mellow tone. Every note he played was mellifluous. He couldn't believe the difference between the sounds he could produce on this beautiful violin, as opposed to playing the old three-quarter-sized model he was used to. He couldn't wait to share his excitement with me, especially as he felt I would share in his justifiable pride in his flawless rendition of 'An Chúilfhionn' (The Coolin) that night. Indeed his performance was talked about in hushed tones of admiration and appreciation for years afterwards. During his stint in Birr Ambrose had gained in self-confidence and so it was a more mature and assured Mr Corley who presented himself for work at the Roscrea branch of the bank in September 1947.

PART IV

11

Ella and Constance

We, Ambrose and May's children, had always called our parents Mom and Dada. As a family we were close to each other and our parents. So we all had our shared recollections of our happy childhood home and Ambrose as a loving father. I knew some of my siblings thought I was Dada's favourite. Of course I had my own individual and cherished memories of him. From conversations with Mom over the years I also had good idea of her perspective on him as a newly married man and a young father. Now I had Shay's version of Ambrose as both child and young man. I longed to learn more. The only one who could fill me in on the missing years of his youth and adolescence was Constance. So in July I determined to visit her at her home. I hoped that she could also answer some questions for me about Shay, who intrigued me. I approached Kiltyroe in the townland of Knocknashee in County Clare from the south. The village nestles in the lee of a hill, with its main street winding around a gentle curve of a valley road. There's a handful of shops and houses flanking the Roman Catholic Church on the right-hand side of the street, and a public house stands sentinel at either end of the village. On the opposite side of the street there is a supermarket with petrol pumps recessed a little from the road with a further two pubs as its nearest neighbours. A few more houses, mostly single-storey cottages, straggle along for a further half mile or so on the southern approach road. The only change to the village in over a hundred years is the recent accretion of an estate of forty houses built at the northern end of the village. The old village school, long since abandoned, has been superseded by a modern glass and steel monstrosity, thankfully tucked away on a side road well away from the village street.

On the western edge of the village stands the old rectory, surrounded by thirty acres, where Shay was born. Nowadays the farm is run by his nephew, my cousin Barry, Constance and Brendan Walsh's eldest son. On this lovely spring afternoon in early April 1979, I parked my car on the roadside. To buy some time before meeting with Aunt Constance, I got my camera and took some shots of the ruins of the little church opposite the old wrought iron gates of the rectory. It was the week after Easter, and I was on holidays from school. Over the previous few weeks I had been reading Uncle Shay's copybooks with great interest and fascination. I marvelled at the way he could draw the reader into a world long gone. I loved the way his descriptions of his youth with his family made me feel that I knew them all intimately. I hadn't been to Kiltyroe in over fifteen years, but between my own memories and Shay's lively prose, I was amazed at how familiar it all seemed. The only difference I could see was a row of plane trees lining either side of the recently tarmacadamed driveway. Other than that, the house and surrounding fields looked exactly as they did when Shay and his siblings lived there. Behind the post and rail fencing, to the right and to the left of the driveway, hundreds and hundreds of golden daffodils still grew, 'fluttering and dancing in the breeze'. These I remember well, but the fence along with the trees must also have been relatively new. The house was south facing. Its tall windows glow golden, basking in the April afternoon sunshine. The three tall, oddly spaced chimneys still pierce the clear blue sky with their pointed stacks. A scribble of smoke rose directly skywards from the nearest one. The ancient Virginia creeper was beginning to come into leaf along the spidery skeletal remains of last year's trellising, attaching its little suckers upwards and outwards in ever-expanding growth. The façade of the house was exactly as I remembered. Six limestone steps led up to the front door, now painted poster red, with its sunray fanlight overhead. The door was flanked by one eight-foot-high sash window to the left and two matching ones to the right. On the level above there were four similar sash windows, but these were only five feet in height. Beneath the tall windows of the reception rooms were windows corresponding to those at the upper level, but these were partially obscured from view, as the rooms below were at semi-basement or garden level.

On that April day I had the weird sensation that if I were bold enough to walk down the driveway and enter the house through the back door, I would find my grandmother, Florrie, in the kitchen removing a tray of fruit scones from the oven of the cast iron stove just about then. I had to shake myself to dislodge the image as I continued to stare at the old house. There was perhaps a little more foliage screening the backyard than I remembered, due no doubt to the more recent addition of shrubs to the garden's perimeter fence line. And of course the older trees, the Chile pine or monkey puzzle to the left of the front door, the horse-chestnut inside the garden gate, and the bay tree opposite had all grown enormous in the intervening years. The monkey puzzle and the horse chestnut in particular now loomed like protective arms above the height of the house. The ancient magnolia still stretched its gnarled boughs upwards, offering its lovely blooms aloft to the blue arch of the sky. The garden was now completely surrounded by sheltering trees and shrubs, providing a glorious suntrap to the front. Behind the house the original cobbled yard had at some stage been covered over with tarmac. A number of cars were parked there, and the old coach house has been renovated. The enormous arched doorway now contained what appeared to be double doors, the upper two-thirds of which were glazed. As I parked my car I noticed that the stonework had been expertly pointed and the little upstairs windows painted a dark ivy-green colour.

I made my way to the front of the house and ascended the short flight of steps. I noticed in passing that the old rickety wooden ramp had been tastefully replaced with cut stone to match the granite steps. I admired the neatly planted ceramic tubs on either side of the steps as I waited for someone to answer the doorbell. I was relieved to hear the swish of the approaching wheelchair before Aunt Constance turned the key, withdrew the bolt, and swung open the heavy oak door. She smiled her welcome and then reached up to give me a hug.

'It's so lovely to see you, Ella. Lordy lord! It must be fifteen years or more since you were here last. Come in, come in, my dear. Shut that door behind you and follow me. I was just about to sit out in the conservatory to catch what little sunshine I can for a few minutes.'

I followed her as she manoeuvred the wheelchair expertly around the large oval dining room table through the delicately furnished regency drawing room to the modern sunny conservatory beyond. Here we sat in the warmth of the early afternoon sun.

'As you probably remember, Aunt Constance, I missed Dada's funeral. But I know from Mom and my brothers and sisters what a rock you have been for them at the time, and indeed down since. I must apologize for not coming to see you in the interval, but I've had a good deal of trouble in coming to terms with all that has happened.'

'Ella, my poor darling, we understand very well how difficult life has been for you. Of course we haven't expected you to make the long journey to see us. But now that you have, I'm delighted, as I'm sure everyone else in the household will be as soon as they see you. Barry and Tessa are around and hard at work as usual. Their eldest, young Brenny, is now helping run the farm. Maria is downstairs with her mum, as it happens, and Jody will be sure to call in later on. He always does on Tuesdays and Thursdays on his way home from school, so he'll not break a tradition just because he's on holidays. Now let's get the family news out of the way first. How is your mother bearing up? But before we get to that, my dear, are congratulations in order? You look positively blooming. Oops, I'm sorry. Am I out of order? Jumping in where angels fear to tread.'

Reaching up to enfold me in a warm hug, she continued.

'Bless you, my love, and the new life. Congratulations. I am so happy for you.

You must be absolutely over the moon. And of course the dad too must be delighted.'

When I recovered my breath, I admitted to my shrewd aunt that I was surprisingly and blissfully pregnant.

'So far only Mom knows, and Greg of course and he is even more excited than I am and pressing me hard to get married. Recently at last I have agreed. I never wanted to go there again after what had happened with Richard, but five years on I've finally decided to move forward.'

At this point the unmistakable sound of rattling teacups on a tray could be heard approaching. Then there was a tentative knock on the door before Tessa's head appeared.

'Constance, I've just brought tea for you and your guest—oh! It's you, Ella. Let me have a look at you, my dear. You look stunning. Doesn't she, Constance? It's great to see you again. If you'd both like to come inside, I've set the tea tray by the fire. I'll leave you both to have your tea, and when you've finished just give us a tinkle. Later on, ye might like to join Barry and the rest of us for a chat in the kitchen. Ella, can you stay the night? It's no problem; we've beds aplenty, especially since we did up the old coach house.'

As was her wont, Tessa left the room swiftly, leaving a sense of welcome as well as unanswered questions in her wake.

Constance poured the tea from a silver teapot into elegant china cups, which I admired. They were from one of her many fine bone china tea sets, some of which were family heirlooms. The others she had been collecting avidly over the years at auctions and at antique shows. She offered to show off her collection later, but right now she was engrossed in encouraging me to enjoy Tessa's array of home-baked scones and biscuits, reminding me to be sure to leave some room for a slice of the delicious-looking apple cake that she herself had made that morning. After a while I got the chance to explain my unexpected arrival in Kiltyroe that day.

'Although my Dada has now been dead for almost two years, it was only recently that I had finally summoned up the courage to return home to Mountbrien. This is the first time since his death,' I told her. 'More to the point, only a few weeks ago I came into the possession of a copy of Uncle Shay's memoir. It had been left to me by Dada and I found it fascinating. Now I hoped that you, having always been very close to Ambrose, would help me to understand him better by filling me in on what he was like growing up. I also hoped for your perspective on your other siblings, Shay and Hannah in particular.'

12

Constance's Version of the Corleys

As a family, the Corleys had always been close, particularly as we were growing up. Music and Irish dancing were the bonding and the binding agents among us and with our parents. As children most of us had looked up to our Papa as the musical genius he undoubtedly was. We appreciated his strong work ethic in the classroom, his exacting insistence on perfection, and his undoubted supportive love for our gentle mother. For Michael and me, as the two older ones, especially, though we found him distant and demanding, we assumed that this was normal paternal behaviour. But almost from the beginning Shay and our father seemed to rub each other the wrong way. They could not be in the same room together without getting on each other's nerves. Papa saw his second son as deliberately trying his patience, and Shay complained bitterly that Papa always picked on him. Though he was probably not aware of it, Shay was not the only one in the family to have a difficult relationship with Papa. Kitty too had always clashed with James, but she had learned very early that she couldn't hope to win, so she avoided confrontation. But by then Shay had long since left home. Shay couldn't help himself; he just couldn't stand our father's overbearing ways. In a sense they were too alike. They were both straight talkers, at times direct to the point of rudeness, and they didn't suffer fools gladly. Though extremely clever and academically bright, they shared a type of emotional disconnect. The significant difference between them was that James was blissfully unaware that he had a fault. As far as he was concerned, he was the normal one. Anyone who did not think or act like him was either deficient or odd in his view. In fact Michael was like him in that, but Michael was never confrontational. Shay, in contrast, recognised his weaknesses in the areas of personal relationships and interpersonnel skills and strove to overcome them. In the case of Ambrose and Hannah, however, they were both cripplingly self-conscious and retiring. They performed to the high standard expected of them but were probably motivated as much by fear of Papa and the desire not to stand out as they were by a love of music or dance. As in many large families where the older ones were clever and motivated, we earned scholarships and bursaries. Armed thus with academic success, my siblings went on to challenging and demanding jobs. The younger Corleys handled the success of their elders in a variety of ways. Despite the age gap, Nora tried to ingratiate herself with her older siblings. She saw herself as on a par with them, and she competed vigorously with them. Kitty, on the other hand, had a very independent streak. She had great self-belief and didn't really care what others thought. If she was sufficiently interested in the subject matter, she studied hard and excelled, but if not, she didn't bestir herself in the slightest. Her sense of self came from within. She would be successful or otherwise on her own terms, not because she was a Corley and it was expected of her.

Our youngest brother, Ambrose, was a very sensitive little boy, born when we the older three, were sixteen, fifteen, and fourteen years old. By then we were away in boarding school for the bulk of the year. His earliest memories of his brothers therefore were only as visitors to a predominantly female household. Inevitably he was spoiled, not just by his mother and grandmother, but by us, his older sisters, as well. Being his eldest sister, I was his favourite. Like Mama and Grandma, I was one of his willing slaves. We all doted on him, but compared to Mama and Grandma I was young and full of fun. I was also physically on his level. He couldn't remember a time when whizzing around with me in my wheelchair wasn't an integral part of playtime. At the age of three Ambrose contracted diphtheria and was lucky to survive. For several years thereafter he was not in the best of health and needed constant monitoring. He grew up in the shadow of his two older brothers. They were his role models, bright, intelligent, academically successful, athletic, strong young men who were a credit to their parents. Young Ambrose compared himself to these 'gods' and found himself wanting. He knew he was not robust and therefore unlikely to be sporty, and somehow from an early age he had internalised this negative view of himself. Worse still, as he progressed through school he doubted his own academic abilities. He knew that, because of his frequent illnesses and hospitalisations, less was expected of him. Therefore his expectations of himself were commensurately low.

Ambrose had been the baby of the family for five years when Hannah was born in November of 1925. Far from resenting her arrival, young Ambrose was thrilled. He loved having a baby sister and enjoyed no longer being the youngest. He appointed himself her guardian almost immediately.

He never tired of watching over her and watching out for her. Mama was relieved of the tedium of keeping the baby amused and was free to get on with all her chores as well as her teaching duties. As soon as Hannah could walk, she followed her brother around like a little shadow. As far as she was concerned, the sun rose and set in her brother Ambrose. As they grew up, this close bond was maintained. Hannah continued to idolise her brother, and Ambrose for his part always supported and protected her. Hannah loved him unconditionally. He was her haven when troubled, her protector from bullying, and her only confidant in a houseful of busy and driven people. She emulated Ambrose in every way. She modelled her behaviour on his, read the books he recommended, mirrored his opinions, and strove always not to let him down. Somehow they became a little duo against the world, safe in their cocoon of love and respect. When Papa died at Christmas in 1937, Hannah was only twelve, and of all of the Corleys she was the one outwardly least affected by his passing. Whatever feelings of love she had had for her distant and somewhat scary father had long since transferred to her beloved Ambrose, whom she trusted would always act in her best interests. She depended totally on him for love, affection, and understanding. When others in the family ignored her, grew impatient with her childish questioning, or were downright dismissive of her, she fled to Ambrose for solace.

After the death of their father, these two were thrown together even more as Florrie tried to cope with her own grief and the endless demands on her time and resources. With her two oldest sons away and Kitty and Nora at university and the attendant financial drain on her resources, her focus had to be on making ends meet. Without Papa's support she was very concerned about Ambrose's future. Because of his ill health he had missed out on a lot of schooling. Unlike his siblings, he had not attended boarding school. Instead he had enrolled as a day student in Ennis, where he had attained his qualifying certificate the previous summer. He was now seventeen and had been helping out on our uncle's farm while deciding what he wanted to do for a living. Since Christmas he had also taken upon himself a lot of our dead father's duties, including the driving and maintenance of the family car, an old Ford Model T. As summer approached, Florrie took her youngest son aside and talked seriously with him about his plans. As a result he applied for a clerkship to the Oriel Bank. He was invited for an interview in June, and being successful, he was offered a job in Birr, County Offaly, starting on July 1.

Ambrose was looking forward to the challenge and to the independence he craved. Mama was delighted for him, and we his older siblings were pleased that he would finally have to cut the apron strings and fend for himself. Hannah was devastated. She had been so looking forward to spending time with her brother, helping out with the farming chores just as soon as school would be out in the early days of July. Now he'd be gone. She was so upset that she actually became physically ill. Ambrose immediately volunteered not to accept the job. He would stay at home to look after his dearest sister, who had worked herself into a tizzy and was in danger of having a nervous breakdown. Immediately a family conference was called. The upshot was a resounding 'no' from the rest of the Corleys. Their advice was incontrovertible. Ambrose would take up his job offer, and Hannah would accept the necessity of the separation. As far as they were concerned Ambrose must face up to his responsibilities, and Hannah needed to 'grow up', 'cop onto herself', or 'quit acting like a spoiled brat' as they variously put it.

And so it was that Ambrose set off for Birr, and Hannah had to make the most of her solitary life at home. As all the others had moved away and were living their own lives. She only had our mother and occasionally myself for company as the long lonesome days of July and August stretched ahead. Mama tried to cheer her up as best she could. Knowing that Hannah was to go to boarding school in September, Florrie tried to arrange a few outings to Ennis and to Limerick, ostensibly to kit her out but really in an attempt to distract her. Along with that, Ambrose had promised to write to her often and keep her up to date regarding his new job. True to his word, Ambrose ensured that Hannah received letters twice or three times a week. This was the beginning of a lifelong habit for them both. Hannah appreciated these early letters, which kept her spirits up and gave a focus to her lonely days. At first she railed against her mother, resentfully refusing to be mollified by any attempts at reconciliation. Then she took to punishing Ambrose. She would sometimes not answer his letters at all, or else she would send terse notes acknowledging receipt of them. Worse, she would often answer in detail everything he had written, pedantically commenting on his language usage or arguing churlishly with whatever position he had adopted. These rude missives were occasionally interspersed with real letters where she opened her heart to the only ally she had ever had. Ambrose understood her pain and continued to write lovingly and supportively, despite the hurtfulness of her behaviour.

Eventually the tide began to turn. By the end of August Hannah had begun to accept that her childhood must be left behind. Like it or not, she'd have to face the future. The first step on that road was not far away. Soon she would be heading off to boarding school. This would be the first time she'd be really on her own, with no family member to talk to. Also of course, it would be her very first time being away from home. With a mixture of determination to become independent and trepidation at the challenges ahead, Hannah vowed to face her September deadline with as much courage as she could muster. It was the beginning of a long and difficult struggle, but looking back years later Hannah could pinpoint this decision as the key to her survival in the harsh world of an enclosed community of teenage girls.

Ambrose continued to support our little sister by keeping up the correspondence on which they both came to depend. They exchanged details of their everyday experiences, and more importantly they were able to confide in each other about how they were feeling. Shy as they were with everyone else, they had no secrets from each other. Hannah never hid the fact that, but for Ambrose's letters, she would never have made friends at school. And many years later Ambrose admitted that these same letters had saved him from severe homesickness and excruciating loneliness in his early months in Birr.

—⁓—

Ambrose was by nature and inclination a solitary person. When he started his working life in Birr he was sick with apprehension. In the early weeks away from home, he was so miserable that he was barely able to function. He couldn't sleep and had no desire to eat. He dragged himself to work, where he spent his hours monotonously filing papers. He worked alone in the eeriness of the bank's basement, in the bowels of the earth, with no natural light. By the time he got upstairs at lunchtime, everyone else had either already left or was busily heading for the exit, avoiding making eye contact with him. No one ever invited him to join them or asked him what his plans were. He had lost weight dramatically in the first few weeks. But for his responsibilities to his beloved mother and his little sister, he may very well have succumbed to an untimely death from malnutrition and depression. He had always taken his duties seriously, and as his body weakened, he realised that he needed to look after his own health to be in a position to look out for Hannah. Luckily he came to also realise that his unnecessary death would break his poor mother's heart. The last thing he wanted was to add to her burden, so he vowed to seek help.

Father Dan Conneran was a young curate in the village of Killinaclogh, just outside the town of Birr. Ambrose had cycled out to Mass there one Sunday, and Father Dan had made a point of talking to him after Mass was over. Having made his decision to seek help, Ambrose thought of confiding in Father Dan. After all, outside of the bank manager and his landlady, Father Dan was the only person who had exchanged a word with him since his arrival in

Birr six weeks before. He was lucky that the person he chose to be his confidant was such a well-balanced and approachable man. The priest immediately put him at his ease by questioning him gently and sharing details of his own background with Ambrose. They found that they had quite a lot in common. Aside from their shared rural background, they were both sons of teachers. They had a mutual love of gentle mothers and came from large families. Father Dan had lost his dad when he was young as well. But whereas Ambrose had always been somewhat in awe of his distant Papa, Father Dan had had a close and loving relationship with his warm and cheerful father. They also shared a deep and lasting love of Irish culture. They often conducted their exchanges in their native language, in which they were both proficient and comfortable. Ambrose loved to play the violin. Unusually he was adept in both classical and Irish music traditions. Father Dan loved music in a wide range of genres. He too was a talented musician. His chosen instrument was the Irish flute. It wasn't long before Father Dan moved on from being mentor/confidant to becoming good friends with Ambrose. When he discovered that Ambrose hadn't played the violin since his father's death, he encouraged him to send home for it. Ambrose protested that the instrument on which he had learned to play was only a three-quarter-sized violin on which many other learners had already left their mark and was hardly worth the cost of postage. The ever-pragmatic Father Dan assured him that half a loaf was better than no bread, and as he could not afford anything better at the moment, he should be glad of the well-loved if somewhat battered instrument. Once it arrived, they spent many a winter's evening companionably playing tunes together as well as enjoying listening to music on the radio or on Father Dan's prized phonograph. Soon the pair became a commonplace sight all over the county, cycling, walking, and playing music together at local concerts. This friendship was beneficial to both young men. In the case of Ambrose, it proved to be the ideal antidote to his tendency to depression. As for Father Dan, it was a welcome relief from the solitude of his calling. Over the next while at the bank, things improved for Ambrose. After two months of nonstop filing in his 'out of sight out of mind' underground bunker, he was at last offered a little reprieve. Now he only spent the long mornings alone. In the afternoons he was assigned a number of marginally less boring tasks. Immediately after lunch each day, he had to count, sort, and bag all the coin received in the bank the previous day. This job was carried out at a section of the counter not open to the public but within earshot of what was going on. Best of all another slightly more senior trainee banker was seated alongside him, engaged in counting and sorting the paper money. When Ambrose was finished with this work, he had to go from office to office and desk to desk to collect the post from the out trays. Next he had to sort, weigh, and frank each envelope before taking it all up the road to the post office for posting. The immediate advantage of the new duties was that Ambrose slowly began to feel part of the bank's large staff. Secondly, he was now in a position to exchange the odd comment with his co-workers. Finally, he enjoyed the opportunity to get a breath of fresh air and have a walk in the afternoons. Meanwhile he and Hannah continued to exchange letters at least once a week. Hannah's letters were full of detail about her lessons, her friends and the minutiae of boarding school life and questions, questions and more questions. Ambrose's letters were always cheerful and supportive and initially consisted of replies to Hannah's endless questions which were often fictional to hide his own loneliness and increasing desperation. After he met Father Dan his letters were peppered with references to his new friend. He would tell his sister what Father Dan said and thought, on everything from the weather, music, the state of the nation to theology and the beauty of nature. Soon he was encouraging her to read poetry, so they could share their views on favourite poets and poems. Then followed invariably Ambrose's reprise of Father Dan's opinions to which, with increasing confidence Hannah would respond analytically.

Ambrose was anxious to contribute to his sister's education and Father Dan was pleased to assist in this process. Ambrose proposed that for the coming term, one in four of the letters they exchanged would be through the medium of Irish. He also suggested that for the following term, she should endeavour to correspond in French on a fortnightly basis, with Father Dan. He and Father Dan would then return her letters with comments and suggestions for correction included. This arrangement, a development of Florrie's practice, continued happily until Hannah did her Leaving Certificate exams four years later.

At the beginning of July, as was the Bank's practice, personnel transfers were announced. Two new trainees arrived along with a fifty percent change in all other grades. Now Ambrose found himself on the first step of the promotional ladder. He was delighted to bid farewell to the filing, counting and even the postal run and to start learning the business of banking. Over the summer, he was busy at work and beginning to enjoy it and equally busy in the long sunny evenings with tennis, cycling and hill climbing either alone or with his friend. But disappointment loomed. Little did they know but these summer excursions would be their last. Father Dan's bishop had other plans for him than the curacy in Killinaclogh. On August 31 Ambrose pedalled out from Birr in great form to meet his friend. They were going to play a practice set of tennis in preparation for the following weekend's tournament. They would be contestants, having qualified both in the singles and the doubles at the county finals. On his arrival at the Parochial House, Ambrose was surprised to find that Father Dan wasn't ready and waiting for him. When he noticed that his car was also missing, Ambrose settled down on the sun-warmed wall to wait. Almost immediately the parish priest arrived at his elbow and invited him to come inside. Seated behind a desk in his study Father Murphy explained that Father Dan had been called to Bishop's House earlier that afternoon. He expected that he would return soon but perhaps he might have been invited to remain for dinner with His Lordship, in which case it could be very late when he'd return. He advised Ambrose to accept that their tennis game would have to be cancelled and he'd be as well to cycle home. On his return Ambrose settled down to write to his mother. He poured out his fears to her, regarding the outcome of Father Dan's visit to Bishop's House. By midnight he was so worried he couldn't sleep so he got out of bed and wrote a letter to Hannah. Then he read for several hours before falling into a fitful and exhausted slumber. When he emerged from the Bank the following evening Father Dan was standing outside waiting for him. By his demeanour Ambrose knew that the news would not be welcome.

'Hi Ambrose, have you a minute? Can we take a walk? I've got something to tell you'.

They fell into step and walking the length of the street soon found themselves heading out the road towards Kilcormac. Father Dan started to relate the events of the previous day. When he had got the summons to Bishop's House he had first been apprehensive. On his arrival he was shown into a waiting room by the Bishop's clerical secretary, who despite having been a classmate of his at the seminary, barely exchanged a word with him before leaving him to kick his heels for over forty minutes. Then he heard the front door close and hurrying footsteps. He was shown into the presence of His Lordship Very Reverend Bishop Ryan. After Father Dan had kissed his ring the Bishop said

'You are very welcome Father Dan. Please take a seat. I've called you in today because I have a new and interesting assignment for you. Your parish priest Father Murphy has written a very good testimonial for you. As far as he is concerned you have the makings of an excellent priest. He can find no fault with your work, your commitment or your dedication to your parishioners. However he has approached me to transfer you from your curacy in Killinaclogh, effective immediately. Father Festus Murphy is a good and conscientious priest whom I hold in high regard. Therefore I really must heed what he has to say. To date he has been a wonderful mentor to a number of young men. No one has ever complained about his treatment of his subordinates. Indeed to a man they have praised him for his example, his non-judgmental nature, his good humour and his kindness. He has never before asked to have a curate transferred from his parish. But he has now. He is concerned that your exclusive friendship with a young man who works in a bank in Birr, is giving scandal in the area. For your own good, therefore, I am advising you to listen to and accept what I'm proposing for you. I am not punishing you nor am I judging you. I am offering you a wonderful opportunity in a new setting that is all. I want you go as curate to a brand new parish on the outskirts of Tullamore, but only on condition that you agree that you must break this friendship. Now over to you Father Dan, have you anything you'd like to say or any questions you'd like to ask'?

'Your Lordship I want to state categorically and on my honour that there is nothing inappropriate in my friendship with young Ambrose Corley. He is a devout practicing Catholic who happens to be vulnerable and sensitive. He came to me for advice and because we had a lot in common we became friends. As far as my behaviour goes, I have nothing to apologise for. I am sorry that some person or persons unknown chose to see evil where none existed. I fully understand the nature of scandal and am happy to accept your offer.

However I respectfully suggest that I be allowed to explain the position to Ambrose, whose mental health could very well be at risk, if he finds I have suddenly and inexplicably disappeared without trace. I merely ask that I be allowed to meet with him, in a public place just once, and thereafter in accordance with your wishes I promise not to meet up with him again'.

Bishop Ryan, being a fair-minded man, had sanctioned the meeting, Father Dan explained as they walked along. They approached a wayside pub, but when Ambrose suggested they'd go inside for a mineral, Father Dan insisted that one of them should enter the premises to buy the bottles and they would drink them outside in the open. By the time they were back in Birr, Father Dan had filled him in on the whole story. He had however, purposely omitted any reference to the implication of inappropriate behaviour. Ambrose was devastated at the thought of losing his friend and mentor, particularly when Father Dan explained that he would be unable to meet up with him once he had started work in the new parish. When he asked the priest if this meant that he would no longer be in a position to assist Hannah with her French studies, Father Dan reassured him that he saw no reason why that arrangement should not continue. Ambrose then asked if they could at least keep in touch by letter. Because no mention of corresponding with Ambrose had been made in Bishop's House Father Dan decided that if Ambrose wanted to write to him he would be happy to respond. Outside Ambrose's digs they bade each other farewell. Then they went their separate ways with heavy hearts. Father Dan consoled himself with the thought that he had signed up for a life of poverty, celibacy and obedience and therefore had no legitimate excuse for feeling hard done by. But the implied criticism still made him smart. As for Ambrose, he felt bereft and abandoned.

13

Ambrose and Shay

In mid-September 1943 about two weeks after the departure of Father Dan, a pale and hollow eyed Ambrose, was called into the Bank manager's plush office. Mr Albert Rutland was concerned for his young employee. Ambrose had recently started work at the front of house. He was now a junior cashier, dealing directly with the public. Though painfully shy, he didn't mind this contact with customers. He felt he was providing a useful service to the best of his ability, assisting people in lodging and withdrawing money from their accounts. He dealt efficiently and courteously with people and most clients were very happy to deal with such a polite if somewhat serious young man. Older women in particular were happy to make a point of queuing at his counter. Some of them tried to wheedle a smile from him by teasing him that he must be saving his smiles for someone special, maybe someone young and gorgeous. One tiny old lady, who reminded him of his Grandma Maud, used to insist that such a good-looking fellow ought to practice his smile on her and make an old woman happy. It transpired that this nice lady happened to be Mr Rutland's mother. She mentioned to her son that she felt that young Mr Corley appeared to her to be very unhappy. In typically maternal fashion, Edel Rutland wanted to know what her Bertie was going to do about it. On that September morning Ambrose presented himself at the Bank manager's office with a good deal of trepidation. The upshot of the interview was a recommendation from his boss that Ambrose take two days of his annual leave. These days were to be supplemented by three extra rest days and he was to go home for a week to recover his health with a bit of pampering and feeding from his loving mother. Ambrose was at first taken aback and then grateful to Mr Rutland for his thoughtfulness. Mama was overjoyed when he showed up unexpectedly in Kiltyroe, the following Friday night. He was heartily welcome. I was thrilled to bits. We hadn't had a decent chat in ages. After the happy greetings were over Mama said

'Let me have a good look at you Ambrose, my love. First, you seem to have grown taller since we saw you at Christmas. But oh my dear you look so thin. You are positively skeletal. Are you feeling alright'?

Seeing how uncomfortable he was I interrupted and reaching up gave Ambrose a hug saying

'I'm sure he's fine Mama. Like most young fellows he probably needs just a bit of your wholesome home cooking and maybe a bit of rest and attention. Isn't that right Ambrose'?

I remember vividly that early autumn visit when Mama and I had both Ambrose and Shay home at the same time to spoil and cosset for nine whole days in a row. Ambrose was badly in the need of feeding and some consolation after a tough time at work and Shay had just discharged himself from the psychiatric ward of some London hospital. It was lovely to see how well they got on together and how they had bonded again after so many years apart. Shay had taken

Ambrose under his wing and they had spent the bulk of their days hunting and shooting and enjoying each other's company outdoors. Ambrose was lucky that at this juncture he was able to confide in his older brother. To give him his due Shay was very supportive and pleased to be able to help. Mama and I were glad that they could confide in and share their concerns with each other. By Sunday, when my brothers were due to leave Kiltyroe, Ambrose was feeling much better about himself. He had enjoyed the time he had spent with Shay, getting to know him and also learning to shoot and hunt. He was also very pleased that he had been able to share his woes with Shay who not only understood his problems but was immensely helpful in alleviating his fears. When Ambrose started to confide in him Shay listened. He encouraged him to tell the whole story.

He put him at his ease by saying that he wanted to hear from his younger brother all about life in Ashdene in the eighteen years he had missed. Little by little Ambrose brought him up to date. Shay was surprised to learn just how often Papa had mentioned him and wondered and prayed that he would be safe.

'I think that despite your differences and whatever caused you to remain away from home Papa actually missed you. I'm sure he felt guilty about you. I think he just didn't know how to fix it without losing face'.

Shay didn't reply to this startling revelation. He couldn't. So he insisted that Ambrose continue with his tale and tell him all about his life in Birr and specifically why he was currently so stressed. Ambrose told him everything, about meeting Father Dan and their friendship. He was fulsome in his praise of his friend. He told of their shared interest in music, tennis, cycling and the fun they had together. It was the first time that Shay had seen any sign of animation in him since his arrival home. When he mentioned Father Murphy Shay interrupted

'Ambrose, what was the parish priest's name?'

'Father Murphy, I just said.'

'Yes I know. I just wondered if you knew his first name.'

'Sorry Shay, I think it was Festus. Is that a real name? I never heard of it before but I'm pretty sure that's what Dan said.'

'So Festy is still up to his old tricks.'

'What did you say? Do you know him?'

'I used to a long time ago. Now Ambrose don't you worry about him. Sorry I interrupted your story, please go on'.

Ambrose explained that he had only recently come to the conclusion that his depression dated all the way back to his first stay in hospital. In those awful early days of being away from home he began to suffer from insomnia. He recognized even then that his inability to sleep was as a result of the terror he felt at the racket going on around him. At some stage he had realised that even when he did manage to fall asleep the quality of his rest was poor due to tension. He would wake stiff and sore and conscious that even in sleep he had been too stressed to relax. Even long after he had returned home, he found himself waking often in the dead of night, tense with dread and trembling with terror. This continued to happen for years, even at home and many miles and years removed from the trauma. The day following these disturbed nights he would find himself miserable, lethargic, and often feeling that the world was pressing down on him. Eventually the stress began to take its toll on his health. He developed various allergies and conditions. For several months in his teens he had suffered from alopecia. Later he suffered from eczema, and also from time to time he still suffered from psoriasis. When it all started of course he had no idea that these were stress-induced medical conditions. Back then all he knew was that he itched unmercifully. Scratching gave some initial relief of course, but tearing at his flesh until it bled created further problems, blood stained sheets and shirts, scabbing, flaking skin, weeping sores, and insomnia, among others.

Having exhausted himself in the telling Ambrose was pleasantly surprised that for the first time in ages he got a full night's sleep. There was no tossing and turning, no scratching himself raw and best of all no nightmares. By the time he was due back in Birr he felt more relaxed and rested due in great part to Shay's support. He knew that it was highly unlikely that he would ever go hunting on his own, but he was delighted at the prospect of accompanying Shay on his jaunts if ever they found themselves in Kiltyroe at the same time again. Mama and I had ensured that they were well-fed and occasionally over-fed on their return to the house each evening. That coupled with the hearty breakfasts, which were always served in Ashdene House were more than sufficient to keep them 'stothered with grub' as Shay put it, even without the packed lunches which I insisted on preparing for them before they could leave the house each morning. Added to that the ubiquitous cups of tea and lashings of homemade bread liberally spread with country butter they were forced to eat, in every neighbour's house they called to, meant that their poor stomachs were looking forward to a rest. Ambrose set off for Birr in much better physical and mental shape than he had left it. As for Shay he was heading back to London. No one knew what he did in London, where he lived, who his friends were if he had any and what he did for a living. He point-blank refused to leave a forwarding address with us. He reassured Mama and me that he would always return to Kiltyroe, for his annual holiday and that we should just ensure that there would always be a bed ready for him. That was all we needed to know or do, he insisted. Bidding farewell to her two sons, took its toll on Florrie. It was poor consolation to her that Shay had promised to be home for his holidays, because in her heart she knew that Shay only returned home, when he was at the end of his tether. He suffered from deep and dark bouts of depression, which he tried to control with medication. Sometimes the pills worked. At other times however, his suffering was so great that he yearned for Mama's unconditional love and the comfort of his home in Kiltyroe. Wandering the haunts of his youth brought him some peace of mind he said. Kiltyroe and its surroundings were where he felt somehow safest. He could be himself in the easy company of his beloved mother and his lovely sister he'd tell us. We understood his need for solitary walks. We didn't intrude, when the 'black dog of depression' as he put it, was in permanent residence. We listened to him when he was inclined to talk and included him sensitively, in our reminiscences and chit chat about local events, when he didn't. As well as that he was grateful for the unspoken part of the bargain that when he was home he should be fed and looked after. So we outdid each other in preparing his favourite meals and tempting him with tasty meals and tidbits. As his home and family worked their magic on him, and he began to improve in spirits, the atmosphere in the house lightened and usually Shay's last few days were a treat for everyone. Not knowing when we'd see him again was difficult for Florrie and me. But harder still was the realisation that, if and when we'd meet again, chances were that Shay would again not be in the best of health. By contrast, parting with Ambrose was a cake walk at least for us ladies. Not for him though, he hated having to leave home again.

14

Hannah

By September 1942 Hannah was beginning her third year at boarding school in Derryarramore, County Galway and had finally come into her own. Gone forever was the shy, introverted, retiring and scared little girl with the mousey look, constantly afraid of her own shadow. Now her classmates were beginning to see the character that up until now, only her mother and Ambrose knew. From the cocoon of childhood now emerged a grounded, quietly confident lovely girl with a sunny outlook on life. In her first year, Hannah had kept pretty much to herself, drawing strength and support from Florrie and Ambrose, via their letters. She was far too afraid of being bullied to trust anyone, let alone to make friends. Things might very well have continued in this way indefinitely, if a new girl hadn't joined Hannah's class half way through the second term. Hannah was called into the Head nun's office the very first day that Eda Holohan had transferred from a day school in Nenagh. Sister Immaculata wanted Hannah to take Eda under her wing, look out for her and make sure she settled in well, or so she said. She had deliberately chosen Hannah Corley for this task she explained, because she felt that being shy herself and a bit of a loner, she would be able to empathise with the newcomer. In truth, the wily nun felt that these two lonely and introverted girls would be good for each other and hoped that they would become friends as well as confidantes. It was obvious that

Eda's circumstances were unusual from the start. In living memory, no other student had enrolled midway through the year. But Eda had suddenly arrived in the middle of February 1943. Her beloved father Jack Holohan had dropped dead suddenly on his farm in Mountbrien the week before. Gerry was only 39 years old at the time. Therefore, Eda was not only very shy by nature but she was also extremely traumatised when she arrived at her new school. She had not had a very easy life to date. Her mother Edith after whom she had been named, had died in childbirth. She had no memory of a time when her dad was not the centre of her world. He had raised her by himself. Now unbelievably, he too was dead. She wondered if she would ever get over the shock of finding herself so suddenly fatherless. Her first days in the boarding school went by in a blur of pain and disbelief. She was walking about in a daze, trying not to think about what had just happened to her. The other girls, knowing her circumstances, were doing their best to be friendly and supportive. But she was finding their endless curiosity overly intrusive. She just wanted to be left alone. After a few days, as a result of being ignored, the bulk of her classmates lost interest in Eda and most of the unwelcome attention declined significantly. It was only then that she realised that Hannah Corley had become a low-key, benign presence constantly in her peripheral vision. She never intruded on her grief, but was always there to direct, accompany and quietly support Eda in finding her way about in those difficult early days. By the time she had lost her novelty value for the other girls Eda was ready to accept Hannah as her friend. From then on they were inseparable and until they finished their schooling rarely out of each other's sight.

When the summer holidays came around the two friends were heartbroken at the imminent separation. Hannah was due to go home to her family in Kiltyroe, Knocknashee for the break. Apart from looking forward to being at home with her mother Hannah was longing to spend time with her favourite brother Ambrose who would be home for his holidays. She was also extremely excited about her older sister Constance's upcoming wedding in July. This meant that the Corley clan would be gathering for several days to see Constance marry her childhood sweetheart Brendan Walsh. But Hannah knew how much her friend was dreading the holidays. She knew what it was like to be lonely and isolated. For her part she knew how much she would miss Eda's friendship and companionship. Eda was to divide her time between her father's young widow Roseanne on the farm in Mountbrien and her Aunt Nancy's boarding house in Kilkee. The two girls promised each other that they would persuade their families to allow them to spend at least some of the holidays together. Hannah was confident that she would be able to wangle an invitation for Eda to Constance's wedding and Eda was equally optimistic that her Aunt Nancy wouldn't refuse to allow her to invite her friend for a few days in Kilkee.

As the end of term approached the girls were full of plans. They would write to each other daily and whenever possible try to make contact by telephone in the first days of their forced separation. They were two of only four students who were taking Art as a subject for the Intermediate Certificate Examinations, so they would be the last to leave the school on the afternoon of June 21 1943. Eda was to get a bus from Galway to Limerick. Here she would board another bus which would take her to Mountbrien. From the village it was only a walk of less than a mile to Willow Farm. Hannah was to be picked up at the school and driven home to Kiltyroe. On the day, much to her delight it was Ambrose who arrived to take Hannah home. With great excitement she introduced her brother to Eda Holohan. Immediately Ambrose heard the name Holohan his mind went into overdrive and he started asking questions.

'It's nice to meet you Eda Holohan. The only Holohans I know are from Tipperary.

Are you from Mountbrien by any chance? A family friend Jack Holohan died there last February? Don't tell me you are related to Jack?'

'Jack Holohan was my Dad' whispered Eda. Remembering his manners he formally sympathised with his sister's friend on her recent bereavement. But uncharacteristically he immediately returned to the questions?

'Are you going back to Mountbrien today? How are you getting there? You must know my good friend Father Dan Conneran, he'd have been a cousin of your Dad's the Lord have mercy on his soul'.

All this time Eda just stared mesmerised at Ambrose, nodding her head in answer to the questions as appropriate. Ambrose seemed to make up his mind about something and turning to Hannah he asked

'Who do I need to see Sis, to get permission for me to drive Eda home?'

Then turning back to her friend he said

'Eda would you like to come with us rather than take the bus? We can drop in at home first and I'll introduce you to the family and we'll have a bite to eat. Then we can drive over to Mountbrien and still be there before the bus is due. Now lead me to Sister Immaculata please.'

Within a few minutes all three of them were in the Corley's Ford Anglia Popular and on the road heading south. The two girls were chatting away like their lives depended upon it. By the time they reached the outskirts of Galway Eda had recovered from her shyness sufficiently to address a few questions of her own to Ambrose. She was curious to know how he knew so much about her circumstances and her family. He told her about his friend Father Dan Conneran whom he had befriended when first he went to work in Birr. He explained that they were in constant correspondence and that he had heard her story without realising until today that Father Dan's cousin Edith and Hannah's friend were one and the same person. Hannah was fascinated too that when she had talked to Eda about her pen friend and mentor in French, that neither of them had noted the coincidence of each of them having a Father Dan in their lives. The rest of the journey passed pleasantly in regaling each other with their experiences of the kindness and friendship of Father Dan. So much so that Ambrose promised the girls that he would arrange for the three of them to visit Father Dan at his home in Carralisheen in the next few days.

True to form, no sooner had they arrived in Kiltyroe but Florrie and Constance had ushered them to a table groaning with food. Eda was welcomed as if she were another family member and not someone they had only just met. Over the course of the meal Ambrose filled the others in on the coincidence of Eda being related to his friend before they set off for Mountbrien. Hannah was delighted that Eda had been made so welcome and felt hopeful that she would be able to persuade Constance to agree to invite her to the wedding. As they got nearer to Mountbrien Eda grew quieter and quieter. Glancing in his rear view mirror to check if she had perhaps fallen asleep Ambrose noticed the tension in her pale face. Close beside her Hannah had already dozed off.

'What's bothering you Eda? Are you not looking forward to seeing your stepmother Roseanne and baby Lucy again? Surely you'll be glad to be getting home and sleeping in your old room'?

Smiling bravely Eda responded

'I'm sure everything will be fine when I get there. I'm a small bit afraid that everything might have changed. Maybe all traces of Dad will be gone. Maybe it will be like our lives in Willow Farm will have disappeared as if he and I were never there? I'm sorry Mr Corley I'm probably just being silly. Anyway, we'll be there soon now. Thanks so much for giving me the lift. It was lovely to meet you and your family. I had heard so much about ye all from Hannah I felt I knew ye all already'.

The sun was going down as they arrived at Willow Farm and the beauty of her home place as usual took her breath away and lifted Eda's heart. There were two cars parked near the house. One was Jack Holohan's old Ford Anglia and the other was a brand new rather ostentatious looking two tone Ford Coupé which had been pulled across the doorway with the front wheels in the flower bed. Eda didn't recognise the car but the way it was so inconsiderately parked made her think immediately of Roseanne's dad. She had only met Jeremiah Meehan on the occasion of her father's funeral. She hadn't liked him on first meeting him. His behaviour over those next few days did nothing to improve her opinion of him. Now her stomach knotted in dread that he might be visiting or worse still staying over in the house. Now she realised that not only did she not trust this man she actively disliked him. She hated the fact that when he was around Roseanne was terrified. His presence seemed to suck the life as well as the joy out of the air she breathed. Ambrose watched as Eda made her way to the door. Her progress was slow and measured. She seemed to diminish as she approached her childhood home. Ambrose followed with her bag. Raised voices could be heard from the kitchen as Eda opened the back door. Her heart sank. Jeremiah in all his bullying bulk was addressing his daughter in a hectoring tone. Roseanne with a cowering Lucy clinging to her knees was uncharacteristically standing up to her father.

'I'm sorry Dad but this is my home now, mine and Lucy's and I am not leaving it.

Besides I must be here for Eda when she gets home, it's her home too'.

'Not for much longer if I have anything to do with it … … … … …'

Eda stood in the doorway looking from one to the other before Lucy spotted her and hurled herself towards her. Instinctively Eda bent and took the quivering little girl in her arms. Ambrose witnessed the scene from his vantage point in the scullery. He was embarrassed at what he had seen and heard. He was puzzled as to what his older sister Kitty's husband Jeremiah was doing here before he recognized with a shock that the young mother was in fact his niece Roseanne. She was barely recognisable. Gone forever was the carefree, bubbly girl he remembered to be replaced by this frail figure with careworn features in the gaunt face with the saddest eyes he had ever seen. Coming through the back door Hannah wondered why everyone was frozen silently in standing positions. Her arrival seemed to break the tension. Everyone began slowly to move, each of them busily avoiding making eye contact with the others. Jeremiah was annoyed at being interrupted. Recognising his wife's siblings he was further aggravated to have been caught berating and bullying his daughter. Roseanne was ashamed and Eda was overwhelmed with the realisation that she had to remain here to act as buffer between Roseanne and her father. Hannah was just puzzled by the whole strange atmosphere. Eda attempted to introduce her friend Hannah and Ambrose to the Meehans until Roseanne intervened and explained the relationship. Hannah was immediately entranced with little Lucy who was delighted to add another adoring fan to her ever-increasing coterie.

15

Mass in Mountbrien

Sixteen years later after the early morning Mass on the last Sunday of Advent 1962 Hannah was sitting in her Volkswagen outside the church in Mountbrien. It was the twenty fifth anniversary of her father's death and as usual the Corleys would gather to mark the occasion. For over twenty years they had gathered in the family home in Kiltyroe. To ease the burden on her mother Florrie and her sister Constance, Hannah had been volunteering for years to undertake the task of organising the family get-together and the catering afterwards. This year she had at last persuaded them. For the first time in years the entire family would be together. Even Shay had agreed to attend the Mass and everyone was pleased to know he would be there. Florrie would be here in Hannah's home surrounded by her children and grandchildren. Constance and Brendan, Michael and Betty, Kitty and Jeremiah, Nora, Ambrose and May were all looking forward to a reunion with Shay at the centre of things. Hannah had planned everything in meticulous detail. She had deliberately opted to go to the early Mass at 8.30 so that she would have time to get breakfast ready for Florrie, Shay, Constance and Brendan, who had all arrived the night before. While the others would be attending the anniversary Mass at 11.00, she could be getting on with her preparations for dinner at one o clock. She had been pleased to have her son Edwin's company as he had been rostered to serve the early Mass. Now she was getting increasingly impatient. She was in a rush to get home to her guests.

Harold Henderson whom she had married the year after she left school was the best husband in the world, but farming was his life. She allowed her mind to wander back to those heady summer days when she had spent several days a week with her friend Eda in Mountbrien. Roseanne, Eda's stepmother who was only a few years older than the girls was anxious that they would enjoy the last summer of their school lives. She didn't want her step-daughter to be burdened with worry. She understood that Eda was still trying to cope with grieving for her father. She had therefore enlisted the aid of Father Dan to ensure that the two young women would be escorted to whatever social events the locality had to offer. So Eda and Hannah had a wonderful time attending fetes and fairs, race meetings and garden parties and a plethora of afternoon tea dances as well as more formal evening dances. Here they met up with young men and women of their own age and a little older. With the exuberance of youth they danced into the wee small hours and soon the good Father Dan's services as chauffeur/chaperon were no longer required. The two young women were inundated with offers of lifts. Sometimes with Roseanne's approval they accepted a lift but as often as not they preferred to go with groups of their peers on bicycles or on foot. The fun and banter that was part and parcel of this experience was far too good to be missed. Among the regulars were two young men in particular who never missed an event irrespective of how much work their busy farming lives demanded. One was Harold Henderson, known to his friends as Hendy and the other his best friend Luke Power. They farmed adjoining properties in Glashabawn and had been friends all their lives. Hendy was the only son of a Church of Ireland family who had been farming two hundred acres in the Mountbrien area for hundreds of years. His parents Harry and Myrtle kept pretty much to themselves and socialised only with members of their own small Protestant community. Luke was the eldest of nine children and couldn't remember a time when he was not helping out his dad Kevin on their fifty acre farm. Luke's mother Marnie was earth mother not only to her own brood but to all the waifs and strays her outgoing children turned up with from time to time. Hendy was the first and favourite of these. His mother used to have to come and get him so often of an evening that she used to joke with Marnie that maybe if she were to adopt Luke the Powers would not just have one but two mouths fewer to feed. But the boys preferred the noise and chaos of the Power's kitchen to the comfort of the 'big house'. That summer as soon as Luke laid eyes on Eda he was instantly smitten and followed her about like a lovesick calf. Hannah remembers that she and Hendy were mere onlookers to this developing relationship. And then as they were thrown more and more into each other's company they realised how much they liked each other. Before the end of summer they had both known that, whatever difficulties might lie in their path and no matter what obstacles they might have to overcome, they would spend the rest of their lives together. It took two years to persuade their families that they were serious about each other. The fact that they came from different backgrounds and religions was only part of the problem, their youth was another. But in the end, love prevailed. With the assistance of Hendy's sympathetic mother paternal approval was at last secured. Nineteen year old Hannah employed all her powers of persuasion to enlist her brother Ambrose's aid in talking her mother round. In the end Florrie gave her blessing and an ecstatic Hannah was allowed to marry her beloved Hendy on his twenty first birthday.

On this morning as she looked back fondly on their sixteen years of marriage she thanked God as she did on a daily basis for the wonder of their happiness. She had loved Hendy from the moment she had set eyes on him and now with the passing of the years she realised that she had come to appreciate his good qualities more than ever. But she also understood that housekeeping had never been a strong point of his. As her thoughts drifted back to the situation at home she thought that when it came to cooking breakfast or even remembering that there were guests in the house, poor Hendy was absolutely useless. As she checked her watch she became increasingly impatient as she had specifically told Edwin that she was in a hurry. By now the car park was empty. Hers was the only car remaining. At least five minutes had elapsed since the last of the altar boys had left. They had all tumbled out together and within seconds had dispersed in all directions, some walking, some on their bicycles and the rest of the out-of-towners to their parents' waiting cars. By now Hannah was beginning to get cross. Edwin, usually a thoughtful, considerate boy had never given his parents an ounce of trouble in his ten and a half years. So why did he pick today of all days to be awkward. She waited another few minutes and then getting out of her car she strode purposefully towards the church to see what on earth was delaying Edwin.

There was no one in the body of the church. In fact there was an eerie emptiness about the long aisle. The scent of recently extinguished candles still lingered, underlaid by the distinctive cold smell of damp stone. Hannah made her way quickly towards the altar which was flanked by two arched doors. Stepping onto the carpeted sanctuary area, she approached the door on the left which she knew opened directly into the sacristy. Turning the brass doorknob she was about to ask the priest seated facing her in the doorway if he knew what was delaying Edwin Henderson. Her eyes nearly popped out of her head in amazed stupefaction when she noticed an altar boy still clad in his soutane and surplice kneeling in front of the man. She grasped the door jamb to steady herself and an involuntary squawk escaped from her locked throat. The noise caused the boy to turn around. With horror Hannah recognised her son's stricken face and anguished eyes. Before she was aware that she had recovered her wits, she had caught Edwin by the arm and swung him to his feet and propelled him out the door.

'Wait for me in the car son' she called after his fleeing form. Turning back to the monster before her she felt her face flush with anger and disgust. She didn't know that she had lashed out until she felt the warm liquid spurt over her hand. Somewhere in her over-burdened brain she realised that the sound she had heard seconds before was cartilage snapping. She swivelled on her heel with the intention of following her terrified son outside. But instead she found herself removing the silk scarf from around her neck. As the man attempted to rise from his seat she stood behind him and pulled the scarf tight across his throat. It was over in seconds. He collapsed heavily back into the chair with the faintest of gurgling sounds. Without a backward glance she rushed out through the church to find her son. A shivering Edwin was crouched in the front passenger seat when she sat in. She went to put her arm around him when shrinking from her he asked what had happened to her hand. She looked down and found her knuckles grazed and that her right hand was spattered with blood.

'Come here my pet, don't you worry about my hand, I probably just banged it off something. It's nothing. Much more to the point Edwin, are you alright'?

Taking her distraught boy in her arms she held him as their tears intermingled. When his sobs subsided she kissed his forehead and said

'Let's get along home now Edwin and try to put all this out of our minds. You know your cousins will all be here later on, as well as all the rest of the aunts and uncles. We'd better go now or there'll be no breakfast and everyone will be late for the Anniversary Mass at 11.00'.

Hannah started the car and taking a steadying breath, she headed slowly towards the exit. Glancing briefly to her left she saw the road was clear. But distracted by the tension emanating from Edwin's stiff shouldered posture, she was looking in his direction as she drove straight out on to the road indicating right.

Back at home Hendy was about his morning chores. With Brendan Walsh's help he was getting through the work as quickly as possible. Contrary to his wife's expectations, he was aware of how important the hosting of this event was to Hannah. He had planned to finish early, so that he could have the fry-up underway, by the time she returned from early Mass. When the men returned to the kitchen they found Florrie and Constance already up and sipping tea companionably, by the range. Hendy set to immediately, preparing the breakfast. Florrie cut the homemade brown bread into neat slices, while Constance set the table. All were conscious of the time but no one said anything about Hannah's tardiness. Eventually when everything was in readiness and afraid that they'd be late for Mass Hendy suggested that they should sit down and eat. He was carefully serving up when he noticed that Shay was missing. He couldn't be found and no one had seen him leave. Florrie thought that perhaps he had gone to early mass with Hannah and Edwin and was disappointed that he would have chosen to do so. However Brendan reassured her that Shay was definitely still in the house after Hannah had driven off. Perhaps he had decided to walk to Mountbrien Constance suggested placatingly. Hendy served breakfast for the five of them and plated up for Hannah, Edwin and Shay on their return. Then he stowed the extra portions in the bottom oven to keep warm, while he and his guests ate theirs. Glancing at the clock he reckoned that something must have happened to delay Hannah so he decided to put the joint of beef in the oven. Hannah had boiled a ham the previous day and as far as vegetables and potatoes were concerned there was no immediate rush. By now Hendy was getting seriously worried. If Hannah didn't turn up soon with the car then they'd be unable to get to the church on time. Just as Brendan had offered that he'd drive instead, a car could be heard driving into the farmyard. Hendy breathed a sigh of relief and hurried outside. But it was not Hannah's Volkswagen in the yard. Instead it was Doctor Findlay's wife Maureen who emerged from her fashionable red sports car. Before she had a chance to open her mouth he knew with a sinking feeling that something awful had happened. Brendan appeared in the doorway flanked by Constance in her wheelchair and Florrie in her good coat and hat.

'I'm afraid there will be no 11.00 Mass today in Mountbrien' Maureen stated as she tried to indicate to the trio in the doorway that they should all return indoors. Linking a stumbling Hendy she followed them into the warmth of the kitchen. Once inside she put the kettle back on the hob and produced a bottle of brandy from her commodious handbag.

'I'm so sorry Mr Henderson but there has been a terrible accident. Gerry rang me at home a few minutes ago and asked me to come over immediately to tell you that Hannah and Edwin have been involved in a collision outside the church. Gerry has gone with them in the ambulance to the hospital. I understand that Father Murphy is dead too'.

Into the stunned silence that followed this Florrie eventually whispered

'I don't understand, why did you say Father Murphy is dead too? Do you mean that Hannah is dead or is it Edwin? Please, please say it is not true'.

The ensuing silence was broken by Brendan grabbing a handful of mugs which he placed in front of Maureen on the table. Maureen decanted generous measures of brandy, which she insisted that they should all drink, to help deal with the shock. She picked up her story and gave them what little detail she had gleaned from her husband's phone call. It would appear that Hannah had driven out of the church car park straight into the path of an oncoming truck. The unfortunate truck driver had done his best to stop but couldn't avoid hitting the car broadside on. He too was now at the hospital, being treated for shock and a broken leg. As it happened Doctor Findlay had been the first to arrive at the scene. He was on his way home from a sick call and had actually witnessed the truck jack knife just ahead of him. He found both Hannah and Edwin in the crushed and distorted remains of the car. Hannah had been killed instantly. Edwin was unconscious but Gerry had detected a weak pulse. He then asked his wife to go to the Henderson farm and break the tragic news to Harold. Just before ringing off, he had added that Father Murphy was also dead. When Maureen asked how, her husband had used just two words tersely 'separate incident' in a tone she recognised to mean 'don't ask'.

Gerry Findlay was upset at finding that there was absolutely nothing he could do for his neighbour and friend by way of medical help. Hannah's body was a shattered mess of mangled flesh and shattered bone. Even in death she had instinctively tried to protect Edwin from harm. When Gerry had established beyond doubt that Hannah had no life signs he had to move her body in order to find her son. Edwin's practically unscathed body was sheltered underneath hers. The boy wasn't dead but his pulse was faint and threadlike. It was impossible to gauge whether or not he had internal injuries. The doctor whispered an act of contrition for the deceased and went in search of help for the living. He made his way to the nearby Parochial House to seek assistance from Father Murphy. The priest's housekeeper told him that Father hadn't yet returned home after early Mass. First he used the phone to alert the hospital and ordered two ambulances to the scene. While waiting for the ambulances to arrive he offered what comfort he could to the truck driver. Some twenty minutes later when the ambulances had set off for the hospital he hurried across to the church in search of Father Murphy. The sacristy door was open but no one responded to his call. He hurried forward to find the priest lying slumped and unmoving against the sacristy wall. Father Murphy appeared to have fallen asleep beneath the window. The doctor checked for vital signs, but the priest was undoubtedly dead. Doctor Findlay noticed a number of things about the body. One was the broken and bloodied nose. The second was sickeningly inappropriate. The man's flies were undone. His first instinct was to cover the man's shame and then he noticed that the priest's hands were already attempting to hide his private parts. Feeling shocked and disgusted Gerry then noted that the cord from the window blind was embedded in the man's neck. Finding the key to the sacristy door he locked it behind him. As he returned to the Parochial House he concluded that the priest had attempted to end his own life. He broke the news of Father Murphy's death to the priest's housekeeper and giving her the key to the sacristy suggested that she immediately inform Bishop's house that Father Murphy's body was in the sacristy. He warned her not to enter the sacristy under any circumstances and not to relinquish the key to anyone other than the Bishop or his representative. By this time a crowd had already gathered. The car park at the church was filling up with the 11.00 o clock Mass goers. As luck would have it Father Dan Conneran had travelled with Ambrose and May and their family to attend the anniversary Mass. When the priest's distraught housekeeper tried to explain that due to the sudden death of Father Murphy there would be no 11.00 Mass Father Dan stepped in and volunteered to say the Mass.

Back at the farm the ever practical Constance and her mother Florrie had come to a decision. They thanked Maureen for her handling of the unenviable task she had just performed. Then they asked her for another favour, which she was more than happy to oblige with. While they would go ahead with the preparation of the food for the family they asked would Maureen bring Harold to the hospital. Meanwhile Brendan would make his way to the church and explain what had happened and invite the extended family and friends to return to the farm where they might face the trauma together. When Brendan arrived at the church he found that everyone had gone inside. The congregation were waiting patiently for Mass to begin. He hastened towards the altar to intercept Father Dan and ask him if he could make a short announcement at the end of Mass inviting the extended family of James Corley for whom the Mass was offered to please congregate at the Henderson farmhouse. Then he made his way as quickly as possible to the hospital to offer what comfort he could to his friend Hendy. Married, as they were, to two sisters who were close, they had long since become great friends. Right now Brendan couldn't begin to imagine the horror that faced poor Harold at the hospital alone and unsupported. When he arrived he found the poor man slumped in a chair in the waiting area outside the morgue. Staff members were still preparing Hannah's body for identification. Brendan suspected that whoever was behind the closed doors was perhaps holding off in the hope that the poor Harold would not have to face the ordeal alone. Accustomed as they were to their work this aspect of it was always demanding and difficult. Their hearts went out to the families of accident victims. In Harold's case they were aware that he had the heart-breaking task of identifying not only the body of his beloved wife but that his only son had also been involved in the accident. Brendan was relieved to have arrived in time to share the horrifying experience with his brother-in-law. It crossed his mind that since Maureen Findlay had broken the tragic news the man they had known as Hendy for more than fifteen years had become in all their minds the more formal Harold.

Within a few minutes the doors to the morgue were opened a crack and a senior nurse emerged. She explained that the body was now ready for viewing for the purpose of identification but counselled that the circumstances of death often rendered accident victims practically unrecognisable. She stressed that the need for a relative to make a definite identification was merely a formality as both Hannah and Edwin had been travelling in the family car. In fact if Mr Henderson preferred he could postpone the task for at least twenty four hours if not longer. Brendan came to Hendy's aid. Whatever it cost him to be here Hendy had steeled himself for the challenge ahead. Heaven alone knew if he could bring himself to summon the courage to return. Knowing this, Brendan helped his friend to his feet and together they made their way into the silent and sterile morgue. The task of identifying Hannah's remains proved very difficult for Hendy. In fairness to the hospital staff they had risen admirably to the challenge of preparing the very badly mutilated body for identification. But nothing can prepare a spouse for the changes wrought by death from full impact trauma on the person of a beloved partner. As far as Harold Henderson was concerned the body lying on the slab could have been anyone. In truth he couldn't have hazarded a guess at the age of the accident victim. Only for the clothing he couldn't be sure whether the body was that of a female or a male. After staring in horror at the mangled remains Hendy turned in confusion to Brendan and said piteously

'Help me Brendan I can see no trace of my beautiful Hannah here'.

Brendan had had a quick word with Hannah in the kitchen that morning. She was wearing a light wool beige skirt and jacket with a cream blouse. She was about to put on her best winter camel-hair coat with the mink collar in preparation for her departure to early morning Mass. She was also wearing a silk scarf, one of her favourites in various shades of pink. But before leaving she had insisted on making a pot of tea for Brendan and apologised that he would have to wait for her return for his breakfast. Picturing her now in his mind's eye, he was able to recognise the blood-stained coat. He quickly identified the body as that of his sister-in-law before hurrying the devastated Hendy from the morgue.

Then they had to make their way to the Intensive Care Unit where they had taken the unconscious boy. Edwin looked like he was sleeping but to both his father and uncle he appeared oddly younger than he had just a few short hours before. His face was miraculously unmarked by the horrendous accident but had acquired a deathly pallor. They were told that preliminary x-rays suggested that no bones had been broken but that there were signs of significant bruising. There was really nothing to be done now but wait patiently for Nature to take its course and for Edwin to come round from the trauma induced coma. Brendan was advised to take Hendy home. On their way out he insisted on stopping at the little restaurant adjoining the hospital. Here he bought a large pot of strong tea which they drank heavily sweetened cup after comforting cupful in silent preparation for what lay ahead. Then with heavy hearts they set off for Glashabawn to face Hannah's assembled family in all its diversity. On arrival they found everyone crowded into the kitchen. Hannah's mother Florrie and her sister Constance were sitting either side of the range. Michael and Betty, Kitty and Jeremiah along with Ambrose and May, Shay and Father Dan were seated around the kitchen table. Nora was busying herself with topping up the mugs of tea that everyone was clutching. The conversations immediately ceased at the appearance of Brendan and Hendy. Ambrose and Father Dan leapt to their feet and insisted on ceding their places at table to them. Hendy and

Brendan sat down and accepted the tea proffered by Nora. After toying with it for a moment or two Hendy cleared his throat and addressing his brothers-in-law and sisters-in-law thanked them for coming and invited them to adjourn to the sitting room where they would be more comfortable. Knowing Hannah as they all did he stated that they must know that she would be itching to feed them all. It was the last thing on her mind before she left for Mass and was no doubt her main priority as she left the church for home. Suddenly Hendy noticed the absence of children. He was assured that all the youngsters had been rounded up by Kevin and Marnie Power and brought to the adjoining farm where they would be fed and comforted by these good neighbours who would be happy to hold on to them all for as long as was necessary. Meanwhile back at Hendersons, typical of Hannah's organised efficiency there was plenty of food prepared and if they would give him a half an hour or so Hendy would like to dish up a meal that she would be proud of. He was trying to usher the menfolk and Florrie out of the kitchen when Constance quietly took him aside. She explained to him that she understood why he wished to fulfil Hannah's chores but it would be more appropriate to allow herself and her sisters to accomplish what was second nature to them for Hannah's sake. Reluctantly he allowed himself to be persuaded and followed the others. At the last minute Kitty excused herself and quickly accompanied him to the sitting room.

The change of location not only altered the dynamic but also loosened tongues. The Corleys had started to talk among themselves and try to come to terms with the catastrophe that had befallen the family. They had formed into small groups in the large formal sitting room. Florrie was seated closest to the fire in the company of her sons Shay and Ambrose and Ambrose's wife May. Kitty made her way immediately to Jeremiah's side. They always stuck together and Jeremiah had already managed to pull Michael and Betty into his company so now they were all seated around the sofa table. Brendan and Father Dan were hovering near the drinks cabinet in case anyone needed a drink. Shay was trying to comfort his mother by regaling her with stories of childhood pranks of her older children to distract her from the loss of her youngest daughter. Ambrose despite his own overwhelming grief understood what Shay was about and he and May struggled to support him by providing an interested audience for the anecdotes. Father Dan and Brendan were holding a quiet conversation while keeping a close eye on the two groups. And so it was that they were the first to hear the raised voices of Jeremiah and Michael on the sofa.

Immediately after Mass was over Michael had made it his business to talk to Gerry Findlay whom he had known since they were at university together. Seeing the doctor at the back of the church he had slipped out the side door so he could intercept him on the way out. Gerry had immediately offered his condolences and was obviously upset. In an effort to divert his mind from the trauma he had recently experienced Michael asked him about the other death that morning. As soon as Father Murphy's name was mentioned Gerry's face suffused had with anger.

'Don't talk to me about that fellow and how he had us all fooled the so-and-so. I blame him for this whole sorry mess'.

But when Michael wished to pursue the matter further Gerry refused to comment and abruptly took his leave. Michael was surprised at the uncharacteristically rude behaviour of the doctor and of course he was curious as to the reason for Gerry's anger. He had been mulling over what had been said ever since. Just now he had related what had happened to his wife, sister and brother-in-law. He was seeking to make sense of what he had witnessed. Betty and Kitty were intrigued but before they could venture a comment Jeremiah started to declaim in stentorian tones

'I knew it, I bloody knew it. Kitty haven't I always said that that fellow was a lousy blackguard. I never liked him but of course the bloody Corleys wouldn't have a word said against a man of the cloth. But you see I was right all along. These fellows think that just because they wear their collars back to front that they're above the rest of us. In their arrogance they think that they can do what they bloody like. I bet that bollix was a dirty little shirt lifter. I for one am bloody glad he got what was coming to him … …'

Before he could say another word Shay and Ambrose had converged on him and catching him by the elbows escorted a struggling Jeremiah into the hallway and out the front door. Father Dan indicated to Michael that he should follow his brothers and then set about restoring calm. Outside the brothers asked Jeremiah what he had been about to say before he was so unceremoniously removed from the company of Hendy and the grieving women. Sulkily he said that if as he suspected the priest had been interfering with young Edwin and that if Hannah had got wind of it then he for one would commend her for killing the bastard. Ambrose was dumbstruck at this appalling scenario. Michael looked like he'd had his worst nightmare confirmed. Shay for his part said nothing. He appeared to be angry and disgusted that Jeremiah, whatever his suspicions, could be so crass as to voice them in such crude terms. He was further incensed that Jeremiah had so little empathy that he could and would have done so in the presence of Florrie, his own wife Kitty and their sisters-in-law. Neither Ambrose nor Michael could bring themselves to entertain the thought that gentle Hannah could be capable of murder. Each of them in turn tried to persuade the churlish Jeremiah that he must be mistaken. They were united in the view no member of the Corley family should ever be burdened with Jeremiah's suspicions. Michael in his authoritative fashion said 'since you have absolutely no proof to support your theories you should keep your half-baked opinions to yourself.' Ambrose carefully and kindly emphasised that there was no point in worrying the womenfolk with idle speculation and begged Jeremiah not to repeat his slanderous assumptions regarding their beloved Hannah. And Shay impatiently growled 'Jeremiah you shouldn't try to paint others in your own evil image especially not our youngest sister. Now don't be such a plank and think for a minute what devastation you'd cause poor Hendy who surely has more than enough to contend with as it is.'

Constance and Nora having already prepared and cooked the vegetables and potatoes were busy getting the dinner to the table. They had noted Kitty's dodging out of the work and acknowledged that they were as well off without her help. They had agreed that allowing Hendy to carve the meat at table would be a helpful distraction for him. Meanwhile they occupied themselves with heating plates and setting the table. Fifteen minutes later the Corley brothers and Jeremiah were called to their dinner. Soon everyone was seated around the kitchen table eating. The distraction had helped. Hendy encouraged them to eat and even managed a wry joke about how the Hendersons of previous generations would be so horrified by the notion of waste of food that they would haunt them if they didn't eat every scrap. He then busied himself ensuring that everyone was served but still he found his eyes straying to the door in the forlorn hope that Hannah and Edwin would somehow breeze in on the wind of their combined energies as they had every day for as far back as he could remember. Each time he did this or cocked his ear to the sound of a passing car it hit him like a crushing blow that Hannah was now part of his past and no matter how much he wished it, it would never be otherwise. With enormous effort he strove to overlay the horrific image of the body in the morgue with this vibrant image of his lovely wife bursting into the kitchen already talking about where she'd been and what she'd been doing followed nine times out of ten by their beautiful boy as lively and energetic and open as his mother. From the very early days of their courtship he had told Hannah that she reminded him of a little bee. She was always so industrious, buzzing with energy and activity and humming with sweetness and vibrancy. His pet name for her had been 'Buzzy'. Now he'd never see his beloved Buzzy in the heart of their home again. Before his thoughts could stray towards the chasm into which his only child had plunged Hendy threw himself into hosting duties that heretofore he had only observed from the side-lines. For now the best he could do was to ensure that Hannah's family would be looked after as well as he could possibly manage while they came to terms with what had happened. He was glad that the Corleys were all gathered in the one place so that they could support each other. The realisation that this blessing too was due to her family's high regard for his beloved Hannah almost unmanned him. He saw the busyness required of him as a gift from his dearest Buzzy to help him cope and so it proved at least in the short-term. Whenever grief threatened to overwhelm him and he felt his heart flutter with panic at the prospect of facing the future, he tried to calm himself with the thought that the sensation he was feeling was his beloved Buzzy keeping close to his heart.

After the dinner had been eaten and everything in the kitchen restored to order they all crowded into the sitting room again. Once seated, the more gregarious chatted among themselves in subdued tones while the quieter ones were content to blend into the background. There was a certain comfort in being physically together even though they were all preoccupied with their own thoughts. The women left the room at intervals during the evening, returning with endless cups of tea with which they tirelessly plied the others. As night drew in, and without any apparent planning all present came to be aware of what arrangements needed to be made. Hendy had been on the phone to the hospital to enquire about his son and also to ask when Hannah's body would be released for burial. The duty nurse explained that there was no significant change in Edwin's condition. His pulse was still weak and he was showing no signs of emerging from his coma. As for Hannah her body could be removed for burial whenever it suited Hendy and the undertaker to do so. When he shared the information with the family Father Dan asked quietly

'Hendy what are your wishes with regard to religious ceremonies and the burial of our beloved Hannah? I ask only that I may be able to assist you in whatever arrangements need to be made.'

Hendy hadn't given it much thought but now suddenly realised the full implication of the priest's enquiry. Coming from different religious backgrounds he and Hannah were aware that at some stage they would have to make a decision regarding their burial arrangements but as they were still young it hadn't seemed urgent. When they married they had each continued to worship in the church of their family traditions. When Edwin was still only a baby Hannah had begun taking him with her to Sunday mass and Hendy had raised no objection. Then as he grew up Edwin began to show an interest in Catholicism and Hendy being the understanding Dad he was, appreciated his son's fervour and supported his decision to practice his mother's faith. Now despite the weight of expectations of generations of Hendersons that his wife should be buried with his Church of Ireland forebears Hendy knew in his heart that Hannah would prefer a Catholic ceremony. And so it came about that Hannah would be buried in the Corley family plot in Kiltyroe, Knocknashee in County Clare almost fifty miles from the Henderson farm in Glashabawn.

He prayed as he had never prayed before that he would not be called upon any time soon to make a decision about burial arrangements for their only son.

PART V

16

Robert meets Constance

Having read Constance's letter Robert suddenly had a focus for and a sense of purpose to his day. He busied himself tidying up. Then shrugging himself into his coat, he accompanied Clara down to the street. 'Let's have a quick bite of lunch together Clara. The café will do me, if you don't mind. I need to get myself to Holborn as quickly as possible'.

Once seated, he ordered the special of the day for both of them and making short work of his own meal, he was soon on his way, having bid a hasty farewell to Clara. He hurried towards the nearest London Underground station at Knightsbridge and within ten minutes was aboard a train on the Piccadilly Line heading southwards for six stops. He passed through Hyde Park Corner, Green Park, Piccadilly Circus, Leicester Square and Covent Garden before alighting at Holborn Station. Here he enquired how he might get to Whetstone Park and discovered that he was a mere five minute walk from it. He set off at a brisk pace and it didn't take him long to locate the address Constance had sent him. Delighted that it had all been so easy, he approached the door at garden level. There was no name on the bell push but Robert was in no doubt that he was outside Shay Corley's flat. He rang again and again but no one answered. As the little light on the bell push was obviously working and he could hear the bell buzzing within he concluded that Shay must be out. He was a bit disappointed as he headed home but also pleased that he now knew where to find Shay. He made up his mind that he would return the following day. Next day being Sunday, he was free to visit at any time. So to avoid missing Shay again Robert set off the following morning and was ringing the bell of the flat a little after 11.00 a.m. He had reckoned that if Shay wanted to attend Mass he would be more likely to select an early morning service and should be back at the flat by 11.00. If as Robert suspected, Shay was still drinking heavily, it was unlikely that he would go to the pub until at least early afternoon. So it was with a sense of confidence that he approached the house and again rang the bell. Again he was disappointed. No one came to the door. Feeling a bit let down by his second wild goose chase, Robert turned away and went for a stroll in Whetstone Park. The weather was crisp and dry and the sun fought valiantly to brighten the day. He enjoyed his walk. After an hour and a half he emerged on the north side of the park. He went in search of somewhere to have a bite to eat. He wandered the unfamiliar streets until he found a hostelry. Here he enjoyed a pub lunch, drank a glass of merlot and decided to retrace his steps in the hope that Shay might have returned in the meantime. On his return to 47 Whetstone Square South, a little after 3 o' clock there was still no answer when he rang the doorbell. He decided to write a short message on the back of one of his business cards and drop it through the letter box. He also underlined his phone number, in the hope that Shay might ring him. Then he headed back to Knightsbridge. He was busy the next day and by the time he was finished at work it was too late to go to Holborn again. He checked with Clara that Shay had not rung the office number during the day and made his way home. He switched on his answering machine but no call from Shay had been recorded either. He would be away from the office at a two day conference on Tuesday and Wednesday so he knew he wouldn't get a chance to call to Holborn again until Thursday evening at the earliest. As things turned out he didn't manage to call until after work on Friday evening. It was about 8.15 as he approached the house and was surprised to note that there was no light coming from the uncurtained window of the downstairs flat. He rang the bell anyway and as expected no one came to the door in response. He mulled over it for a while, debating whether or not he should be worried at his failure to contact Shay. In the end, he decided that it was worth the risk of disturbing the residents of the other flats in the building in an effort to establish whether or not any one had seen Shay in recent days. He climbed the flight of granite steps to the imposing front door and selected the top of the five bell pushes. No one responded from there either. He thought he'd work his way down the row of bells until he elicited a response. He had no luck with the next one and was about to press the third when he heard hurried footsteps rush up the steps behind him. A young man almost collided with him in his hurry to insert his key in the front door lock.

'Sorry' he muttered 'but I'm in an awful rush. I don't want to be late for my night classes.

'I won't hold you young man, I just wanted to enquire about my friend Shay Corley in the ground floor flat' said Robert hastily. 'Who is asking? You surely don't expect me to discuss my neighbours with random strangers' said the youth as he firmly closed the door in Robert's face.

Recovering himself Robert decided to hang about for a while in the hope that the young fellow might reappear soon on his way to his night class. Sure enough within a few minutes the door opened and the young man hurried back down the steps. Robert fell into step with him and proffered a business card, explaining that he was worried about his friend. Stopping under a street light to examine the card the young man confessed that he hadn't seen Shay for the bones of a month. In fact he hadn't taken any notice until Robert had asked. He added that Mr Corley, though invariably polite to his neighbours, had always kept himself to himself and wouldn't have welcomed intrusions on his privacy. He then introduced himself as Tony Malone and said that he had fully intended to ignore Robert if he found him still hovering on the doorstep. But mentioning it to his wife Lillian as he hurriedly changed his clothes she had expressed concern that neither of them in their comings and goings had seen Mr Corley in a long while. Tony then accelerated his pace and hastened towards the underground station. Robert followed at a more leisurely walk lost in thought. He decided he would return to Holborn in the morning, to see if he could extract more information from other residents. Perhaps he could find out if there was a resident janitor, or if all else failed he'd try to find the owner of the building. On his way home on the train Robert thought over the events of the past week. He found it hard to believe that less than a week ago he had no idea where Shay might be and now he was almost as familiar with his address as he was with his own. Furthermore he couldn't credit how confiding in Clara Tilsley had lifted his spirits. In the thirty two years since his arrival in London he had never opened up to another human being. Although Shay Corley had befriended him in his youth the combination of the fact that he had been Robert's boss and the Kiltyroe connection had resulted in a certain reluctance on Robert's part to confide and on Shay's part to pry. Since the previous Saturday it was as if a huge weight had been lifted from his shoulders. Not only that, but he had been sleeping more soundly at night. And he had been waking feeling more refreshed. Each morning for the past week he had felt invigorated and ready for anything that the day might bring. Of course he still had secrets and he certainly wasn't ready yet to share some of his innermost horrors with anyone and certainly not with a member of the fairer sex. But nonetheless, sharing his burden, insofar as he had with Clara, had been a surprisingly cathartic experience.

On Saturday morning Robert woke early and with a sense of urgency. He set off for Holborn feeling optimistic that today he would be lucky. He rehearsed in his head how the conversation with Shay would go. He was looking forward to catching up on the missing years, but more than anything he was dying to renew the friendship, open up more and stop keeping Shay at arm's length. He made his way to the door, convinced that this time he would get an answer and cheerfully pressed the bell. But once more after several attempts no one came to the door. This time he decided to make his way to the front window and peer inside. The curtains had not been drawn so he was able to see into the room. He could see the little kitchenette in the corner, the table and two chairs. As he leaned in on the right hand side he was able to see the lower end of what he took to be a single divan. He had a feeling that someone was still in the bed and the hump in the middle was covering the shape of a sleeping figure. He knocked sharply on the windowpane but still there was no response. Taking a coin from his pocket he rapped even harder but still the sleeper didn't stir. By now he was sufficiently worried to go for help. He hurried up to the main door and found Tony Malone's bell push and pressed it insistently for several seconds. Almost immediately he heard Tony tripping down the stairs in his bare feet and muttering to himself.

'For God's sake will you keep your hair on 'tis only a quarter to nine on a Saturday morning? Bloody hell, the one day you have a chance of a lie in, some busybody has to sit on your bell at first light'. He threw the door open and growled 'Oh not you again! Of course I haven't seen Mr Corley since last night. I intended to look him up later today. Anyway what's the panic at this hour of the morning'?

'Tony, I'm so sorry to have disturbed you and Lillian but I've been ringing Shay's bell for ages and getting no reply. I peeped in at his window and to tell you the truth I'm very worried. I think he's in bed but no matter how loudly I rap there's no movement. Is there any way we can get into the flat to check on him? Do you have a key? If not do you know who might have a one'?

'Whoa there Robert, step inside for a sec and let me try to answer a few of your questions.

On second thoughts come on up and let me get dressed. I'm sure Lillian will have the tea made by now'. They made their way upstairs to the back first floor apartment where Lillian offered them tea. While Tony was throwing on some clothes, Robert told Lillian what he had noticed.

'Tony doesn't the guy in the front ground floor flat have a master key to all the apartments in case of an emergency? I've heard he has been able to let people in on occasion when they've managed to lock themselves out'. The three of them made their way downstairs and knocked on the door of the apartment directly inside the front door. The door was opened straightaway by a rather dour looking older man. When they had explained their errand Phil Williamson left them standing in the hallway for some time, while he telephoned the owner of the building. Eventually he reappeared and told them they would have to wait for at least half an hour until Mr Evans arrived. They waited in the Malone's living room. When Tommy Evans turned up Robert and Tony accompanied him outside. Tommy opened the outer door and the three men entered Shay Corley's basement flat. It was immediately obvious that something was seriously amiss. The stench was overwhelming. Tony rushed back outside and vomited violently. The two older men proceeded into the bed-sit knowing only too well what awaited them. Poor Shay had been dead for some considerable time.

Bodies begin to decompose shortly after death. The first of five stages begins immediately after the heart stops beating. Because the heart is no longer pumping, the blood drains to other parts of the body creating an overall bluish-purplish discolouration usually called livor mortis. Within three to six hours, the muscular tissues become rigid and incapable of relaxing and what is commonly called rigor mortis sets in. Putrefaction then begins, leading to the second stage of decomposition known as bloat. This is when the accumulation of gases within the bodily cavity causes the distension of the abdomen and makes the corpse appear bloated and sometimes indeed to rupture. If flies or insects then have access, maggots hatch and begin to feed on the bodily tissues. Escaping gases and fluids result in the overpowering distinctive stink associated with the third stage of decomposition known as active decay. It is at this stage that the greatest amount of disintegration and mass loss occurs. It happens as a result of both the voracious feeding of maggots and also the leakage of decomposition fluids into the surrounding environment. The end of active decay is signalled by the migration of maggots away from the body to pupate. At this juncture the fourth stage called advanced decay occurs followed by the final dry remains stage.

The mortal remains of Shay Corley were at the latter end of the active decay stage, suggesting that he could have been dead for anything up to three weeks. Neither Tommy nor Robert had any knowledge of death at first hand, so finding a body in such an advanced stage of putrefaction was a profoundly shocking experience for both of them. The trauma was exacerbated by the fact that it was not just any cadaver they had found but the corpse of a lodger and a friend. Poor Robert was further troubled by the fact that he had neglected the friendship. He blamed himself for not having tried harder to locate Shay in recent years. His nights would now be haunted by nightmares and the nagging feeling that if only he had been there for Shay he could have at least saved him from the saddest of all deaths 'Bás gan cáirde', death without friends. But at 11 o' clock on the morning of November 15 at 47 Whetstone Square South there was a lot to be done. Tommy Evans and Robert were forced to retreat from the flat, before they were overcome with noxious fumes. They were both feeling queasy as a result of what they had just witnessed. They were also conscious of the urgency of setting things in motion as quickly as possible. As a matter of compliance with health and safety regulations, arrangements must be made immediately for the removal from the premises of the badly decomposed body of Shay Corley. The Coroner would have to be notified. An undertaker would have to be selected and of course Shay's family must be contacted without delay. Tommy undertook to get on to the Borough Council straightaway to alert the Health and Safety Authority and the Coroner. Robert took on the unenviable task of informing Shay's mother Florrie, his sister Constance Walsh and the rest of the Corley family. At first he was tempted to write to the Kiltyroe address but admitting to himself that this was the coward's way out he steeled himself to get the number from directory enquiries and face the trauma of ringing Constance and speaking to her in person. When he had broken the sad news he offered to look after the funeral arrangements. Constance thanked him for his kindness and on behalf of her mother and the family accepted his offer of help.

Constance wanted to come over to London immediately so Robert knew he had to delay her at all costs. As Shay's nominated next of kin she expected that she would have to identify the body. Robert didn't want her to have to face such a gruesome prospect and felt that if he could put her off, even for a few days, he might be able to spare her the horror of what he had already experienced. Given that both he and Tommy Evans had been present when the body had been found, and that Shay was well known to both of them, Robert was confident that the authorities could be persuaded to accept their identification as sufficient for the record. Unfortunately, he was mistaken and the authorities insisted that the body must be identified by a family member. As things turned out however Constance was spared the trauma of this most harrowing task as her brothers Michael and Ambrose were adamant that they would fly over immediately to deal with it. Robert went ahead and made the funeral arrangements. As the Corley family, in accordance with Shay's own wishes wanted to lay him to rest in his native Kiltyroe, Robert had to hire a London undertaker as well as hiring Dowlings the local firm of undertakers in Kiltyroe. The London undertakers were responsible for preparing the body for burial and placing it in a lead-lined casket for transportation to Ireland. All this took some time so it was December 12 when the casket was finally ready to travel by air-freight from Heathrow to Dublin Airport where Dowling's hearse would meet the mourners and proceed to Kiltyroe for the interment the following day. Robert was the only one to accompany the body on the London to Dublin flight. And he it was who had the task of ensuring that the casket was reclaimed at the Dublin end.

When he arrived at the mortuary Robert was surprised to find that quite a number of mourners had already gathered. Shay's brothers along with several of his nephews and nieces, many with members of their families were there.

The intention was to accompany the funeral procession home to Kiltyroe. Also in attendance were some of Shay's former classmates from St. Cosmas's College, as well as a scattering of politicians and senior civil servants who had worked with him long ago in Dublin. The cortege leaving the airport was followed by about twenty five cars facing the miserable hundred and forty mile journey. About thirty miles out from Kiltyroe the first car joined up. And soon they were waiting at almost every crossroad; augmenting the procession by at least another thirty cars. By the time it had reached Ennis that number had swelled to over eighty. More and more cars joined the cortege and finally the bikes, down the narrow, winding road in the dusk so that when it finally arrived at St. Ruan's church there were more than a hundred vehicles clogging the village street and the approach roads for a mile or more on either side. It was more than an hour after the scheduled arrival time of 8 o' clock when the coffin was carried shoulder high into the church. There Florrie, a slender and tiny lady with snow-white hair, a soft voice, and clear friendly eyes, took her place at the head of her family as the coffin was moved within the church door. This was the third time she had come to bury a loved one, first her dear husband James, then her beloved Hannah cut down in her prime, and now poor troubled Shay. She struggled to keep her composure while feeling grateful at the huge turnout. By now the crowd was large, too large a crowd for the village church. Many of the sympathisers were forced to remain in the churchyard throughout the ceremony. After the rosary and the prayers for the dead, Father Dermot Ryan the parish priest announced from the altar that the Walsh and Corley families would be happy to welcome all members of the congregation, especially those who had travelled long distances, to partake of some refreshments at Shay's childhood home. When people emerged from the church, they were shepherded by the younger generation, both relatives and neighbours, in the direction of Corley's as it was still known in the locality. The youngsters explained to the visitors, that they were better off leaving the cars where they were, as Ashdene House was only a couple of minutes' walk away. Constance's young grandson Jody a favourite of his Uncle Shay waited patiently until Robert emerged to ensure that he would be accompanied home.

'Excuse me Mr Fitzmaurice. Will you come back to the house for a wee bite to eat'? he asked.

'Oh no, not at all young man, I'll be heading off now but I will see you in the morning; sorry I don't know your name' Robert replied.

'I'm Jody Walsh, Shay was my uncle. Please Mr Fitzmaurice, you really should come home with me for a couple of good reasons. First, Uncle Shay would never forgive me if I failed to invite his friend and probably more importantly Granny Florrie wants to talk to you and lastly Mam will skin me alive if I make a botch of the one small job she gave me to do'.

'Okay Jody. I take it that your mother is Constance Walsh and I have no wish to upset the good lady so against my own instincts I'll go with you. I will not overstay my welcome I promise you'.

So they fell into step and by the time they reached the house they were relaxed with each other and chatting away companionably. Instead of going in the front door as he had been directed Jody insisted on bringing Robert directly to the kitchen where he knew he'd find his dad Brendan. His mother and sister and his Granny Florrie, would be upstairs supervising the supply of tea and refreshments for the crowd of visitors. Brendan would put Robert at ease as only he knew how. Jody was certain that no matter how busy the kitchen was his dad would find a quiet corner to sip tea with and make Robert welcome and comfortable. It would be time enough for meeting with Florrie and Constance when the crowd had thinned out upstairs.

17

Shay's Homecoming

On arrival at the wake house, the visitors were ushered in the front door and into the dining room to the right, where an abundance of food was arranged buffet style. Having helped themselves to a selection of foods, people drifted through to the sitting room where others were already seated and eating. Tea in china cups was promptly served and sweetened and cooled to taste by an army of local women, who remained on hand for top ups as required. The family members circulated, welcoming and speaking with all the callers. Some people moved on rather quickly while others were in no hurry to leave. By midnight only family and close friends remained. At this stage Brendan and Jody had brought Robert upstairs to meet Florrie. They were getting along very well, having some quiet words together when Barry called for everyone's attention saying

'If you don't mind I've noticed that there are a lot of individual conversations about Shay going on. Everyone is busy reminiscing and as lots of people are anxious to share their own best memories of Shay, I wondered if it wouldn't be better if we all gathered in. We could all settle down for a bit of storytelling and later maybe we'd have some music and give Uncle Shay a proper send-off'.

So they all sat around the fire and Constance began by paying tribute to her beloved brother. She spoke of his great love for their mother Florrie, his generosity of spirit, his innate kindness, his unwavering sense of justice and fair play and his love of mischief. Her brothers Michael and Ambrose and sisters Nora and Kitty soon joined in and illustrated these traits with stories from their childhood. This opened up the floodgates and soon everyone in the room had an anecdote to tell, a joke to share or a witticism of Shay's to repeat. Some of the friends of his youth in Kiltyroe were delighted to fill the family in on some of the escapades that had involved Shay locally. All agreed that Willie Hurley's stories about school under the tutelage of Shay's austere Papa as school-master were hilarious. A born entertainer as well as a skilled impersonator, Willie enthralled his audience by reliving the experiences complete with 'voices'.

'You remember the day your father decided to do a competitive seven-a-side oral spelling test. I was team captain for one of the teams, and you'll remember Michael you captained the other. Your Papa assigned two contestants to each team and we as captains were allowed to pick the rest. When my turn came the first one I picked was of course Shay, not just because he was a good speller and I couldn't risk you getting him on your team, but more importantly because he always brought fun to every occasion. Anyway we were doing fine despite your dad's best efforts to nobble us with the poorest spellers in the class'.

Michael interrupted

'Willie you can't be serious about your team being nobbled? Do you not remember who he landed our team with? Anyway go on with your story'.

'Well after six rounds with only a point between the teams your dad announced the final round. On the face of it the two teams were evenly enough balanced. We had four good spellers each and two passengers and we were the point up going into the last round. Anyway my team mates had spelt ARITHMETIC, QUANDARY, EXCELLENT and BICYCLE correctly.

Michael's team had come up trumps with PHILOSOPHY, IMMIGRANT, CRYSTAL and TIPPERARY.

With two spellings to go and a good and weak player per team left we were still one up.

Michael's weak player who shall remain nameless correctly spelled ANKLE. Our man was asked to spell KNEE.

He looked stupefied with confusion until the bold Shay started to prompt him, 'a' said Shay sotto voce 'A' repeated our man aloud, 'r' said Shay, 'R' repeated our man, 's' followed by 'S' and finally 'e' followed by 'E', knee followed instantly by a proud and loud KNEE.

The entire class burst into sniggers, giggles and guffaws of laughter depending on how close they were to the apoplectic schoolmaster. When your Papa had restored order he completed the test. The teams were even but when Michael's final player had correctly spelled MOUSTACHE everyone confidently expected a draw as Shay was the only man left to complete the round. With a baleful glare Mr Corley then asked Shay to spell BLACKGUARD. Knowing his goose was cooked, Shay feeling that discretion was the better part of valour misspelled the word thus saving a tie breaker round. Your Papa acknowledged the gesture with a wry smile but I believe Shay got his due punishment at home that night'.

This yarn went down so well that Willie was persuaded to tell another one. This time he reminded his audience of an incident when a younger Shay had proven a trial to his worthy Papa albeit unwittingly. One October afternoon very shortly after young Shay had transferred to third class, and therefore into the senior section of the school to be taught by his Papa, a schools' inspector arrived. It was unusually late in the day for such a visitor, but he was welcomed nonetheless by the headmaster. Mr Grogan enquired as to what he had interrupted as he sat down at the master's desk to scrutinise the roll book and register. He then requested Mr Corley to proceed with the lesson. The lesson was on English grammar and Mr Corley had just begun to introduce the concepts of comparative and superlative forms of adjectives. Mr Grogan had been listening for a while and then decided that he would take over and test the pupils on what they had learned to date. Things went well for a while, and the pupils were answering successfully if somewhat shyly. It was only when the inspector started to challenge the pupils with more difficult questions that they began to get nervous and freeze up. Shay could see that his Papa was unhappy so when no one else seemed willing to answer the question 'Can anyone give me the comparative and superlative forms of the word good'? He took it upon himself to volunteer. Raising his hand he proudly announced

'Sir that would be GOOD, DAMN GOOD and DIVIL A BETTER'.

When the laughter had died down, these stories were augmented by those told by his friends from Dublin's music scene and further added to by his ex-colleagues in the civil service. The stories were mostly about drinking, carousing and the kind of larks, that young fellows are prone to get up to, when they get away from home and discipline for the first time. All the men present could empathise. The younger ones as always were surprised that their elders from previous generations, had been involved in such nefarious activities. Niall Finn, who had joined the Civil Service the same day as Shay had, then shared some of his memories with the gathering. Shay and Niall had worked side by side in their probationary year and for a further eighteen months thereafter. Niall always felt that he couldn't have had a better friend or more supportive colleague than Shay. He too paid tribute to Shay's work ethic, his wit and his antic sense of humour. He told a story of when they both worked for a spell in the Department of Lands in the Land Registry Office. As young Executive Officers, commonly known as EOs, between them they handled the correspondence for the twenty six counties. Shay had been dealing for some time with a case in County Leitrim. A small farmer had applied for a grant, in respect of growing some wheat on his small holding. For some reason, he had failed to provide the paperwork properly, which resulted in a visit from a land registry official. This visit was undertaken by a more senior member of staff an Assistant Principal Officer (APO). By the time the visit eventually took place the poor man had died and his widow, with her brood of small children were in dire straits. The official found that, although the minimum amount of land decreed by the Department to avail of the grant was two acres, when he inspected the crop it was short by a rood. The farmer had sown a rood of rye instead. The widow was then told that she would not now receive the grant aid. When she protested the APO advised her to write a letter of appeal to the Department. The letter ended up on

Shay's desk. Shay felt that the situation had merit, and sent
it up the line recommending the payment of the grant, as an
exceptional matter in the circumstances. The APO agreed,
added his signature to the suggestion and sent it on to the
Principal Officer (PO) Tim O Connor. Here it sat for several
months until Shay received another letter from the widow.
He decided to follow up and made it his business to seek out
the PO at the earliest opportunity and ask him about it. A
few days later, on a Friday night Shay found himself in the
same pub having a few drinks after work. He approached
the PO and reminded him of the case. Mr O Connor was
not amused and told him in no uncertain terms that he
never discussed work matters in a pub and neither should
Shay. Within a few days he was summoned to the PO's office
for a dressing down. When the PO had finished bawling
him out, he asked Shay to outline the case. When Shay
was finished Mr O Connor asked why the PO was being
bothered by such trivialities, and why the decision had not
been dealt with by the relevant APO. Shay explained that he
had followed the protocol and that the APO had forwarded
it with his recommendation to Mr O Connor.

'Which APO was this? And when is all this supposed
to have happened?' barked Mr O Connor. Shay was then
summarily dismissed. He returned to his work station and
tried to figure out what had just happened. The case dragged
on and on until a few weeks later, he received a memo from
the PO's office requesting him, as a matter of urgency, to
forward the file to the newly appointed APO Mr Kenneth
Bates. More delays ensued, and then the correspondence
started all over again. By now Shay was thoroughly sick of
the time wasting, and the wholesale lack of consideration for

the poor widow. Things came to a head, when after several letters back and forth, another visit was proposed. Then this visit was cancelled, in an effort to save money. Meanwhile the file grew bulkier and heavier and Shay grew more and more frustrated. The final straw was, when after several more letters, he was advised that no decision could be made regarding the payment of the nugatory grant, until it could be established what had become of the rood of rye. In a fit of impatience Shay wrote

'Maybe the goat ate it' and returned the file to Mr Bates' office. This time he didn't have long to wait for a response. Mr Bates had reported him to Mr O Connor for insubordination and within days Shay was to be sacked. Shay pre-empted the action by resigning that very evening. Niall had provided the Corleys with an answer to another mystery in the life and times of the recently deceased.

As the wake was taking place in Clare, the evening inevitably turned into the sharing of music and song. The Corleys in turn sang their favourite songs which had been taught to them as children by their exacting father. Nora sat at the old upright piano and accompanied the singers. As a tribute to their parents Florrie's favourite *'Eileen a Rún'* was sung by Constance and *'Some Enchanted Evening'* was reprised by Michael. Soon the instruments were produced and the old tunes played on concertinas, fiddles, accordions, flutes and tin whistles. Young Jody Walsh went off and got a bodhrán he'd made himself and joined in the music. This caused his mother some embarrassment, as she was very conscious that their father hated bodhráns with a passion. In fact he would have thoroughly agreed with Séamus Ennis's much quoted sentiment that '*the best way to play a bodhrán was with a penknife*'. The senior members of the Corley clan overtly consoled her with reassurances that boys will be boys and time had moved on while secretly enjoying her discomfiture. When the impromptu concert was over and it was time for all good people to be in their beds, Constance and Brendan saw the last of the visitors off the premises. Earlier that day Constance had rung the Bed and Breakfast where Robert had booked in, explaining that he would be her guest until the obsequies were over and that the room should be re let. Before retiring for the night, she had taken Robert aside and asked that after the funeral he would return to the house so that she and her mother could have a proper chat and catch up with him.

The 13th of December dawned a freezing cold morning with temperatures nationwide in the minus levels of centigrade. The requiem Mass took place at 11 o' clock in Saint Ruan's. The church was packed to capacity, with most of the people who had been at the removal the previous night as well as neighbours and locals who were unable to attend. Added to this were friends of all the Corleys and Walshes. Robert was surprised and pleased to see four well-dressed gentlemen that he recognised from his days in the Department of Justice in London. Father Ryan had organised a prayerful funeral service. The local choir sang a lovely mixture of traditional and modern hymns in both Irish and English. At Communion Seán Hurley Shay's childhood friend played a plaintive air on the Irish flute and Ambrose gave a poignant rendition of the family variation of 'Danny Boy'. When the Mass ended the mourners followed the cortege and Shay Corley was laid to rest at last in the adjoining cemetery in Kiltyroe. As they emerged from the church Nora turned to her mother and said 'It was a lovely Mass; sure, it would send anyone to Heaven'. Then Michael and Ambrose, Hendy and Brendan, arms locking them into pairs, shoulder to shoulder, carried the coffin up the ridge, up past the ruin of the old cabin church, and down over the graves to where the neighbours had dug the new grave. When the priest had finished the prayers, Florrie turned and said, 'Now, I'll be the next, and I'm glad that my poor lonesome Shay is here at rest in peace beside our lovely Hannah'. When she left the church yard a few tears came and she berated herself for her weakness. Constance dried her tears and tried to emulate her mother's stoic behaviour. When the lone uileann piper had piped Shay home, the mourners made their way on foot to the local Gaelic Athletic Association sports hall, to which everyone had been invited and where refreshments would be served. The friends and neighbours had surpassed themselves in providing a sit down meal for the large gathering. People were seated and waited upon swiftly and efficiently. In less than two hours, over a hundred and sixty people had been well fed and were on their homeward journeys. Shay's siblings and their families remained until all their guests had left. It was only then that the women who had done such a wonderful job at catering for everyone else were at last able to sit down and have something to eat for themselves. Having thanked everyone for their efforts, the Corleys returned to the family home. Here they took their leave one after the other until only Robert and the Walshes were left. An exhausted Florrie went to have a well-earned rest.

18

Constance and Robert

Constance and Robert sat companionably by the cosy fire in the upstairs sitting room, where they wouldn't be disturbed. Constance set about putting Robert at his ease by explaining that being in a wheelchair had certain advantages. For example people tended to confide in her a lot, once they got over their initial tendency to feel sorry for her. She had noticed this from a young age and always told people on first meeting them that she hadn't always been so confined. She had great memories of running, dancing and playing robust games with her siblings until she was struck down with polio at the age of nine. She had never allowed her disability to come between her and her dreams and had gone on to hold down a fulltime job as a bookkeeper for a couple of years until she had married her beloved Brendan and settled down to raise a family. She told Robert that her role as confidante and agony aunt dated back to her teenage years when her siblings found in her a sympathetic and patient listener. Brendan Walsh a classmate, who had known her all their lives, was the first one to accept that what had happened to her had in no way diminished her. He accepted her change in circumstances as a mere blip in her journey and initially helped her in not allowing it to circumscribe her life. As one by one her siblings fled the nest, she had with her mother's encouragement trained as a bookkeeper. When Brendan came a courting, Florrie it was who first noted his interest and encouraged him in pursuit of her charming and independent daughter. From then until Florrie's death at the age of 97 the Corley/Walsh home had been a welcoming haven of family harmony. Now Constance wanted to share some long overdue information with Robert. She started by saying

'First of all Robert I want to thank you for all your help in making the arrangements and for smoothing things for us at the London end. Honestly we wouldn't have known where to begin with the paperwork, never mind the logistics of transporting a body from one jurisdiction to another. My brothers are particularly in your debt and have asked me to reiterate their sincerest thanks to you, not just for your help but also for your kindness and hospitality when they had to go to London for the identification of poor Shay's remains.

But the main reason I needed to talk to you, was to thank you for returning with him to his final resting place. I know that this gift to us was above and beyond the call of friendship.

Also I know how hard it must have been for you to return to Kiltyroe. Believe me I know only too well what courage was required of you to set foot in these parts again, and how traumatic these last few days must have been for you, revisiting the scenes of your childhood. You see I know the circumstances of your departure from Kiltyroe. Shh! a stór do not worry I am not re-opening old wounds thoughtlessly. You are not now, nor ever have been the subject of gossip in this house, or in the village either, as far as I am aware. Your own mother is my source for what I am about to tell you. You will not be aware that I nursed Eliza in her last days. When she knew she was dying, she confided in me that she really hated the idea of having to die in either a hospital or a hospice. Her preference would have been to die at home in her own bed. After your father's death, she had donated all their savings to the Catholic Church. She had also arranged to donate the proceeds from the sale of the house after her death. She had retained only a small amount of money to live on, and unfortunately she later discovered that it was not sufficient to pay for a home nurse.

To prevent her hospitalisation, she agreed to spend her last days here in Ashdene House in my care. In fact she died in this very room over there on the chaise longue. Before she died, Eliza talked frequently about her beloved Frank and also you'll be interested to hear she talked a lot about you. I asked her if she would not like to be reconciled with her only son and she admitted that it was her dearest wish. But in the end she refused to allow me to contact you, saying she could not risk her immortal soul, even to fulfil her own greatest desire. I tried to reason with her but she was immovable. Her favourite quotation was from Matthew Chapter 5 Verse 29

'If your right eye causes you to sin, gouge it out and throw it away. It is better for you to lose one part of your body than your whole body to be thrown to Hell'.

I was surprised at her rigid views, and pleaded with her, suggesting that many devout and God-fearing Catholics nowadays, did not agree with wholesale condemnation of gay people. I reminded her that scripture also directed us to hate the sin, but to love the sinner, and that after all you were being condemned without evidence of any sin and without trial. But Eliza believed her stance was the correct one, especially from what the parish priest had told her and

Frank the night before they had banished you forever from their home.

After that, she said she didn't wish to talk about it anymore, and begged me not to raise the subject again. As far as she was concerned the matter was closed and would remain so. Whatever it was that Father Murphy had accused you of haunted your mother until the end and it's no wonder she died a very conflicted person. From what I myself remember of you growing up, and as the child of such an outstanding couple as your parents I find it hard to accept that you could have committed a crime so heinous as to deserve the punishment meted out to you. I must admit that I had my own reservations about the story, as I had never seen eye to eye with that priest. There was something about him that set my teeth on edge. But in accordance with your mother's wishes, I didn't refer to you again in her presence and she slipped away quietly and we trust peacefully in the end. I didn't make contact with you either, as I knew that's what Eliza wanted but it didn't stop me worrying about you and praying for you. Shay, on his visits home kept me up to date on your progress in London and was able to reassure me and Florrie that you were leading an outwardly happy and successful life. But your mother's words continued to disturb me, and eventually I decided to try and trace the old man who had poisoned her mind against her only son. Recently I decided to trace the horrible old geezer. My conscience was niggling me to try to make some amends by giving you some information at least which might lead you to seek some form of redress. At my request, Brendan drove me to Bishop's House and knowing well he was redundant for a few hours he left me there to be collected later. I enquired of the good bishop where I might start to find out the current whereabouts of Father Festus Murphy. First of all I wished to establish whether or not he was still ministering as a priest'.

'He should never have been a priest in the first place' interrupted Robert. You know that the hardest part of my realisation that I was different was the fear that people would compare me to that horrible man. And much as I disliked him it was nothing to the venomous hatred he had for me. He never tired of his favourite sport of baiting me and making me look bad in front of my parents who in turn berated me endlessly for not showing proper respect to a man of the cloth. Anyway I haven't wasted a thought on the old reprobate in years. Sorry I interrupted you Constance.'

'Well I was shown into a small reception room in Bishop's House. I wasted no time in asking him what had become of Father Festus Murphy who had served in the parish of Kiltyroe from 1940 to 1944 him. I asked him straight out what part he had played in your banishment. First he blustered and pretended not to know what I was talking about. But I was in no hurry so I let him sweat it out. Even as long ago as 1944 there were questions being asked about his behaviour? No one wanted to talk about it then but there were suspicions that he had behaved inappropriately with young boys. Eventually the bishop admitted that around the time you were doing the Leaving Cert the net had begun to close in on Father Murphy. In a last ditch effort to divert attention away from himself, when a nine year old boy had made a complaint against him, the unscrupulous blackguard had persuaded the boy's parents that the child was mistaken. To cover his tracks he had hinted to them that the incident the youngster had described could indeed be true and he would root out the perpetrator. He then went to his parishioners the Fitzmaurices and led them to believe that you my dear Robert were not just gay but were also a paedophile. He then played on their emotions by suggesting that it was only a matter of time before the police would arrive to arrest you. Terrified for your safety both physical and moral, they came to their heart-breaking decision and the rest of course you know'.

Poor Robert was speechless with horror. He couldn't believe that anyone could be so evil as to make such an accusation against an innocent teenager. His brain swam with conflicting emotions. His eyes filled with tears of pity for his unfortunate parents who had been so cruelly duped. At last he began to reach some understanding of why they had done what they did. He cringed with shame at the thought of their suffering, in trying to come to terms with the fact that they had raised and loved a son, whom they had been assured was a pervert. Then he marvelled at the strength of their love for him, that they were prepared to give him the benefit of the doubt, to the extent that they allowed him to escape the pursuit of the law. This must have been very difficult for such law abiding citizens as his parents. He wondered at how such a religious couple would have battled with their consciences to facilitate the escape of a paedophile. Part of him hoped that they didn't really believe the accusation made against him. He was still reeling from the shock of Constance's revelations and the dawning realisation that his poor parents had suffered as much, if not more than he himself had, from their enforced separation. When he recovered his breath Robert said

'Oh Constance! Can you imagine how my poor parents must have suffered'?

Constance's response was to open her arms and give him a comforting hug. Then she said

'I'm sorry to have upset you my dear, and I hope you will forgive me for pursuing the matter. But it plagued me to see how conflicted your poor mother was, and as time went on I felt I couldn't just stand idly by and do nothing to get to the bottom of the mystery. And for some reason, I always felt that that evil cleric was somehow involved. It raises my blood pressure to think about the torture he put you all through. Robert I am so sorry'.

Struggling to steady himself, Robert replied 'my dear Constance thank you so much for all you have done. It will probably take me some time to absorb what you have told me, and maybe even longer to come to terms with it. Anyway how could you have known'?

'All it needs for evil to prevail is for the good to do nothing, or whatever that old adage is. We were all shocked at your disappearance, but no one made any attempt to find you. We just sat idly by wondering what had happened, or else we judged your poor parents for their apparent insensitivity and their very real unwillingness to talk about it. In fact we chose to ignore it and forget about you. I blame myself most of all. Even when Shay was home that first time and mentioned that he had met you and that you worked with him I did nothing. I didn't tell him about your abrupt disappearance. Worse I never told poor Eliza that I knew where you were. In fact I sat on my hands and did absolutely nothing. Oh my God to think that I could have spared you all such anguish'.

Robert smiled and in spite of the circumstances started to chuckle which caused Constance to look at him sharply.

'We make a priceless pair you and I Constance. Here was I dreading this meeting, because I felt so guilty about neglecting Shay. I've been berating myself for not having done more to seek out your brother and see what had become of him over the past eight years. I was so ashamed of the way I had done nothing for the man who had been such a good friend to me, and fearful of having to explain myself to your good self. So Constance, please stop beating yourself up about failing me. Can we now agree to be kind and to forgive ourselves and each other for the failings of our past? I've no doubt Shay has forgiven us, and I'm sure Eliza and Frank are looking down on us happy in the knowledge that we have brought some comfort to each other'.

Later the same day, Robert took his leave of the Walshes, promising to keep in touch. This time, as he made his way back to Dublin in his hired car, he had the comfort of knowing that he would be welcome back in Kiltyroe whenever it suited him. Not only had Constance insisted that he return at any time but her kind invitation had been supported in turn by Brendan, Barry and even young Jody. So it was with a feeling of warmth and inner peace that he boarded his flight and headed back to his London home.

PART VI

19

Ella's Story

Going back to school in September, was the best possible therapy for me. My little four year old charges kept me fully occupied all day long. The amount of preparation necessary to maintain nearly forty little ones focused and enthusiastically involved in their own learning, kept me busy late into the evenings. My colleagues were wonderful at this time, especially Lucy Holohan my closest friend on staff. Lucy Holohan and I had first met in Teacher Training College and because we were both country girls we often found ourselves hanging about with a group of other Tipperary students. Over our three years in college we often met on trains and buses, as we went to and fro, visiting our families. It was only in our third year that we had become real friends. We were amused to find that we had both applied for teaching posts in Saint Andrew's School in Dublin's expanding north side. We were even more thrilled to discover that we had both been successful. So, we had started our professional lives in close support of each other. In the early days we had shared a series of dingy bedsits and had moved several times over the years to better accommodation until eventually Lucy wanted to invest in a place of her own. This coincided with my engagement to Richard, so we parted company but still remained friends and continued to work happily together in Saint Andrew's until my disappearance in November 1975. Poor Lucy hadn't heard a word from me until the following July when at last I felt well enough to meet up with her. After my return to work, my colleagues quietly and patiently weaned me back into school activities. By degrees these merged into quasi social events until I found myself less reclusive, and beginning to face the occasional social outing without too much trauma. I was still uncomfortable and sometimes panic stricken in public. I wondered how I could possibly have survived this awful time without Lucy's friendship and support.

It was at one such event that, after prolonged searching, Greg Mahon had finally tracked me down almost two years later.

My mother May and my siblings were of course thrilled that I had managed to join them all for the family Christmas. Those of my family, who had already met him, liked Greg and were delighted that I had invited him to be part of the festivities. They had all been pleased when I had eventually seen the light and begun to reciprocate his obvious love for me. The extended Corley clan in Mountbrien knew how to party and a wonderful time was had by all. Greg was made to feel so welcome that he had accompanied me on another visit soon after. I had been down twice on my own since the previous Christmas. On my last visit Mom had given me a box containing papers and some items that Dada had wanted me to have. Among the odds and ends I had found a sizable envelope wrapped up in a silk scarf. The envelope contained a handful of copybooks. First I flicked through them desultorily, wondering where they had come from and left them aside for perusal later. Weeks on, as I was rooting through Dada's things, I found the solution to the mystery in a letter he had written to me many years before. He must have intended giving it to me on the occasion of my twenty first birthday, not too long after Uncle Shay's death. Now, taking the packet of notebooks from my handbag and showing them to Constance, I said

'Aunt Constance, aside from your mother Florrie, whom he loved more than life itself, you were the closest one to Uncle Shay. The last thing I want is to upset you, but I've been over and over it in my mind since I first read the notebooks. I'm blown away by Shay's story. The reason I came down was to ask you an enormous favour. Please Aunt Constance would you mind reading the notebooks. I'd really value your opinion.'

Before she had a chance to answer, Barry and Tessa followed by Maria came upstairs and the conversation turned general. Soon after that Jody arrived, and as usual within minutes he had everyone in stitches with what he laughingly referred to as his tales out of school. He and I had a lot in common despite the twelve year age gap. Like our grandfather before us, we were both primary teachers. We spent a good while swapping views on educational trends and sharing stories on the similarities and differences between urban and rural schools and urban and rural kids. Later, over dinner we all reminisced and shared family news, told yarns and enjoyed each other's company. Of course, by the time we were finished, it was far too late to consider setting off on the long journey back to Dublin. Tessa had already made up a bed for me, so after a nightcap of hot chocolate for Constance and me and hot whiskeys for some of the others, we all retired to bed. I texted Greg to tell him of my decision to stay overnight, and he immediately responded with a loving message, telling me how relieved he was that I was not driving late at night. Tessa showed me upstairs to bed. Having admired the new décor, I prepared myself to settle down for the night. It was only then that I realised that I was in my father's childhood bedroom. Remembering holidays in this house soon banished sleep, and I spent quite a while recalling happy days here. Inevitably my thoughts turned to memories of Dada. I was very close to my father. I could not remember a time when we had not understood each other perfectly. Honest to a fault, we shared many other character traits both positive and negative too. We were both clear-eyed and self-critical about our own faults and consequently rather hard on ourselves. Both of us were headstrong, loyal, passionate, sensitive, strong, inclined to be rigid, occasionally to hold grudges and to cling to first impressions. We were also equally likely to hide feelings of shyness and inadequacy with a tough exterior. Ambrose was sometimes self-righteous, which I understood but did not suffer from. Fortunately for me, I did not share my father's shaky sense of self-esteem. What all who knew me, appreciated most about me, were my helpfulness, empathy, common sense and my intelligence. All of these qualities I had inherited in huge measure from Dada. But luckily for me I had also been blessed with my mother May's pragmatism and innate kindness. Eventually, I fell asleep, warm in the love of my father. I awoke refreshed and looking forward to the day ahead.

After a leisurely breakfast in the cosy kitchen I handed over the packet of copybooks to Aunt Constance before setting on the long drive home. As I made my way happily back to Dublin I was glad to have made the journey to Clare and very pleased with the kind reception I had received from Aunt Constance and her family. It was lovely to have re-established contact with my extended family, and wonderful to hear, at first hand, the high esteem in which my dear dada had been held by my cousins. I was delighted too, that I would have the benefit of Constance's opinion on Shay's prose. I had been enjoying better health in recent times, but today was the first day in a very long time that I was experiencing the pure joy of living. The realisation that my depression episodes were becoming not only less frequent but also shorter-lived, was also to be savoured and celebrated. Today the weather was glorious and the traffic light as I drove through the Curragh. My heart lifted at the thought of sharing all my news with Greg, later that evening. I suddenly realised that I was happy. I began to appreciate the feeling of contentment that warmed my spirit, as the spring sunshine warmed my body. I hastened homeward with a broad smile on my face. On arrival at our end-of-terrace home in Clontarf, I hastily unpacked the car and hurried indoors. I had stopped at a large shopping centre just off the M50, to buy the ingredients for a special dinner that I wished to surprise Greg with, when he came home from work. While there, I had bought some gorgeous flowers, as well as some good wine and a lovely variety of Greg's favourite cheeses. Now as I prepared dinner, I realised just how much I had to be thankful for. My sense of contentment remained with me, and I found myself talking to myself and my unborn baby as I worked. I really loved the new house that Greg and I had recently moved into. Shortly after Greg had found me, he had put his apartment up for sale, knowing how hard it was for me that he lived at our old address. Because he had sold in a very buoyant market, he had made a nice profit. He had re-invested some of the money in a smaller apartment, near his office. The rest he had invested in his expanding architectural business.

20

Laying a Ghost

Greg and I had been passing the Clontarf house, on our regular walks for quite some time, before we noticed the for sale sign in the overgrown and neglected garden. Then one Sunday afternoon in August, we were caught by a sudden squall. Being inadequately clad, we had taken shelter under the awning of a little restaurant opposite. When the shower had passed, we had crossed the road and peeked in the windows of the abandoned and neglected house. We were both happy with what we saw. Next day Greg talked to the auctioneer and arranged a viewing. When we had thoroughly examined the house from top to bottom, we were both equally excited about its possibilities. When the auction came around we were lucky that the only other couple bidding against us had withdrawn quickly. When our offer was put to the vendor, we were thrilled that it was accepted. There was a lot of work to be done of course, but the house was structurally sound. Greg was delighted with the challenge of converting it into a comfortable home. With the addition of a light-filled extension to the back, while preserving the redbrick façade and the house's many period features he had planned a stunning home. The conversion had taken longer to complete, than we had at first anticipated. This was initially because of Greg's attention to detail and his almost obsessive insistence on having everything just right, but was also because he had become increasingly busy at work. He was spending all his waking hours rushing from one work project to another, and then heading to Clontarf to devote what little leisure time he had left, to lovingly restore what would be our family home. I laughingly said that I would like to be party to some of the decoration stage decisions or otherwise I might never see him at all. Greg was pleasantly surprised when I proved to be an able assistant, as I had had plenty of experience over the years at painting and wall papering. I also had a very good eye for colour and a natural flair for interior design. I had always loved antiques and going to auctions. After I had acquired some beautiful pieces, and made some very good investments in the process, Greg had become enthusiastic in his support of my ideas. It wasn't long until he agreed that we should both be involved in all the decisions regarding décor and finish. In this way, the house conversion became a real joint venture, and the focus changed from an architectural project to the preparation of a family home. It was November of the following year before the house was finally ready for us to move in. We had been spending so much time together, working on the house that we had neglected both family and friends, and hadn't had a social night out in months. So we decided to throw a house warming party at the earliest opportunity after moving in.

On the last Saturday of November then, a large crowd of family members, our co-workers, friends and neighbours gathered to wish us joy of our new home and our new life together. I had surpassed myself with the catering. With some help from an enthusiastic Greg, we put on a wonderful spread for our guests. We were busy pouring wine; serving food and giving guided tours while making our guests feel welcome. The groups were mixing well and some couples were beginning to dance. At some stage Greg had an uneasy feeling that he was being watched. He turned around and was absolutely flabbergasted to see none other than Richard Benton, lounging against the mantelpiece casually observing the comings and goings. Greg couldn't believe his eyes but his first thought was for me. He looked frantically about but luckily I wasn't in the room. His relief was instantly replaced with anger. He made it to the fireplace in a couple of strides, grabbed Richard by the elbow and frogmarched him unceremoniously to the nearest exit, which happened to be the front door. He didn't pause until they were outside the gate and down the street out of sight of the house. He was so furious that he had to physically restrain himself from shaking Richard until his teeth rattled. He took a deep breath before hissing

'What the hell do you think you're at? How did you know where to find us? You are so bloody lucky that I haven't called the guards already. And don't think that I won't. You should be locked up for what you did to Ella'.

'Okay Okay! Keep your hair on Greg. I'm not here to make trouble. I just came around to tell Ella …'

'You what? How dare you even think of talking to Ella! Have you taken leave of your senses? Ella never wants to lay eyes on you again in her life. Are you completely mad? How could you even think of traumatising her with the thought of, never mind the sight of your ugly mug? You sicken me. Get out of my sight before I call the guards. I promise you if you ever, ever come within five miles of this place again, I'll have you arrested or worse.

Scram! Before I change my mind and hand you over right now'.

'Ah Greg don't be like this. I only wanted to tell her I'm off to Australia in the morning. I thought you at least would be pleased. After all I'm leaving you a clear road'.

As Greg stepped towards him with bunched fists Richard turned and hurried away. Greg shouted after him

'Remember what I said, if I ever see you near either of us again, I'll not hesitate to call the authorities'.

When Greg returned to the party I hurried towards him. I had been on my way downstairs as he was bundling someone who looked uncannily like Richard out the front door. I'd almost fainted with horror, but managed by clinging to the banisters to sink to a seated position on the stairs. Here, after a few minutes I attempted to recover my equilibrium. I made my way shakily to the drinks cabinet and poured myself a small measure port and brandy, to settle my stomach and my nerves. When I saw Greg return alone a few minutes later I pasted a smile on and said

'I wondered where you'd got to. Has something happened love? You look upset'.

He told me there was nothing to worry about, and that he'd just been seeing off some of our departing guests. Then taking me in his arms, he waltzed me round the floor. If anyone else had seen or recognised Richard, no one mentioned it in the course of the evening. As the party progressed Greg began to relax, and hope that I need never know a thing about our unwelcome visitor. The remaining guests continued to enjoy themselves and when they tired of dancing, settled down around the fire where soon the chatter was replaced by the inevitable singsong. When only the friends with designated drivers, family and neighbours were left and the singing had petered out it was nearly four a.m. We were both exhausted, and deciding to leave the tidying up until morning we retired contentedly to bed. When Greg hadn't made any reference to Richard's presence in our home, I didn't either. Over time I began to wonder if indeed it was really Richard I had seen, and decided to dismiss the matter from my mind.

I had returned to Saint Andrew's after my recovery. I loved my job, and found my current cohort of eight year olds a joy to teach. Recalling my recent conversation with Jody, I was pleased that my cousin and I shared such an appreciation of our pupils and such enthusiasm for our chosen profession. Buoyed up with this realisation, I had gone into school that first Monday morning, with a sense of excitement and anticipation. My friend Lucy had often said that the best kind of distraction anyone could hope for from any sort of worry was a class full of lively youngsters. Aside from their all-encompassing need to be watched every second of the day, there was the hilarious incident potential of every lesson. Like for instance young Tim who boasted he'd got a wonderful birthday present of a toy with the '*destructions*' printed on the side of the box. A little girl announced one morning that she had a new baby brother, and when asked what the baby's name was, volunteered that he was to be named '*Spot*', only to explain the following day that he was in fact to be called '*Mark*'.

Not to mention the wonderful parental boobs, such as the note which read '*Partick doan't feel very well if he gets any sicker send him home he incested on going to school'.* Or the lovely mother who was happy to pay to have inoculations done privately, because she didn't want her daughter *'examinated by them public health doctors. You wouldn't believe what they call poor underprivileged kids. They call them siblings'.*

I had often used such quotable gems to lighten a moment or liven up a flagging conversation, on social occasions. In earlier days such stories had earned me quite a reputation as an entertaining guest.

Now that my depression had lifted, I felt that it was high time for me to reclaim some of the lost ground and to re-join society. Since the night of the housewarming party, over five months earlier, life had improved dramatically for me. I had had a wonderful Christmas with my family and my beloved Greg. For the first time in ages, I was relaxed and happy. Now I also had that lovely warm and happy feeling of hugging the knowledge of my pregnancy to myself. As yet only Greg and I, my mother and now Constance were privy to this wonderful secret. Added to this was the relief of having handed over Uncle Shay's writings to his sister Constance, and the comfort of heading off each day to a job I loved. In this happy frame of mind I could now turn my attention to the future and particularly to planning our wedding and the birth of our baby. At first, Greg and I had difficulty in reaching a decision as to which event should come first. We would have liked to be married before the birth, for the sake of my family. But this decision was complicated by the circumstance of my previous marriage. As I had not applied for a Church annulment, or for a divorce, we now faced the realisation that starting either process at this stage would be too late, to allow for a marriage, prior to the expected birth date in late October. June was a lovely month with fine sunny days and a great stretch in the evenings. Greg and I, although busy, managed to do quite a lot of entertaining in our lovely new home. We enjoyed especially the opportunities the clement weather allowed for eating al fresco, and watching the sun set, replete and relaxed after imbibing some summer wine. Towards the end of the month, as the school term was winding to its close, I was beginning to wonder why Constance had not got back to me with regard to Shay's writings. I had taken to watching out for the postman in the mornings, in the hope that I might receive the packet with Constance's comments. Several weeks had gone by and I was becoming impatient with the delay. Knowing that I had eight weeks holidays coming up, followed by maternity leave, I was growing increasingly anxious as I had expected to be able to make a start on preparing the manuscript for publication as soon as possible.

June 23rd brought a packet in the post at last. I tore it open excitedly, before I had time to notice that it was far too small to contain the expected copybooks. What the package contained knocked me off balance for a few minutes. The sheaf of papers it contained was not from Constance at all. I searched for the familiar address and Constance's covering letter, only to discover that the letter in my hand was typed on heavy cream vellum. It bore the heading of a firm of solicitors from Brisbane, Queensland in Australia. Attached to the letter were several legal documents and what appeared to be a cheque. Scrabbling through the papers for a clue, my eye was caught by the name Richard Benton. Overcome with panic and nausea, I threw the papers from me and rushed out the door to school. Once in class, I managed to put it completely out of my mind. Later on, as I was about to head home at the end of the school day, I suddenly remembered it and decided to ring Greg. I explained what had happened, and my reluctance to face reading whatever was in the letter alone. Immediately Greg suggested that he would leave the office straight away, and meet me at home in fifteen minutes. As soon as we arrived, Greg gathered up the scattered documents and we retired to the dining room table, to peruse them. First, he scanned the covering letter, before reading it aloud to me. It contained the surprising news that Richard Benton was dead. When the documents were re-assembled and the packet was examined, it was found to contain along with the letter the following; a death certificate, Richard's last will and testament and a cheque. He had died, as a result of an industrial accident in the pharmaceutical facility, where he worked in Brisbane. Tragically he and two co-workers had been killed in an explosion. Because the firm had been found to be negligent, there was a large pay-out in compensation. But most surprisingly the cheque for Aus$100,000 enclosed, had been made out to Ella Benton née Corley. The letter explained that I was the sole beneficiary of Richard's will. After we had got over the initial shock, we sat for a while in the garden swing with our arms around each other. Suddenly Greg straightened up and started to pace excitedly up and down.

'Ella my love, do you realise that there is now no impediment to our marriage in the Catholic Church. If we wanted to, we could even do it during the summer holidays. Wouldn't it be grand if we were officially and legally married, before the baby arrived? Tell me my love what do you think'?

With tears in my eyes I walked into the circle of his arms and said

'Greg my dearest man, there is nothing I would like better. You needn't worry; these tears are not tears of regret. Bad as he was, I cannot believe that even Richard deserved such a horrible death. My tears are a mixture of sadness for his wasted talent and relief that I'll never have to set eyes on him again. How about Friday July 30 as a date for the wedding?

That'll give us nearly five weeks to make arrangements, and please God I won't be too obviously pregnant, with still three months to go'.

'Are you sure sweetheart? There's no rush really Ella on making this momentous decision, maybe we should sleep on it? You might need more time to adjust to all this information.

What do you think'?

'Greg, I think we should move forward with the best decision we'll ever make in our lives. If you are happy with July 30, let's waste no more time in organising our perfect wedding day. Come on let's just go for it.'

'Okay my love, but only if you are absolutely certain. Right now we'd better have a bite to eat and then we can discuss matters'.

We started to put together some cold meats and salads and when we were seated again in the garden I said

'There's just one detail I'd like to get out of the way first, if you don't mind Greg. I'm concerned about the money, and what to do with it. I suppose we should be grateful to

Richard for allowing us to go ahead with our wedding plans, but I do not want his ghost casting a shadow over the day, by being in any way connected with it. Aus\$100,000 is roughly 70,000 euro which is a sizable sum, but even if we needed it Greg, which we don't, I couldn't bear to profit in any way from Richard's death. Also I can't help wondering why he'd leave all this money to me. But now that I think about it, since Richard's parents are dead, and he had no immediate family, and as we were not divorced, I can only conclude that I must be his next of kin. If you have no objection Greg, I'd like to use the money to erect a headstone on his parents' grave and bring his ashes home to be buried with them. I'd like to donate the remainder to *The Miscarriage Association of Ireland*, a voluntary body, to help them in the wonderful work they do to support bereaved mothers and parents. Richard also lost a child, and even though I have no idea how or even if, he was affected by it, I'd like to think that this would be a fitting way to spend the money and to help to bring closure for us all, at last'.

Greg stood up and kissed me on the cheek, whispering tenderly in my ear

'You have to be the kindest, sweetest person in the whole world. I understand completely, and I am 100% behind you, in what you want to do. Not only that, but I am overwhelmed by your generosity of spirit and strength of character. I pray to God I will always appreciate you, and I want you to know that I will always love you. Selfishly I am pleased that Richard's taint will not be on our wedding plans. You'll have no opposition from me love.

I couldn't have imagined a more fitting way of using the money'.

21

A wedding

As soon as school was out for the summer holidays, I threw myself into the twin projects of laying Richard's ghost and organising our wedding. I was so busy that for a while I managed to put to the back of my mind, that as yet I'd got no word from Aunt Constance about Uncle Shay's writings. For the next couple of weeks, I hadn't time to think beyond the next urgent detail that needed sorting. I had persuaded Greg that, in light of my condition and because it was my second time around we should have a small family wedding, with as few guests as we could manage, without offending people. Greg reassured me that whatever I wanted was fine with him. His only interest in the day itself, he insisted was the moment when I would consent to be his wife. Of course he would be on hand to assist me in every way, but the 'what and where and how' of the organisation he was more than happy to leave in my capable hands. I wanted our wedding day to differ in as many details as possible from my first one. In the first few days of July, I was happily making arrangements for an intimate marriage ceremony. The marriage was to be followed by a very special reception, for a small select group, in an exclusive city centre restaurant called 'Chez Francois'. Everything was beginning to fall into place, and buoyed up with the excitement and busyness of it all I was delighted to put my feet up in the evenings. Then I could relax and regale Greg with the details of the progress I was making. At first all seemed to be going well until it came to deciding on the exact number of guests to be invited. Difficulties only began to emerge, when we tried to match names of guests to the limit of forty places which the elite 'Chez Francois' insisted was all it could accommodate.

Coming as I do from a large family, I was conscious that forty was a particularly small number, so I was well aware of the challenge facing us. Greg, on the other hand was an only child who had lost his beloved mother when he was only thirteen. His father had died only three years later. Greg had been left reasonably well provided for, and had been a boarder in Clongowes Wood College in Kildare. After his father's funeral, Greg had returned to school, where over the next three years his classmates became his substitute family. By the time he had finished his schooling, he had no living relative left in the world. Understandably, Greg wished to invite his coterie of school pals to celebrate with him on this very special day. The problem as far as the guest list was concerned, was that not only were there seven of them but also all seven friends were now married and Greg had been a guest at all the weddings. So even before looking at his partner Jeff and Jeff's wife Louise, not to talk of co-workers and friends fourteen of his scarce twenty allocated places were already accounted for. My own situation was equally problematic. Just accommodating my mother and siblings with their significant others accounted for thirteen places. Reluctantly, I had to go back to the drawing board, give in to the inevitable and forego my dream wedding plan. After a lot of discussion we decided that the realistic number of guests would have to be at least 80. At Dublin prices this was going to blow our budget out of the water. Even worse, with so little time to find a suitable venue the organisation of the wedding moved from difficult through problematic to trauma in short order.

Seated in the garden in the shade of a parasol, feeling very frustrated with the lack of progress and conscious that there were only three weeks to go to the wedding date, I was almost at the end of my tether. To try to distract myself I rang my mother for a chat. Recently May had embraced wholeheartedly the new technology. She had been absolutely thrilled with our Christmas present of a mobile phone. She had learned to text almost immediately. For me it was a great luxury to be able to chat to Mom at will. May was now instantly available, as she always had her mobile charged and on her person, wherever she happened to be. On this particular day she answered with a cheerful

'How are you love? I deliberately haven't rung you over the past few days, knowing how frenetically busy you must be? Where are you? And what are you doing right now?'

On hearing her voice I burst into tears

'Oh Mom it's all falling apart here. The number of invited guests is increasing daily. I've had to cancel 'Chez Francois'. I've spent all morning ringing around and cannot get anyone to take us on at such short notice. I'm so hot and sweaty and flustered, I've just retired to the garden with a cold drink. I was just settling down for a little weep when you rang.'

'Well stay there for another wee while my dear. Your ever loving ma has a surprise for you.'

Less than fifteen minutes later, I heard the front gate creak. Around the corner of the house appeared my mother with Aunt Constance and Cousin Barry's wife Tessa in tow.

'Mom' I screamed in delight 'and Tessa and Aunt Constance too. I know you warned me to expect a surprise, but this I'd never have dreamt of. You are all so, so welcome. Now that I'm nearly over my fright-induced heart failure, let me get ye something to eat and drink. I know mother will want tea, how about you Aunt Constance and Auntie Tessa?'

'I'm with May on that. I could murder a cuppa thanks' answered Tessa while Constance nodded in eager agreement. Ella asked her visitors why they had decided to suddenly come to Dublin today of all days. It transpired that May had been spending a few days visiting Constance. In fact she had been summoned to Kiltyroe by Constance, who was in quite a state. Shortly after receiving the package from me, she had made copies of Shay's writings and sent one to each of her surviving siblings and to Hannah's widowed husband Harold. She had carefully crafted a letter to accompany each of the manuscripts, requesting the recipients to read and comment on the content. She had recommended that when they had completed the readings, they might get in touch with her with their comments on the literary value and content of what they had read. She also asked that they vote on whether or not they thought the writings should be published as Shay's memoir. Now after several weeks, she had received responses from only four people. Two were enchanted with the work and the other two were violently opposed to its publication now or ever. That's as much as Constance was prepared to divulge at the moment, but it was obvious to May that she was very disturbed by the negative reactions she had received. In fact Constance had been so distressed, that she had sent for May. But on May's arrival, she had been unable to share the depth of her emotional upset with her sister-in-law. Poor Mom had spent nearly three days trying to console a distraught Constance, without any idea what was causing all the trouble. So when Greg had rung her that morning, telling her of the glitch with the wedding preparations, she was actually glad of the distraction. Suddenly, she felt that she could be of some use to me, and perhaps the diversion would help Constance to cope with whatever was bothering her. So appealing to Constance's innate kindness, she persuaded her that a trip to Dublin was the very thing to help them get some perspective on their problems. They could spend the journey in discussion. Their unscheduled arrival on my doorstep would serve two functions, offering me some support while at the same time cheering them all up. Conscious of the fact that Tessa had been worrying about Constance's distress over the previous weeks and had spent the last few days trying to make her feel welcome, at the last minute May had invited her to join them on the trip.

Now sitting in the garden, sipping their tea the three older ladies listened to me outlining my frustrating day and the impasse I had reached, regarding the organisation of the wedding. It didn't take long for the obvious solution to present itself, and soon they were all talking at once, as detail after detail fell seamlessly into place. At first, I was reluctant to accept what was on offer. I felt that the generosity of the Constance and Tessa was too much, and that I couldn't in conscience accept it. I had barely voiced my concerns when

I was eagerly talked out of them by three ecstatic ladies excitedly protesting 'that there was no problem', 'it would be no trouble', 'sure all we're doing is providing a venue' followed by 'sure we wouldn't dream of interfering in your plans love, you go ahead and organise things as you want we'll only be there to give you a hand if you need us'. Mom summed it all up with

'Ella my love it will be PERFECT. A marquee in the garden of Ashdene House, surrounded by all the family and those who love you most in the world; what could be more appropriate?

Why didn't we think of it sooner? What was wrong with us? It was so obvious, it was staring us in the face.'

By the time Greg arrived home, the bulk of the planning was in place, and there was a palpable sense of euphoria emanating from the four happy women sipping cold drinks in the evening sunlight of the garden. Leaning over my shoulder to give me a kiss he couldn't help commenting

'That's my girl. Lovely to see you're back my love. Ladies you wouldn't credit the contrast between the love of my life this evening, and the distraught creature who had stolen her outward appearance that bade me farewell this morning. Now tell me what magic you three have woven in my absence?'

May, Constance and Tessa looked from one to the other before turning to me and declaring in unison 'You'd better fill him in Ella, and let the poor man out of his misery.'

Greg couldn't believe the turnaround of the morning's disaster, and was delighted when I had finished outlining the new plan. The wedding ceremony, to be performed by Cousin Dan, was now to take place in the little church in

Kiltyroe. This had already been agreed with Father Dan, and cleared with Father Dermot Ryan, the Parish priest in Kiltyroe. The reception would take place in a large marquee in the garden of my father's childhood home, Knocknashee. The catering would be done by 'Heavenly Hosts', a local firm which had already agreed to take on the commission. The guest list had already been expanded to include cousins and friends. The preliminary booking of the caterers was for 130 to 150 guests. The details regarding flowers, hair and make-up could all be worked out, without too much fuss, in the new location. All that remained to be done right now was the cancellation of the church in Killester. As it was only a provisional booking, this was easily accomplished by Father Dan, the following morning. After that the arrangements just seemed to fall into place, and everything proceeded seamlessly and smoothly until the morning of July 30 dawned. The auguries were good and references to the old saying *'Blessed is the bride that the sun shines on'* continued throughout the length of the glorious day.

It wasn't just the weather that contributed to making our wedding day as perfect as my mother had predicted. As a couple we were ecstatically happy, comfortable in our own skins and mature enough to realise how lucky we were, to have found each other. Added to this, we were surrounded by family and friends who loved us, and were delighted to see us so happy and fulfilled. And to cap it all the setting couldn't have been better. The gardens at their summer best looked absolutely spectacular, and the balmy day was perfect for guests to go strolling on the lawns. Some were relaxing in the shade of the parasols and pagodas, dotted around the tree-shaded perimeter, while the photographs were being taken. The caterers had come up trumps, the food was delicious and the service excellent. The marquee looked splendid, perched on the upper lawn. Luckily, because the day was so warm, it was possible to tie back large sections of it so that cooling breezes could blow through, and keep it well ventilated throughout the meal and speeches. Afterwards, some of the younger guests got involved in playing croquet on the lower lawn, as the clearing of the tables was underway and before the music for dancing started up. Because almost everyone knew everyone else, the day of celebration soon turned into a wonderfully happy 'anything goes' kind of party. The entertainment included performances by local 'straw boys', set dancing, céilidh dancing and traditional music, culminating in a singsong that continued into the wee small hours of the following morning.

22

Honeymoon

Because the reception had taken place on their premises, Barry and Tessa had insisted that their gift to us would be the hosting of a post wedding barbeque the following day. All the guests were invited, and also any of the younger family members and neighbours who hadn't attended the festivities on the previous day. This event was also a huge success, after which we set off on our honeymoon. We had been extremely careful not to let slip any idea of where we were going, or even how long we would be away. To throw the curious off the scent, we had created the impression that we were planning to go abroad. In reality we had rented a seaside bungalow, outside Duncannon on the Hook peninsula in County Wexford, for the entire month of August. We would spend the first two weeks there enjoying each other's company, in the privacy of our little haven, after which Greg would go back to work, returning to our retreat at weekends. Everything went according to plan. The weather in the sunny southeast lived up to its reputation, and day after day, we awoke to bright sunny mornings, gorgeous ten and a half hour long days on sun kissed beaches, or messing about in boats, followed by sunsets vying with each other in nightly splendour. We thoroughly enjoyed our coastal idyll, wandering along a different beach each day. We had leisurely swims and sunbathed happily on busy Duncannon strand. Other days were spent with a handful of other bathers on

Dollar Beach or on the sands of almost deserted Bella Vista Cove. Sometimes we drove further out towards Hook Head, visiting the golden strands of Fethard-On-Sea, Baginbun and Slade. When the time came for Greg to return to Dublin, I decided to accompany him so that I could attend my gynaecologist for a check-up on the Monday. Greg drove me back down on the Tuesday evening, and set off for work from Wexford on the Wednesday morning. Far from feeling abandoned, I actually enjoyed the silence and independence of my own company. I continued to spend time on the less isolated beaches, taking my swim when other swimmers were in the water and reading under the shade of my parasol in the glorious warmth of the summer sun. Within a few hours, I noticed that because I was alone, people tended to stop to chat as they passed near me. Children in particular were curious to know where I came from and why I was alone. Invariably, a caring parent would appear to ensure I was not being disturbed by their chattering offspring. In this way I got to know a few neighbouring families as well as other holiday makers. Late in the evening, as I was gathering my bits and pieces in readiness for departure, I fell into conversation with a friendly woman about my own age who was walking her much loved and elderly Cairn terrier. I introduced myself and found I had been talking to Agnes O Rourke and her sweet-natured dog Mabel. We accompanied each other up the narrow lane back to the road. On the Thursday morning, before I'd even had a chance to get ready for my daily seaside visit, I had an unexpected visitor. A cheerful voice called out before I got around the corner of the house from where I had been sipping my breakfast tea in the garden.

'It's only me, Agnes. We met yesterday on the beach. I usually walk this way with Mabel for our bit of morning exercise. And as I knew I'd be passing by, I've brought you a wee bit of fresh brown bread and a few of our free range eggs if you don't mind'.

'Why would I mind Agnes? Thank you so much for your kind thought. Would you care to join me in a cuppa, if you're not in too much of a hurry? I've just made a fresh pot of tea'.

A half hour later we were still in the garden, in companionable chat, after which we agreed to take a stroll together later that evening. When Greg arrived on Friday evening, he was surprised to find instead of the home cooked meal followed by a cosy intimate evening together, that he was expecting, I was all dressed up and ready to party instead.

'So where to my lovely, now that you're all ready for action?'

'Come on let's walk. You've spent quite enough time cooped up in a car for one day.

I'll just pop my high heels in a bag, and I'm ready.'

We set off walking, but when we came to the crossroads, instead of turning left towards Duncannon, I insisted that we continue straight on the narrow country road. After a short time I stopped at a pretty roadside cottage and perched for a moment's rest on the wall outside. Almost immediately, and much to Greg's embarrassment, the owners appeared.

'I'm terribly sorry folks my wife needed to take a breather and your wall seems to be where she wants to sit for a moment.'

Agnes and I were smiling at each other conspiratorially when Jeremy stepped forward saying

'You must be Greg. Our two ladies here have cooked up a notion that we should have a night out in 'downtown Duncannon', a meal in a little restaurant followed by a few jars and maybe some dancing in my favourite local pub. If the plan meets with your approval, we'll take a stroll down now. We've already left our car down in the village and Agnes will be happy to drive us all home later, as she doesn't take a drink.'

Greg caught my eye and knew that this little subterfuge had been planned, so he agreed enthusiastically. The little restaurant prided itself on a great variety of fresh fish dishes, as well as a good array of other mains, all served with local organic vegetables. The desserts were wonderfully tasty concoctions, ranging from substantial old time favourites such as gooseberry fool, apple tart and individual sherry trifles, which went down extremely well with the menfolk to frothy creations beloved of us ladies like tiramisu, chocolate mousses and feather light cheesecakes in various flavours. The meals were delicious and all four of us thoroughly enjoyed our selections. Afterwards, we walked uphill towards the church, where the O Rourke's had parked their car earlier. We looked out over the sea and admired the setting sun from this vantage point before heading for Jeremy's favourite watering hole in a nearby village.

On our arrival a little after 10 o' clock, the music was lively and the dancing already in full swing. The traditional Irish music was supplied by two old-timers known simply as Phil and Josie. Phil played the piano accordion and Josie sang in a sweet tenor voice, while accompanying himself on the guitar. They played for hours on end without the use of any sheet music and without ever consulting each other. They had been playing together for so long that they were comfortably aware of which tunes made up a set, and seemed to know instinctively the order in which each audience would prefer them played. How they communicated this information to each other was a secret neither of them was willing to divulge, even to their closest friends. Jeremy insisted on buying a round of drinks for the four of them, before they found themselves '*ringside seats*' as he put it, where they could quench their thirst and admire the prowess of the dancers already on the floor. Soon they too joined the happy throng swirling and dipping in time to the waltzes and gracefully and energetically participating in the quicksteps and foxtrots. When a Plain set was called, Agnes and Jeremy were invited to join three other couples while Ella and Greg were happy to observe in admiration from their vantage point. On their return to their seats an exhilarated if somewhat breathless Agnes and Jeremy insisted that Ella and Greg would have to promise to participate in the set dancing on their next visit.

'But we only know a few sets Agnes, and they're mostly Clare sets. We could manage the 'Plain Set' and maybe 'The Kilcommon' but we'd be better at 'The Kilfenora', 'The Caledonian' or 'The Clare Lancers' wouldn't we Greg'?

As it turned out the O Rourkes also were familiar with the Kilfenora and the Caledonian, so they were happy to agree that as soon as was feasible after the arrival of Ella and Greg's baby the two couples would dance a Caledonian in this venue. Later, when Agnes pulled up at the rented cottage, the Mahons insisted on inviting their new friends in for a nightcap. Agnes and Ella settled for hot chocolate while the men opted for hot toddies. More than an hour and a half flitted by in getting to know each other better, until Agnes's horror stricken face betrayed the fact that she had glimpsed the time on Jeremy's oversized watch. It was registering 02.10 a.m. so the O Rourkes somewhat apologetically took their leave. By the end of August we had become firm friends. When we returned to Dublin, Agnes and I quickly established a habit of keeping in touch by letter, by phone and even by email as matters of common interest crossed our minds. Because Agnes was already a mother of two boisterous boys, Jamie who was now twelve and Ronan who was ten, it was natural that I felt comfortable talking to her about the latter stages of my pregnancy. It was not just gynaecological matters that were of mutual interest of course, we had discovered that we had rather a lot in common. First of all we were both teachers by profession. Then we were both interested in people, and were outgoing by nature. Added to that, we were avid readers, with more than a passing interest in creative writing. We also loved to travel, and unlike most of our friends and contemporaries we both loved the now almost extinct art of letter writing. A shared interest in Regency furniture and antique china was a further bond. Soon we discovered a reciprocated love of visiting antique fairs, exhibitions and the occasional weekend auction, time permitting. Having so much in common, and furthermore being gregarious people, it was no wonder that the two of us would become immediate and lasting friends. Coincidentally, we were also both redheads, Agnes's silken locks were almost a strawberry blonde while my hair was closer to titian in colour.

23

New Beginnings

For me September came and went in a rush of thank you letters for wedding presents and preparations for the upcoming birth. Before I knew it, it was mid-October. Knowing that the last days of Indian Summer were upon us Greg and I had decided to escape to Wexford for a last carefree weekend. We had planned to stay in a lovely little hotel in Fethard-on-Sea and walk the local beaches. We were looking forward to getting away from Dublin's busyness and spending time together. We also intended to surprise our friends, by inviting the O Rourkes to join us for dinner on the Saturday evening. At the last minute, after Greg had finished his own packing and was on his way to the car, he noticed my hospital bag on the landing so on a whim he added this to the luggage in the boot. We left the city early on Friday afternoon, arriving in Wexford with time to spare for a refreshing walk around the lighthouse at Hook Head. After watching the sun go down in all its autumn glory, we booked into the hotel. We enjoyed a wonderful meal by the fireside, in the almost deserted dining room before retiring early to bed. I enjoyed the best night's sleep I'd had in weeks, and therefore we both woke early but very much rested and refreshed. As it was way too early for breakfast, we remained in bed chatting companionably in low tones in order not to disturb other guests. After a while Greg got drowsy and I decided to read for a bit. I opened my book of baby names and started working my way through the girls' section. After a while Greg sat up and joined in. We decided to make a list of the names we both liked and soon the following names were on the list for consideration: Bevan, Caroline, Dearbhaile, Grace and Heather but we weren't enthused sufficiently by any of them. When we came to the names beginning with J we both knew that if the baby turned out to be a girl our daughter would definitely be called Jana. This was a pre Celtic female version of the name John meaning 'the long-awaited'. After that we had a leisurely breakfast over which we agreed that if the baby was a boy he would be called John. Having reached a decision, regarding naming our much anticipated child, gave us an inner glow and we were looking forward to sharing the news with our friends. We decided then that rather than ringing Agnes and Jeremy we would call on them for morning coffee and tell them about our plans for the evening. But first we would take a long walk along the beautiful strand at Duncannon before visiting the bakery to buy some delicious cream cakes to go with the coffee. We found the O Rourkes about their Saturday chores, Agnes busy baking bread, and Jeremy as ever working with his plants and vegetables, in his well-tended garden. Over the coffee Greg explained that he had booked a meal for the four of us at 7.00 in the nearby Dunbrody House. Agnes and Jeremy were pleased to accept and the talk turned more general. I was bursting to share our news about the baby names, when suddenly I doubled over gasping, as a dart of pain shot through me. Agnes reacted instantly

'There'll be no Dunbrody for any of us tonight. Ella my dear, you are in labour or I'm a Greek. Action stations Greg! Which maternity hospital have you booked her into?'

Feeling a bit nauseous and somewhat scared I asked

'Agnes can it really be labour? It is two weeks too early? Couldn't it just be a false alarm at this stage? Ooooh! Ooooh!'

Agnes rushed to my side and pressing me to sit down she lifted my ankles on to the sofa. Then she helped me to lie prone. Next she handed the phone to Greg, telling him that he should ring the gynaecologist immediately for advice, stating that in her view it might be better to head for the nearest maternity ward as quickly as possible. Agnes's instincts proved completely accurate and by the time Greg had finished his call, Agnes had accompanied me to the bathroom, where my waters had broken. When Greg realised how imminent the birth could be, he immediately rang The Coombe Maternity Hospital, to explain what had happened and to enquire whether or not he could proceed to Wexford Hospital maternity unit as an emergency measure. He was immediately reassured that this was his best option, and that all would be in readiness for us, if we got on the road straightaway, leaving the logistics to the hospitals to arrange. As he and Agnes were helping me into the back of the car, I clung to Agnes and begged her not to abandon me. Jeremy offered to follow on later to collect Agnes and encouraged us to be on our way. Greg proved to be very competent and calm, and despite his inner feelings of excitement and panic, he drove carefully and quickly to Wexford General. On the way, Agnes helped me with my breathing and soon I remembered all I had been taught at my ante-natal classes.

Greg reassured us that the bag with all the essentials was in the boot, and that we should be at the hospital within ten minutes or so. At this stage the contractions were only three minutes apart, but they kept trying to console me that first babies were unlikely to arrive in too much of a hurry. It was only much later that Greg realised how lucky he was to have Agnes along, to guide him on the shortest and quickest route to the hospital. As things worked out we only barely made it to the labour ward. We were met at the entrance to the hospital by a nurse and an orderly, who rushed me in a wheelchair to the maternity unit and directly to the labour ward, where within eight minutes the baby was delivered. Young John Ambrose Conor Mahon was born, a robust eight pound ten ounce baby with a shock of dark hair at ten minutes to two o clock on the afternoon of October 16th 2009. This baby had a healthy set of lungs, which he was happy to use to herald his early arrival into the world. In the immediate aftermath of the birth, we his ecstatic and somewhat shocked parents didn't quite know what to do with ourselves and our bundle of joy. I had been so lucky in that I was in great health and had an easy birth requiring no resultant stitches or repairs. I was understandably a little tired after the ordeal of the birth, but my euphoria more than offset this. The nurses were very supportive and rewarded both Greg and me with the ubiquitous tea and toast beloved of maternity wards since old gods' time. Less than an hour after our breakneck journey had ended, we were ensconced in a private room ready to show off our beautiful boy. Our first visitor was of course Agnes, who in all the excitement had been abandoned at the front desk. She had heard from the nurses that it was a boy, so by the time she got to see the little lad, she had managed to buy a baby card, a baby album and a bunch of cheerful flowers to welcome him. She had also rung Jeremy who was now on his way in with Jamie and Ronan to collect her and briefly greet the new arrival.

Within a few days we were all three of us back in our own home in Clontarf. Greg was busy at work and I was enjoying the early days of motherhood, proudly showing off my son to the endless stream of visitors and well-wishers who called to our home over the first few weeks. I was on a permanent 'high' and really enjoying bonding with my baby. I had always been blessed with great energy and was by nature well-organised and efficient. Now I found myself calling on all my skills, both innate and learned to run my home effectively, using the time while my baby slept, to prepare in advance meals for Greg and myself. I baked and cooked and had a well-stocked freezer to cover all eventualities and had time to enjoy every second of baby John's waking hours. I was relaxed and content and the baby seemed to thrive in this happy atmosphere. I was looking forward to going back to work, after my maternity leave was up in the early days of December. I was confident that by then John would have settled into a routine of sleeping through the night. I had been planning ahead since the latter end of August, ensuring that my substitute teacher, Sue Malone knew exactly what I had intended to teach in all subject areas. I had met with Sue the night before school reopened and handed over my term's plan and my scheme of work for the first week. Every Friday evening after that Sue had called after school. I welcomed her with tea or soup and we spent a half hour discussing progress before I handed over the next week's scheme of work. Often the package would include not just my detailed notes, but also charts, pictures or samples of art and craftwork to act as exemplars, to encourage the young pupils' own efforts. It was not all one-way traffic either, as Sue's commodious holdall often contained letters and handmade 'Welcome to Baby' cards or occasionally little knitted toys that the children had lovingly constructed for teacher's new baby. Every aspect of my life seemed to be in harmony and I had never been so content. The only blot on the horizon was that I had heard nothing from the family regarding Uncle Shay's writing. The deafening silence worried me for a number of reasons, not least of which was the fact that I would have so little time to deal with preparing and promoting its publication, once I went back to fulltime work.

24

Lucy Holohan

Lucy Holohan had met Johnno, as he was known to his friends at our wedding. They had been inseparable in the five months since then. Johnno was the Principal of Kiltyroe National School where my cousin Jody taught. He was a strikingly good looking man, who had spent almost four years studying for the priesthood in Maynooth. In the twelve years since he had returned home to Kiltyroe as principal, he had never dated anyone. As far as his family, friends and neighbours were concerned, Johnno was a confirmed bachelor. Though somewhat bookish, he was very personable and outgoing. At first he had caused quite a stir in the locality, and many a young girl had taken a fancy to him. Johnno was good company, very courteous and polite, but he showed no interest in any of the women who had set their caps at him. He never refused an invitation to local dances or other events, but other than a reciprocal gesture, he never seemed to want to see the ladies again. He had only come to the wedding as his mother's 'plus one'. He had been seated between his mother and Lucy Holohan for the reception, and they had spent most of the meal talking about the profession common to all three of them. Once the meal was over Mrs. Angland slipped away, happy in the knowledge that her son and this charming young woman would hardly notice her departure, so engrossed in conversation were they. I was delighted, when I found them still in each other's company late into the night. They had spent most of the following day at the barbeque together as well. By the time Greg and I returned from our honeymoon, Lucy and Johnno were seeing each other practically every day. Because it was during the school holidays, Johnno's continued absence from Kiltyroe had gone practically unnoticed. The relative anonymity of Dublin's apartment living meant that Lucy's movements during her school holidays always went uncommented on. So those early stages of their getting to know each other were not disturbed by unwelcome attention or comments from friends and colleagues. In fact it was well into October, before I got to hear of the situation. One evening I rang to speak to Aunt Constance when the phone was answered by Jody. Before he was willing to hand over to his mother, Jody insisted on filling me in on the latest local gossip.

'Ella you'll never believe what's happened. You know my boss Mr Angland, well Johnno to his friends, has finally fallen in 'lurve'. And guess who the lucky lady is? I'll give you a hint, you know who she is. In fact she's a good friend of yours.'

'Get me out of my misery Jody! It couldn't possibly be Lucy Holohan could it? Oh my God and she's never said a word to me. Are you sure Jody? And how do you know anyway?'

'Yes Ella, I'm absolutely sure. Take it from me, it is true. As for how I know, I have my sources, just believe it girl. Here Mama is dying to talk to you. Bye, bye Cousin.'

I had to be content with that. And when I spoke to Aunt Constance about the writings, I got no joy there either. A few days later Lucy called to see me and we drank tea, discussed my pregnancy, chit chatted about school and admired the changes made to the house since Lucy's last visit. I was on tenterhooks, waiting for Lucy to make some reference to her new boyfriend. She gave nothing at all away, not even when I asked her directly what she thought of Johnno Angland.

'Oh you mean that guy I met at your wedding. He's alright, I suppose. Not bad looking, and for a teacher not too dull. Why do you ask'?

I felt I had no option but to shrug it off as unimportant. Inside I was seething. I couldn't figure out who I was most annoyed with, Jody for telling me about it, or Lucy for not telling me, or myself for feeling left out. Within a few minutes of Lucy's departure my customary good humour was restored by a quick phone call from Greg. I then wondered if maybe Jody had been mistaken, and vowed to mind my own business, until my friend felt the time was appropriate to take me into her confidence. That time came not too much later, but not before young John Mahon had put in an unexpected appearance. The Friday night of the first weekend after our return to Clontarf, as I was finishing preparing for a mass invasion of Corley visitors on the following day, the doorbell rang. Greg answered it, and a few minutes later I heard him welcome two visitors and usher them into the sitting room, before calling out to me

'Ella the first of your baby visitors have arrived'.

By the time I had pulled a comb through my hair and put the kettle on, Greg had taken the visitors' coats and poured them drinks. When I appeared, the visitors were bent over the crib admiring the sleeping baby. It was Lucy and to my surprise and delight her companion was Johnno

Angland. After the congratulatory hugs and the opening of the baby gifts, Greg escaped to the kitchen to set a tray for tea and cakes. As soon as his back was turned, the three of us all attempted to fill the ensuing silence at once.

'Delighted that you named the … …' started Johnno.

'Thanks so much for … …' I began while Lucy said

'Ella I'm so sorry … …'

The ice thus broken we laughed heartily and decided to have another go.

'What were you about to say Johnno?'

'Not a lot really, I was just trying to ease the tension, by joking that you and Greg had excellent taste in naming the wee lad after me. It sounds awfully stupid now I know'.

'Not at all Johnno, I was only reiterating my thanks for your lovely gifts'.

Lucy then explained that for her part, she was about to apologise for keeping her blossoming relationship with Johnno from her best friend. Over the tea and dainties, the two men got a chance to get to know each other better, while we ladies did a quick catch up. When Lucy and Johnno left, it was very late, but young John had already been fed and put to bed. Greg and I were pleased that the evening had gone so well. We were thrilled for Lucy, who was so obviously happy in the company of Johnno. As we made our way contentedly to bed, we agreed that Johnno was a lovely man and that he and Lucy made a great couple. By the time we'd all meet up again at New Year Greg and Johnno were well on their way to becoming good friends.

25

The Project

I was disappointed that I still hadn't heard anything from Aunt Constance by the time I returned to school on 5th of December. For several days prior I had found myself compulsively checking my post in the mornings, and my email messages several times a day. But I had to put the lack of news to the back of my mind for the moment. As far as school was concerned I was more than ready for the challenge. It didn't take me long to settle back into my classroom routines. But now I had to adjust to my after school/fulltime mother way of life, which was every bit as busy. Then as Christmas approached, I became fully absorbed in preparing my pupils for the Nativity play and Christmas concert. At home, I was so occupied with all the cooking, baking, present buying and wrapping, as well as the trimming of the tree and decorating of the house and all the chores happily associated with this special time of year. All this activity helped to distract me somewhat, but still I assiduously checked my email messages morning and evening and continued to be disappointed. I consoled myself with the thought that I would surely hear something by Christmas, and if not I would be in a position to quiz my aunt and my mother over the holiday period.

We had promised to spend Christmas with my family in Mountbrien. But I wanted to establish a family tradition of waking up in our own home in Clontarf. Even though young John was far too young to understand the significance of his first Christmas, both Greg and I were anxious to have him all to ourselves, on this special morning every year, until he'd outgrown Santa's coming. So it was nearly 11 o clock before we got on the road to Tipperary. Christmas dinner was the usual riotous affair, full of good-humoured teasing and mounds of delicious food and a vast variety of trimmings. Dessert had to be postponed, until the lazy ones had a fireside nap, and the more energetic had been for a brisk walk to make room for the delights of May's delectable homemade plum pudding, My famed trifle with its secret ingredient and an alcohol rich tiramisu, not to mention the nutty chocolate Christmas tree cake and the traditional iced Christmas fruitcake. Later that night we played games of Trivial Pursuit, Scrabble and Charades. Inevitably the night ended with a lively 'trad' Music and singsong session which went on until very late. As Greg's birthday was December 31, I wanted to be back in Dublin, so we could celebrate it with our friends. As his birthday fell on the last day of the year Greg had always enjoyed his special day culminating in welcoming in the New Year. This year, as usual we planned to attend the swish New Year Ball hosted by our good friends the Richardsons at their mansion in Howth. The only difference would be that young John would be with them this year. Thelma and Fintan Richardson had always ensured that any of their friends who had young babies would not be excluded from these wonderful parties, and so from the very beginning they had insisted on providing crèche facilities in their home. The food was exquisite and the drinks flowed freely. After the meal, an orchestra struck up dance tunes and the diners made their way happily to the ballroom, where they enjoyed dancing to lively sets interspersed with stately waltzes. Just before midnight, we slipped away and crept upstairs to ensure that baby John was fast asleep, before we joined Thelma and Fintan and the rest of our friends for the countdown to ring in 2010. After participating in Auld Lang Syne and exchanging celebratory kisses with each other, the braver amongst us made their way outdoors. Here they stood in a huddle, to listen to the bells from the surrounding churches peal in the New Year. They could also hear the ships' sirens bleat their lonesome calls from nearby Howth Harbour and across the darkness from not too distant Dublin Bay and Dun Laoghaire further away. Just as they were about to go back inside, they were halted by the unmistakable sound of gunfire. The ladies, in particular, were startled and somewhat frightened until Thelma reassured them, that it was only Fintan and some of his friends from the Gun Club 'shooting the Calendar' an old tradition from his native County Limerick. The group then returned to the ballroom, where they joined in a lively foxtrot, in an effort to warm themselves up after being outdoors in the frosty air. My friend, Lucy Holohan and her new boyfriend, John Angland joined us as we sat out the next set. A waiter offered us some warm punch as we chatted. Lucy was looking terrific and it was obvious that she was very happy in the company of her dashing escort.

26

Meeting Hendy

On January 2 2010, as soon as Greg had left for work, I popped my pre-packed suitcase and all the baby paraphernalia into the car, gathered up the carry cot and placed John on the back seat. Having secured the carry cot I sat in and set off from Clontarf to Mountbrien before most people were awake. I arrived home to my mother as planned, just in time for elevenses. Unable to contain my excitement a second longer no sooner had we sat down with our mugs of coffee in Mom's cosy kitchen, than I broached the subject that had been tormenting me for months now.

'Mom I can't wait a minute longer, what's been happening with Aunt Constance? She must know how anxious I am to get on with having Uncle Shay's writings prepared for publication. I haven't heard a dicky bird since I don't know when. I'd hoped to get started in the summer, or at least in September. Then I waited and waited, hoping to have something done before going back to work. Now Christmas has come and gone, and still no word. Have you any idea what the delay is? Every time I contact her Aunt Constance seems to be more and more uncomfortable and less and less inclined to talk to me. As there were only six of you to be consulted, I cannot understand what the problem is. Surely at least Aunt Constance and you Mom are on my side. And I've always felt comfortable that Uncle Michael would be delighted to see Shay's work in print.'

Noting her mother's stricken expression, Ella stopped suddenly.

'Mom what's the matter? You've gone pale. What have I said that's upset you?'

May cleared her throat and taking her daughter's hand in hers pleaded for understanding.

'Ella my love I know how much this means to you. But please bear with me. Your dada, God be good to him, was so utterly opposed to any of it seeing the light of day, that I feel I really have no option but to reflect his views. Therefore sweetheart I have told Constance that I feel conscience bound to vote against publication. As for how the others have or will vote I'm afraid I have no idea. Aunt Constance has not discussed the matter with me, though I suspect that worrying about it all is the reason she has been so anxious over the past few months. I hope that the position I've taken doesn't come between you and me love.'

I was of course very disappointed not to have my mother's vote but having mulled over it during the night I grudgingly came to understand and accept where May's loyalties lay. The following morning I awoke filled with determination to move on with my pet project. I greeted Mom with a cheery hug and over breakfast outlined what I proposed to do, with Mom's approval. First I wanted to pay a visit to each of the interested parties and discuss with them their individual stances on publication. Then I would like to bring all of them together and see if a consensus could be reached. I promised that I would abide by the majority decision. While I was in Tipperary I would make a start with visiting Harold Henderson in Glashabawn and before proceeding to the Meehan's farm in nearby Carralisheen to hear what Kitty had to say. I was hoping that Mom would volunteer to accompany me especially to the Meehans as I not only disliked my aunt's husband Jeremiah, I had always been afraid of him. But Mom wisely pre-empted any such request by offering instead to mind baby John while I did whatever it was I needed to do.

'By the way when do you intend to visit Constance?'

'Mom I really don't know. I was so confident of her support. After all she was Uncle Shay's closest confidante. But she appears so very conflicted now. I think I'll leave it until I have a better idea how some of the others are thinking.'

'Ella my love, I gather as you are talking to Hendy and Kitty first that you'll see Michael and Betty in Dublin before heading to Kiltyroe, is that right? I'm not criticising your decision love but if you would like me to go with you to Clare I'd be more than happy to do that. Do you think you'd be able to fit in a visit soon? I'd worry that Constance would feel bypassed if she hears you are doing the rounds without speaking to her first. Anyway as I always go down early in the New Year she'll be expecting me so maybe you might be able to come with me? Tell you what why don't you take the train to Limerick the weekend after next and I'll pick you up there and we can drive down together. We can drop in on Nora in Newmarket-on-Fergus on our way to Kiltyroe if you'd like. Now let's get young John sorted out so that you can get over to the Henderson farm as soon as possible. That way you might be able to fit it in the Meehans today as well.'

When I drove into the yard of the Henderson farm I saw that there was another car parked familiarly near the back door. I hoped the visitor wouldn't stay too long so I could talk to Uncle Hendy in private. I fished out the gaily wrapped bottle of whiskey I had brought from the back seat and my packet of Uncle Shay's notebooks and was making my way towards the house when the door opened and a man emerged calling goodbye to Hendy. As he was heading towards his car he stopped and greeted me warmly saying

'I'm delighted to see that the old tradition of dropping in on friends and relatives is still alive and well in rural Ireland. I'm guessing you are one of Hannah's nieces God rest her soul. I'm sure Hendy will be delighted to see you. By the way I'm Gerry Findlay an old friend of the family.'

He offered his hand and I shook it warmly saying

'And I'm Ambrose and May's daughter Ella, Doctor Findlay. I'm not surprised you didn't recognise me, it's been a long, long time since we met last. My guess is it's probably been the bones of fifteen years when I was only one of the mob of young cousins who used to visit before Cousin Edwin and Aunt Hannah's accident. I'm so pleased you were on a social call. For one awful minute I was afraid you were here as Hendy's doctor rather than as his friend. How is he by the way?'

'Hendy is Hendy, as strong as an ox and as healthy as a trout. But as you all know he lives for his farming and the hard work keeps him going. He's never got over the tragedy so don't go upsetting him now Missy with going back over memories of that horrendous day. Keep your conversation to the present and fill him in on what the younger generation are up to. He'll like that and it will cheer him up. Bye now Ella and a Happy New Year to you and yours and all the Corleys.'

I found Hendy in the back kitchen washing up two whiskey tumblers. He was delighted to see me. We sat in the cosy kitchen sipping tea either side of the range. Bearing in mind what Gerry Findlay had said to me I was careful to keep the conversation general so I showed Hendy photos of baby John on my mobile phone. This led inevitably to Hendy asking about Greg and a discussion on the wedding which Hendy had enjoyed. This led in turn to questions about how we were coping with the new arrival and before I knew it Hendy was reminiscing about the birth of his only son Edwin and how he and his lovely Hannah had learned as a very young mom and dad to parent their precious boy.

'Of course we made mistakes but before that awful day we must have been doing something right as he was such a wonderful boy. I guess when a child is as loved and appreciated as Edwin was not much can go wrong. At first I couldn't bear to hear people mention his name. But over the years I have drawn some comfort from the fact that Hannah was spared the pain of seeing him so damaged. Though I miss them both every day of my life I'm glad that Edwin survived even if his life has been so cruelly curtailed. Sometimes when I visit I get the impression that it is still possible that someday he'll recover. I think that perhaps his mutism is temporary. Maybe it is his way of coping so that he doesn't have to live with the everyday loneliness of the loss of our lovely Hannah. Now to happier thoughts. I sincerely wish you and Greg joy of your little boy and I know he'll never lack his parents' love. In many ways Ella you remind me of my Hannah particularly in the way you listen and keep in touch with the extended family. But most particularly you are like her in your interest in people and your boundless energy. You know

I used to call her my 'Buzzy' she was always so gainfully and happily occupied. Now Ella thank you so much for the visit, the chat and the whiskey but I can't help but notice that you brought something else with you. Unless I'm mistaken what you've been trying to conceal there are Shay's notebooks. So I must assume you want talk about the possibility of publication. By the time I got to know Shay he was well on the way to his untimely death. He had suffered most of his life from depression but in his later years his black episodes were occurring more frequently and he was finding it more and more difficult to hold down a job. He was very fond of Hannah and this house was one of the few places he felt comfortable and welcome in. He loved animals so the farm had its own attractions for him. Hannah was a warm and loving sister and he felt safe here away from prying eyes when he wasn't well. And of course this area near the Ballyhoura Mountains was ideal for a man who loved shooting and hunting. He and I got on very well together and shared many a happy hour in quiet conversation or companionable silence. In the aftermath of my own tragedy Shay was a huge comfort and support to me. At considerable cost to himself he came to stay time and again especially in the early years to help me cope with the horror and the loneliness. When I received the packet from Constance a few months ago I was intrigued. Shay and I had often talked about his frustrated ambitions as a writer but until then I hadn't realised that he had actually kept any of his scribblings as he called them. He had often penned sketches, humorous pieces and at one point he had prepared a collection of his poems for publication. He had even been offered a small advance by the publisher. The money was soon spent on drink and as the time for submission approached Shay had a spectacular row with his publisher after which he returned to his flat and in a fit of pique promptly burned the manuscript. Imagine my surprise and delight when I started reading to discover that some of Shay's writing had actually survived. I read on with interest, excited by his ability to tell a tale. Of course it didn't take me long to recognise the autobiographical nature of the work and was hugely impressed with Shay's initial characterisations. But as I read on I recognised that despite their undoubted accuracy many of the descriptions especially those of his father were acerbic and unnecessarily cruel. Furthermore the people he liked were described in overly sentimental schmaltzy terms while those whom he disliked or who had crossed him he tended to demonise. As I continued to read on my intention was to tell you to 'publish and be damned' but then I came to his description of Hannah and Edwin's accident and I had to change my mind. For a long time after I had read his description I had nightmares. Much as I loved Shay I found it impossible to forgive him for his description of the events of that dreadful day. The idea that he would fictionalise his dear youngest sister's passing and the damage to our lovely boy quite honestly sickened me. So reluctantly Ella I feel it would be inappropriate for me to approve the publication of Shay's memoir in its current format. I am so sorry to disappoint you my dear. For what it's worth I do agree with you that the writing is good but I cannot be party to the publication of something that in my view trivialises the memory of my nearest and dearest'. I hastened to reassure Hendy that I fully understood his position. I apologised for my insensitivity and told him that I had no problem with his decision before taking my leave.

27

The Meehans

Next I made my way the few miles from Glashabawn to the Meehan's farm in Carralisheen. I was dreading this visit. As it was now about 1.30 and I had refused Hendy's kind invitation to stay for lunch I now took the opportunity to postpone the inevitable by stopping at a roadside pub for a toasted sandwich and a pot of strong tea. Thus fortified I pulled up at the Meehan farm a little after two o clock in the afternoon. I was relieved to see no sign of Jeremiah's car in the yard. Aunt Kitty greeted me warmly and ushered me into her cosy little sitting room. Kitty was in great form pressing tea, coffee, a drink, Christmas cake on me. Eventually to placate her I promised that I would gladly accept a cup of coffee after we'd had a chance to discuss the matter of the publication of Uncle Shay's memoir. Much to my surprise Kitty was very positively disposed to the idea. She was most enthusiastic about the project and waxed lyrical about Shay's writing skills. We didn't feel the time go by so engrossed were we in the excitement of planning the launch and post publication party. We were brought back to reality abruptly about 4 o clock when the door was flung open by an irate Jeremiah demanding

'What the hell is going on in this bloody house? I come in after a hard day freezing cold to find the friggin' Aga almost out and no sign of my goddamned wife. As for signs of a dinner or a bite to eat not a bit of it. Her Ladyship is far too busy in her cosy hideout entertaining some other useless housewife on my hard-earned money no doubt. Oh! It's you Miss Goody Two Shoes. To what do we owe this unexpected pleasure? No don't tell me; you want something, otherwise you couldn't be bothered to visit. You're like all the rest of your generation too lazy, idle and self-centred to get up in the morning unless someone makes it worth your while. Well you are wasting your time if you think that buttering up your aunt will get you first dibs on any of my money. I'd rather leave all I own to a cat's home than see any of her lot get a sniff of it. Isn't that right wifey dearest'?

This last question was addressed to Kitty's retreating back as she hurried towards the kitchen. I followed in her wake and within a few minutes Kitty had riddled the stove, put on the dinner, boiled the kettle, recovered her equilibrium and poured coffee for both of us. She went to the pantry and returned a few minutes later with some of her own excellent Christmas cake. I thought I heard voices while Kitty was absent; a suspicion that was confirmed some moments later when Jeremiah re-entered the kitchen smiling and welcoming and acting like nothing had happened earlier. He propped himself in front of the Aga thanked Kitty for the proffered mug of tea and proceeded to play genial host. Soon he had winkled out of me the reason for my visit. Taking my lead from Kitty I pandered to Jeremiah's ego by discussing Shay's memoir with him and seeking his approval for its publication. Jeremiah wasn't shy about sharing his opinions on Shay's work and was delighted to pontificate on all the reasons why he felt that 'Shay's opus' should reach a wider audience. I couldn't help feel that though the vote from the Meehans was as I wanted it I really could have done without Jeremiah's sordid speculations and salivations over the few salacious passages in the Shay's work. I wondered how Aunt Kitty managed to cope with living in the company of such an awful man and keep her sanity. It made me even more thankful for my own life with Greg and now the added blessing of our lovely baby. I arrived home to Mom about 5.30 and was glad to be reunited with my baby son after my exhausting day. Once I had played with little John fed and changed him and put him down to sleep I was ready to sit down to dinner with Mom and pleased to have the opportunity to fill her in on the day's events. As usual Mom was supportive and delighted that on my first day out I had garnered at least one positive response. When I ventured the opinion that Kitty was to be pitied May held up a restraining hand saying

'Ella my love I'd rather not gossip about the state of your aunt's marriage and as far as I am concerned the least said about Jeremiah Meehan the better. Kitty made her choice many years ago and wouldn't ever have tolerated never mind welcomed sympathy from anyone. Jeremiah likes to appear like he's in charge especially when he has a captive audience but appearances can be deceptive. It's a good thing they only had the one child to get caught in the crossfire. Poor Roseanne cannot have had an easy time of it with their constant sniping. I sometimes think that they are as bad as each other and who knows maybe they deserve each other. Anyway who are we to judge? Now please let's move on. Come tell me all about your visit to Hendy. Now there's a brother-in-law to be justly proud of'.

So I recounted my conversation with Aunt Hannah's widower in as much detail as I could remember. May was silent for a while after I finished and then she asked

'Were you very disappointed that Hendy didn't want you to go ahead?'

'To be truthful I suppose I was a bit, at least initially but sure you couldn't be upset with Hendy for long. He is always so amenable, so reasonable and so understanding of everyone else's position and perspective you'd want to be a monster to begrudge him his stance on something as important to him as preserving the privacy of his wife and son.'

'When first I read Shay's account of that awful day I wondered about what might have gone on that morning in the church in Mountbrien and how much Shay knew that he wasn't telling. I admit I was very worried about how Hendy might react to dragging the whole traumatic experience up again. There was a good deal of speculation at the time and I do remember your dada and your uncles having to restrain Jeremiah from mouthing off that afternoon. Later at the funeral everyone was careful for Hendy's sake not to indulge in theorising. As far as we were able to ascertain Hendy had been spared this burden. But Shay had visited quite frequently in the months and years following Hannah's death and he spent quite a lot of time in Glashabawn. I know that Hendy appreciated his presence and support. And of course Shay would have met lots of neighbours including the bold Jeremiah who no doubt took pleasure in filling his ear with their speculative interpretations of what might have led up to the tragedy in Mountbrien. Nonetheless it must have been a great shock for Hendy to be presented with evidence of this kind of ugly speculation and gossip about his family after all this time'.

Ella was horrified that she had caused undue stress to Hendy and apologised to her mother.

'Oh my God Mom I never realised that this would be news to poor Uncle Hendy. I should never have interfered. I should have left things as they were. The Corleys will never forgive me. Oh God what have I done?'

May threw her arms around her and said soothingly

'Ella you did what you thought was right by Shay. You couldn't have known how your decision would impact on others. It wasn't as if you set out to hurt anyone. Anyway too many people over-analyse their decisions with the result that nothing ever gets done. So my advice to you is now that you have started the ball rolling you should see your plans through. When you have accumulated as much information as you can then you can make an informed decision as to how to proceed. In fact I think you should sleep on it and if you want to go ahead we could even make for County Clare tomorrow instead of kicking our heels here worrying ourselves silly. Off to bed with you now and we'll see how you feel in the morning'.

I found it hard to sleep with all the worry. Something was nagging at the back of my mind. Something that Hendy had said was not consistent with Shay's account of the tragedy. As I couldn't sleep I decided to reread that section of Shay's narrative. In reading the description of what Hannah was wearing as she left for the church on the morning of the accident suddenly I knew what had been niggling me. Earlier in the day in conversation with Hendy he had talked of his harrowing experience of identifying Hannah's body by the clothes she wore. He had made no mention of the scarf. With growing horror it dawned on me that the scarf I had been given with Uncle Shay's writings matched exactly Hendy's description of what Hannah was wearing on that fateful morning. How on earth had it ended up in Shay's possession? As dawn approached I eventually fell into an exhausted and troubled slumber. I woke up burdened with unwanted speculation. I decided that no good would come of sharing my troubling thoughts. I got up anxious to get on the road as quickly as possible. By the time Mom appeared in the kitchen a few minutes after 7.00 a.m. I had already fed and changed the baby, the porridge already made, the table set and the kettle boiled for the tea.

'You look like you have a busy day planned my dear. What have you in mind?'

'If you are still up for it Mom I'd love if we could head off this morning for Kiltyroe.

Maybe we should ring Aunt Constance first and let her know we are on our way and we have the baby with us and also give her some idea of what time to expect us. Should we call to Aunt Nora on our way there or would it be better to leave that until we are on our way back?'

'OK! I'm with you love. Give me a minute to finish the breakfast and I'll be ready.

I hope you don't mind driving. I'll ring Constance and we can be on the road by 7.30.'

When May rang Kiltyroe Constance was thrilled to hear of our proposed visit and insisted that we'd come prepared to stay overnight. She also suggested that we should call to Nora en route and ensure that she too would accompany us to her childhood home. She professed herself delighted at the opportunity to cook a decent meal for us as she was sick and tired of turkey and Christmas leftovers.

28

Nora

In a little less than two hours I was driving in the gateway of Nora's neat bungalow on the outskirts of Newmarket-on Fergus. A smiling Nora greeted us at the door and ushered us into the warmth of her cosy sitting-room. She welcomed Mom and me and fussed over baby John. By the time I had fed and changed him and put him down for a nap we were all pleased to sit by the fire sipping freshly-ground coffee and nibbling on home-made biscuits. Nora explained that she had been speaking to Mom earlier and would be delighted to accompany us to Kiltyroe. But now that we had a little time on our hands she would like to take the opportunity to discuss my plans for Shay's writings. My first reaction was one of relief that I didn't have to be the one to raise the issue of publication. But my relief was short-lived and quickly followed by concern that Nora was about to outline a whole series of objections to the idea. I was itching to interrupt and put up some arguments of my own but I was getting signals from Mom to bide my time. Nora had produced her copy of the manuscript and I was surprised to see that most pages were heavily annotated. She proceeded to outline her reasons why she was suggesting what she described as some minor adjustments to Shay's text. She had some reservations about his slant on some of the historical detail of family lore she explained. She had done a lot of research over the years and since first reading

Shay's work she had re interviewed a lot of her sources. So now she was quite confident of the real facts. Mom and I listened in wonder as it became increasingly obvious that Nora despite her voiced reservations was actually in support of publication. She also had quite a few ideas about how to bring the project to fruition not to talk of a wide circle of contacts in the publishing business.

'Ella my dear so far who's on board, besides myself I mean.'

'So far I've only been talking to Harold Henderson and Kitty and Jeremiah Meehan.

The Meehans for different reasons are quite enthusiastic about publication but poor Uncle Hendy is hugely concerned about the negative implications of Shay's description of what might have led up to Hannah tragic death and poor Edwin's unfortunate condition. Mom has her own reasons for opposing it and as you know I've not yet discussed the matter with either Aunt Constance or Uncle Michael.'

'What's your instinct about which way they'll vote?'

'I'd hope that Auntie Constance will want to go for it but I think Uncle Michael and Betty will think like Mom and Dad and oppose it. What do you think Aunt Nora?'

'Well I'm inclined to agree with you about Constance. The only problem I'd see is that being the sweet person she is she'll be torn between the two sides of the argument and she'll not want to vote at all. Mind now that she doesn't try to pull the abstention card.

As for Michael you'd never know you could be right or then again he could be talked around I'd say'.

After lunch we set off for Knocknashee, the Corley homestead in Kiltyroe to be precise. May sat in the back where she could keep an eye on baby John and keep him amused if he didn't fall asleep. Nora was happy to sit in front and quiz me to her heart's content.

29

Back to Kiltyroe

We arrived at Ashdene House mid-afternoon in waning daylight and were soon ensconced in the kitchen the heart of the old home being entertained by Constance as she efficiently prepared dinner. All three of us wanted to lend a hand with the preparations but Constance wasn't having any of it.

'Will ye for Heaven's sake sit down the lot of you and relax. Isn't it high time you learned to appreciate being waited upon once in a while? We'll be twelve for dinner I hope you'll be pleased to hear. That's you three, five of ourselves Walshes and I've taken the liberty of inviting two close neighbours and friends. It should be a lovely cosy evening and I'm sure there'll be music and singing before the night is out. The idea that there'd be none with Jody and Maria in the house is inconceivable. Barry, Tessa and Ella mustn't be allowed to hide their lights under a bushel either. As for young John he will just have to learn to get used to the sound of merriment and as Florrie, God be good to her, used to say he'll never learn younger. And by the way Nora and you too May will have to do your bit for the older generation, we can't have it said we'd let the side down now can we?'

Nora ever curious wanted to know who the extra guests might be and if she would know them. But Constance refused to be drawn on the matter admitting only that no one would have any objections to her guests and Nora like everyone else would just have to wait and see.

The evening turned out to be just as Constance had promised, wonderful food accompanied by good wine in excellent company. I was delighted that the mystery neighbours turned out to be none other than Johnno Angland and Lucy Holohan. The dinner passed in a whirl of conversation and bonhomie. Later we played charades for a while and then the music started. Constance and Nora played duets on the piano and also sang in beautiful harmony the old sweet songs of their youth. Jody played a selection of reels on the violin and Maria danced for us. Barry went to get his guitar and Tessa her mandolin while we all sat around the fire singing favourite songs, individually at first and later all the ballads we knew in unison. I was thrilled to have my friends welcomed into the bosom of our family. Both Lucy and Johnno were familiar with the Walshes, Lucy having accompanied me to Ashdene House on several occasions over the years and Johnno as a neighbour, but this was their first invitation as a couple. They fitted in very well and made their own unique contribution to the evening's hilarity. Lucy was a wonderful actress and loved nothing better than to entertain an audience with monologues, sketches or recitations. These would be chosen for their entertainment value and performed with fervour and panache. The subject matter varied from the sublime to the heart-breaking and from the ridiculous to the ribald but Lucy's performances were usually side-splittingly funny and always memorably sincere. She had an unerringly brilliant sense of timing. Johnno had a rich and melodic

baritone voice and as a result of years of training was a joy
to listen to especially when he performed from his broad
and varied repertoire of classical as well as traditional Irish
songs. Everyone thoroughly enjoyed the evening. Waking
the morning after the night before the family gathered in
the old fashioned kitchen for a late breakfast. It was only
then that the subject on everyone's mind could be raised
at last. With May's encouragement and Nora's constant
interruptions and support I outlined my reasons for wanting
to publish Shay's memoir and my progress to date with the
rest of the Corley family. Constance immediately offered
her backing for the idea in general and confessed that
she had been rather miserable over the past few months
worrying about the possible negative impact on others in
the family. But now given my passion for the project she
had finally become persuaded that this was the right course
of action. She wondered aloud if perhaps it might be a good
idea to get everyone together to air their ideas and express
their reservations and suggestions. If the get together was
well chaired as she had no doubt I could do then perhaps
a consensus could be reached. Such an open discussion
would have the added benefit of providing me with a clearer
indication of what I ought to do next. Constance gaining
courage then suggested that Kiltyroe was the obvious place
for such a meeting but immediately Jody shot in

'Personally I think it would be a better idea if ye all went
to a neutral venue for the meeting.

I propose that Ella organise a room in central hotel
in Dublin. That way she can establish from the start that
this is a business meeting and it will be easier for her to
chair it. It will also ensure that the Meehans in particular

will be forced to take it seriously and will have to take their turn like everyone else. As for the rest of you if you organise yourselves well you can combine it with a few hours at the January sales. I'll bet no one else will have the slightest problem going to Dublin. Don't be disappointed Mom that you won't have all the trouble of the organising and feeding. You know you'd love a trip to Dublin. Besides if you're happy with the arrangement don't you know well that everyone else in the family will follow your lead as always. That's my tuppence worth, sorry to have interrupted; I promise not to say another word.'

The idea of the meeting was greeted with general approval and soon the older women in particular were discussing a date for the trip to Dublin enthusiastically as if the venue were never in doubt. By the time May, Nora and I were ready to set off on our homeward journey the date of the meeting had been settled. I had undertaken to book the boardroom of a central city hotel for 2.00 on the afternoon of January 7th. I had immediately rung the hotel and confirmed the booking as I packed my overnight bag. Constance had agreed to notify all concerned of the time and venue. True to her word as soon as her visitors had left Constance got out her writing materials and sent out personal invitations to her siblings and in-laws. Each letter replicated the others only in the detail of the arrangements but differed in tone and content reflecting Constance's relationship with the recipient. Her letter to May for example was a mere reminder of what had been agreed, while Kitty's begged that she and Jeremiah would try not to monopolise the meeting and allow others to contribute. Her message to Hendy was gentle and encouraging in tone and in her letter to Michael she explained that Ella would be calling to see him prior to the meeting so that the same courtesy would be extended to him and to Betty as had been to all the others. At the last minute Constance decided to write one more letter. She had decided to invite Robert Fitzmaurice to the meeting. It would be a good idea she felt to have an interested outsider present at the discussion. Also she knew that Robert had loved their brother and in many ways had a better understanding of him as an adult than his family did. In the absence of Florrie to offer insights into Shay's personality and thinking Constance felt that Robert would assist in bringing balance and clarification to their deliberations. She had found his letters and phone calls hugely supportive when she had no one else to turn to.

30

Together Again

At two o clock on January 7th I was seated at the head of the table in the boardroom. I nervously cleared my throat and called the meeting to order. To my right sat Constance and to my left my mother May. Beside May sat Michael and his wife Betty. On Constance's right were Hendy and Nora forcing Kitty and Jeremiah the last to arrive to occupy the last two seats on opposite sides of the table. Casting my eye down the length of the table I was rather pleased with the way the seating arrangements had worked out. Whatever chance Kitty had of controlling Jeremiah's behaviour had suddenly been made easier by the fact that he was directly in her eye line for the duration of this most important meeting. So faking a confidence I didn't yet feel I got to my feet and said.

'Welcome everyone to the meeting and thank you all for coming. But just before we begin Constance would like to say a few words'.

Constance explained that she had invited Robert Fitzmaurice to join us and begged our indulgence for doing so. She asked if it would be alright to invite him inside. There were murmurings around the table but no objections so I went to fetch Robert. Once he had been welcomed and taken his seat at the foot of the table I began to outline my prepared arguments as to why I felt so strongly that Uncle Shay's memoir should be published. First of all the raw talent displayed in the writing. Second the Corley family history contained in the work. Third the social commentary and the ease with which Shay was able to bring to life not just the events of times past but the nuances and specific tones of a long lost era. Then I acknowledged that being from a different generation than all of the others I had been perhaps a bit insensitive as to how Shay's siblings and their spouses might view some of the content of his writings. So now I would like to open up the discussion to all of them. But first I pledged that whatever form the memoir would take when prepared for print they were all to rest assured that they would each have an opportunity to approve or reject my proposed editorial changes. A silence ensued as everyone took a while to allow my words to sink in. Eventually Constance broke the silence by stating that as yet she hadn't made up her mind which way to vote but she had been very taken with my arguments and was willing to keep an open mind until she had heard what everybody else had to say. She would be happy to go with the majority decision and hoped that over the next couple of hours we would be able to reach a consensus. For what her opinion was worth she pleaded with all of us not to try to veto any suggestions but for the sake of the Corleys who had gone before us and out of respect for Shay's memory that we would listen carefully and courteously to each other and then try to reach agreement as equably as possible. Constance's reasonable tone seemed to loosen tongues and immediately Michael, Hendy and Nora indicated politely that they would like to speak. My chairing skills were put to the test for the bones of the next two hours. In deference to Michael as the eldest I said I would allow him to speak first, followed by Nora whose indication I had noted fractionally before Hendy's. I requested that Robert might assist me if he didn't mind might keep an eye out for the next contributor and keep a list thereafter to ensure the smooth running of the meeting. Michael's input was short and to the point. On first reading Shay's writings almost twenty years ago he had been horrified. He couldn't accept that Shay could have been so cruel in his depiction of his family members. Both he and Ambrose had agreed that it would never see the light of day. They were troubled by the rawness of the prose and what they considered an invasion of privacy in the case of the section concerning Hannah and Edwin. Their immediate concern was for their mother Florrie and also for their sisters and especially for Hendy. But the passage of time and what currently passed for literature as well as his own more recent experiences had mellowed his views. Coming to the work again after all this time he was pleasantly surprised at how well it read. He was also a little embarrassed at the prudishness of his earlier responses not to talk of being deeply ashamed for having deserted and ignored Shay when he had fled to England. He found it hard to defend his youthful reactions and almost impossible to forgive himself for cutting off poor Shay in his time of greatest need. But now that he had had a chance to discuss matters with Hendy he was inclining towards the view that there was merit in the notion of publishing not least as an opportunity to make it up to Shay for his neglect however belatedly. Nora was delighted to add her own words of encouragement for publication. It was obvious to me from her self-satisfied grin in my direction that Nora was thinking 'I told you so'.

Surprised at Michel's positive stance and hardly daring to hope that the trend might continue I welcomed the next contribution which was Hendy's. Hendy opened by apologising to me for upsetting me on my last visit to him at home. Then brushing aside my attempt to contradict him he outlined what had happened in the interim to make him change his mind. Immediately after my departure he had sat by the Aga in the kitchen and started to read again right from the beginning. First he cleared his mind of all emotion and tried to read with a fresh look as if this were a novel recommended to him. He had recently converted the Aga to an oil fired burner so he continued reading in comfort without the necessity of refuelling. In the early hours of the following morning he paused for a pit stop and made himself a mug of tea. When he eventually finished reading he was satisfied that he could and would change his mind about publication. He could now face the fact that his worries about the reputations of his beloved wife and son were unnecessary. The gossip and speculation were long in the past and anyone who knew Hannah and Edwin would never have been troubled by gossip or changed their opinions as a result. Being the compassionate and sensitive character that he was Hendy finished by apologising to all present for what he described as his initial negative and self-absorbed reaction. He then wished me every success with the project which he knew was so close to my heart. I couldn't help but notice the changing expressions on the faces of Kitty and Jeremiah Meehan. Kitty appeared to be happy that the consensus of opinion was in line with their professed view but knowing the perversity of her husband's nature her face had clouded with apprehension as the meeting progressed. It wouldn't have surprised her or me if Jeremiah didn't do a volte face at the last minute just to put the cat among the pigeons and make the task difficult for me and life unpleasant for the rest of the company. True to form he interrupted rudely just as May was about to speak. But Robert calmly and authoritatively but gently restrained him by laying his hand lightly on Jeremiah's shoulder and indicating that he would give him the floor immediately May had finished speaking. Jeremiah was irked to say the least but had to content himself with muttering under his breath, shifting in his chair and fidgeting throughout May's short intervention.

May began

'In light of what Michael and Hendy have said I too am prepared to change my mind and vote for rather than against publication. My own sympathies were always with Ella on this but knowing Ambrose's position I felt I owed it to him to reflect his opinion here. However if Ambrose were here himself now I think that he would surely have been influenced by the generosity of spirit demonstrated by both Michael and Hendy today'.

Taking his chance Jeremiah launched into a tirade of condemnation of the lily livered Corleys. He berated his wife for not being able to make up her mind about anything without his input. He was critical of Shay's prose and at the same time savaged Hendy and Michael for their cowardice in initially opposing the publishing of the work. As he worked himself up into a rage spitting his words harshly and spraying those nearest him I wondered whether I should intervene or not. So as not to direct his wrath in my direction I decided to give him his head and see if he'd wear himself out. Sensing that he had lost his audience by the deathly quality of the silence he abruptly changed tack. Now he smiled ingratiatingly and singling people out around the table he proceeded with great glee to address them one by one. To assist him in maintaining his fiction of reasonable helpfulness he first addressed his wife.

'Kitty my lovely wife and probably the smartest of the clever Corleys, you have been my life's partner for over thirty years. We have made each other happy and miserable in equal measure all this time. Married life was hard at first but when you eventually accepted that a man must be boss in his own home things got a bit better. Nowadays we get on pretty well most of the time. For an intelligent woman it took you long enough to learn the few basic lessons of co-habitation but it has to be said once Kitty has learned a lesson it stays learned. Do you remember how we laughed when first we read Shay's puerile drivel that was being served up as high quality literature no less? It was so amusing to see the high and mighty Corley's suckered in. But of course it's not so surprising when it came from the pen of one of their own. The Corley's always thought that they had a monopoly on God's gifts. In their arrogance and superiority they all believed implicitly in the garbage fed to them as children that they could do anything they wanted to, achieve anything they set their minds to and that the world would fall at their feet. As for the mighty Shay the author. Don't make me laugh if he was any good he could have written a bestseller by simply describing a few of the myriad family secrets. I still can't get my head around whether Shay was hopping a ball and having a good giggle at ye all or if he genuinely thought anyone would be interested in reading this stuff. Let me tell ye about your precious Shay. He was nothing but a hot headed bully. Oh he was intelligent I'll grant you but that didn't give him the right to look down his nose at everyone else. Instead of using his brains to make something of himself he indulged his pride. He was nothing but a vainglorious, arrogant, selfish bastard. He could have been a millionaire and helped us all out of this miserable excuse for a country. He could have been an inventor even, he had the turn of mind for it, but no he'd rather spend his time carping about his superiors and keeping the rest of us in our place. For God's sake he had enough charm to sell ice to Eskimos. If he wanted to he could have made a fortune as a salesman. Ah but that wouldn't have been good enough for the stuck-up Corleys. He was more like his arrogant Papa than he'd care to admit. When I think of the waste of that superb intellect it makes my blood boil. Speaking of which the same fella had no control of his temper. The scenes I've witnessed over the years when he totally lost the box and thoroughly disgraced himself I've lost count of. But would ye believe me or anyone else who had the gall to say anything derogatory about your perfect brother.' Turning then to Michael and Betty he said

'I expected more of you Michael. Surely you should have been able to see through him. After all you were supposed to be the genius of the family or at least the most gifted academically. And you did very well for yourself in a world which loves pomposity and believes that any fool with a plummy accent and letters after his name has the right to be listened to. Oh I forgot, you turned your back on him years ago. Were you afraid the association would taint your chances in Dublin society? But of course if you had the sense you were born with you wouldn't have saddled yourself with an empty headed Foxrock blonde lush for a life's partner'.

With cries of 'For Shame' and tuttings of disgust echoing around the table I jumped to my feet calling the meeting to order and demanding an immediate and unreserved apology from Jeremiah. Recognising that he had gone too far this time Jeremiah grunted sorry to Michael but continued his diatribe.

'Nora my dear haven't you been keeping nice and quiet? For a woman who prides herself on her independence and is never short of an opinion on any subject I'm amazed that we haven't heard a word from you all day. But like all your kind you are full of wind and noise with precious little substance to back it up. As for you Constance we'll excuse you for your misguided loyalty to your family given your circumstances. And May and Ella wife and daughter of Ambrose the Wimp could hardly be expected to have an independent opinion of their own. It did surprise me though given his old maidenly prudishness that ye haven't objected to what I consider the best of the writing. The bold Shay had a way with words when it came to describing sex scenes now hadn't he? It would make you wonder though where he got his inspiration from. I always thought he was a bit queer myself but maybe the dirty old dog swung both ways. Maybe the learned spectre at the feast, the posh west Brit Robert would care to expand on that subject for us later on. There's no need for you to look so shocked Ella you cannot pretend that you didn't know the reason Shay has always been the Corley's dirty little secret. Finally Hendy your flexibility is impressive but then you were always overly influenced by the "sainted in hindsight" Hannah'.

Delighted with himself Jeremiah resumed his seat smugly satisfied that he was leaving a wasteland of wanton wreckage in his wake. After being forced to listen to Jeremiah's rantings no one wanted to remain any longer in his poisonous presence. I swiftly called the meeting to a close promising to keep in touch with all branches of the family after which everybody sorted themselves into congenial groups and hurried from the hotel leaving the Meehans behind. I dropped off Mom along with Constance and Nora in Grafton Street where I knew their customary good spirits would soon be restored. They loved their rare opportunities to visit the stylish shops and I knew that they would savour this chance to be in each other's company. Nora had bolted hot on the heels of Michael and Betty. Within minutes she had texted me explaining that they were heading immediately to Michael's home where they hoped I would join them later. Betty and Michael had planned a festive get together for everyone that evening but given Jeremiah's behaviour hadn't issued the invitation after the meeting as originally planned. Nora had volunteered to text all the others now and apologised for abandoning Robert. I replied saying that Robert was with me and that Nora only needed to contact Hendy as the others were with her too. Nora told me that Hendy had gone over to the hospice to visit Edwin and would join us later at Michael's. When Robert had unloaded Constance's wheelchair from the boot and waved the three ladies off he got back in and we set off for Clontarf. We were all happy to be going out to Foxrock later on but right now I needed the comfort of my own home where I hoped Robert would feel welcome and comfortable enough to share his memories of Shay with me. When we were seated by the fire sipping comforting mugs of hot chocolate I sighed and began by apologising for Jeremiah's unforgivable behaviour. I hoped that Robert was not disgusted with the lot of us after what he had just heard and thanking him for his unfailing courtesy in accepting Michael and Betty's short-notice invitation assured him that he didn't have to go if there was anything else he'd prefer to do in Dublin. Robert professed to be delighted to eat with the Corley family all of whom he would be pleased to spend time with. Now he wanted to hear from me what was eating Jeremiah and why he was so hell bent on punishing the entire family and for what. Unfortunately I was unable to throw much light on the subject. All I could say was that Jeremiah was considered by the older generation to be an embittered man and that he had been even as a young man when Kitty had first brought him home. Because of his own feelings of inferiority Jeremiah was invariably wary of others and insanely suspicious of his wife's successful siblings. From the beginning he had been fascinated and repelled in equal measure by the Corleys. At first he appeared to love Kitty. He was certainly besotted with her as she was with him. But from the outset it was obvious that neither of her parents liked him. James Corley hated his arrogance, his boorishness and his lack of respect for Kitty. Florrie feared that once the novelty of winning her had worn off Jeremiah would inevitably bully their independent daughter.

'Anyway Robert, I'm sure you know as well as I do that the Corleys, particularly my father's generation, were always averse to airing their dirty linen in public as well as priding themselves on loyalty, self-sufficiency and a prideful sense of privacy. But whatever about Jeremiah's self-congratulatory carve-up of the Corleys there is absolutely no justification for his disgusting treatment of you, our guest. I cannot apologise enough.'

'Ella my dear girl you really have nothing to apologise for. Jeremiah alone is responsible for his actions. Aside from that you mustn't think that I was bothered by his childish attempt to embarrass me. If I were to rate him on a scale of one to ten for homophobic insults he'd only get a one. You really would not like to know the vileness I've had to put up with over the years. Even while he was fulminating away my mind was wandering and you'll be amused at what came into my head. T'was a favourite saying of Shay's I first heard on the day he interviewed me. Apropos of my very concise answer to a long and complicated question posed to me by one of his colleagues he'd intoned with a twinkle in his eye 'Blessed is he who having nothing to say refrains from giving us wordy evidence of the fact'. Now let's not waste any more time on that sad little man. I for one would much prefer t spend what little time we have talking about Shay and in particular about his writing'. We spent the next few hours sharing our memories of Shay. In turn we told each other about our experiences of times spent in his company, how he had influenced us before moving on to talking about our impressions of his work. Our perspectives on him though different were those of his juniors. It had taken Robert a long time to get over his awe of Shay and begin to treat him as a friend rather than as his ex-boss and mentor. As for me Shay was so like my beloved Dada in appearance I'd have forgiven him anything. Also my memories of him were much more of the affable, cheerful, loving uncle who visited us as children rather than the more irritable man I knew in later life. So we spent quite a while swapping stories of his generosity of spirit, his facility to empathise with people, his wit and humour and his uncanny ability to communicate on their level with people of all ages, backgrounds and personalities. We each had our own special experiences to relate as well as a huge range of anecdotes and witnessed interactions. It was with strong feelings of approbation and admiration that we chatted excitedly to each other vying to express our common love for Shay and to dispel the miasma of noxious association with Jeremiah's description. But this Shay, the man in the whole of his health, was a far cry from the miserable creature who was constantly trying to outrun his demons and his depressed alter ego. I had little personal experience of his dark side but I had heard stories about some of his more noteworthy episodes many of which had made their way into local lore. I found it hard to reconcile my own experience of Uncle Shay with the man who was the butt of unkind laughter in the pub. One thing we had to agree with Jeremiah on was Shay's reputedly short fuse. Robert had observed Shay's famed outbursts of bad temper on more than one occasion. He regaled us with an account of a spectacular scene he himself had witnessed in the early days when he worked with Shay in the public service. It was an ordinary day at the Department of Justice. Nothing unusual about it as far as everyone at their desks was concerned. The most senior officer overseeing the work of all twenty two souls in the open plan office was Shay. He usually worked in a glassed in section at the back of the big room the door of which was open unless he felt the need for a private conversation with another officer. This kind of encounter occurred very seldom indeed either necessitated by an infringement of some kind on the part of an underling or a rare meeting with top brass. Shay's management style was informal for the most part so the more recent recruits had actually never seen the door closed. Shay had recently been interviewed for promotion but the bulk of staff wouldn't have been privy to this information. Shay himself must have had some inkling that today was the day when he'd hear one way or the other. He'd arrived at the office early and closing the door had kept his head down while the rest of the staff filed in and took their seats at their desks. No one said a word though everyone was taking surreptitious glances at the closed office door. If anyone had been around when Shay had arrived they'd have known something was up. He was still wearing the suit he'd worn the day before but now his clothes were stained and scruffy. It was obvious that he'd not been home and the smell of stale Guinness suggested that he'd had a skinful the night before. He looked like he'd fallen down and slept where he fell. Underlying the overpowering stench of the booze was the lingering smell of vomit. All morning long there wasn't a sound from the glass cage. Over half the workforce had gone to lunch when a dishevelled Shay emerged. All eyes swivelled to stare. At the door Shay turned and glared

'WHAT ARE YOU CROWD OF SNOT-NOSED JERKS GAWKING AT?' he roared. 'HAVE YE NEVER SEEN A MAN WITH A HANGOVER?

FECK OFF OUT OF HERE THE MISERABLE LOT OF YOU.'

Every eye in the room continued to look in Shay's direction not because anyone wanted to embarrass him but because they could see the Secretary General standing directly behind him. Thus ended Shay's career in the British Civil Service. My own experience was much more recent. From the date of Hannah's death Shay had been a much more regular visitor at home. In sickness and in health he came to support Hendy at least twice a year spending all his annual leave between Mountbrien and Kiltyroe. While basing himself at the Henderson farm he spent a considerable time every visit with Ambrose and our family. At this time he had developed an interest in golf and had left a set of clubs at the house. At first Shay had plenty of golf partners but bit by bit people began to fine excuses to avoid playing with him and soon he was reduced to going out alone. I was only about thirteen at the time and one day I asked if I could caddy for him. This was the beginning of my love affair with golfing. Soon I became obsessed with the game. Shay loved my enthusiasm and also was delighted to be able to teach me all he knew. He was most encouraging in mentoring his avid pupil, displaying endless patience and understanding. Like the perfectionist he was he demanded high standards from me. He demonstrated how it should be done and then insisted that I practise, practise, practise until I had internalised every stroke. Uncle Shay and I were a common sight on the golf course at sunrise. I persuaded him that if we played early enough we could get eighteen holes in before I went to school. Once the holidays came around I continued with this early morning schedule so as to make no further demands on his time. Alternatively if he wanted to go shooting in the early part of the day we would play late into the long summer evenings until it got too dark to see the ball. By the time I was ready to start my teacher training I was already an accomplished golfer playing off a handicap of 7 to Shay's 9. At this stage I was winning prizes all over Munster at open days and in tournaments, but I was always available and happy to play with Uncle Shay. On this particular day we had opted to play in the evening as Shay had promised to give Hendy a hand on the farm in the morning. It would have suited him better to play in the afternoon but I wasn't available then as I didn't want to let May down.

When I arrived at the golf club at 7.00 p.m. on that summer Saturday evening Shay already waiting impatiently on the first tee box. He greeted me with a terse

'What's kept you 'til now Ella? I'd booked the tee time for 7.00 not 7.03'.

With that he bent to tee up and addressing his ball drove it hard and straight down the middle of the fairway. I followed suit, first as I had been trained I took a practice swing and then taking a couple of seconds to settle myself I picked a point on the fairway where I expected my ball to land, measured the distance with my eye and only then did I address the ball. With my eye on the back of the ball I produced a smooth backswing, halted at the top and then striking the ball with the sweet spot of my driver on the downswing I followed through cleanly. Not until the ball was at the highest point of the parabola did I raise my head to follow its path. The ball had just begun its descent as it passed over the spot which I had selected so it continued for at least another twenty yards before it landed a good thirty yards beyond Shay's ball. We were both on the green with our second shots Shay's ball on the lower right hand edge about thirty five feet short and mine pin high on the left about a foot from the flag. Barking at me to man the flag

Shay stomped up to his ball. He banged it halfway up the slope where it stopped and then began to slowly roll back down gathering momentum to where it stopped within five inches of where he stood. His next attempt shot uphill at a tremendous rate and flying past the hole continued on its merry way off the green and down the slope where it came to a halt about two feet into the long grass at the back of the green. Shay now had to return to his bag for a pitching wedge in order to take his fifth shot which of course landed on the down slope and drifted several feet downward away from where it had landed. His sixth shot, a putt was only a few inches short but resulted in his scratching the hole. Needless to say I succeeded in slotting my third, short putt home for a birdie. As we made our way back towards our bags I could feel Shay's anger steaming off him like a visible vapour. From my own tee box on the left I indicated to Shay that he should tee off first. He addressed his ball and drove straight into the lake. I could hear him swearing from where I stood. But following protocol I teed off, crossing the lake and landed my ball a few inches to the right of the flag. Shay had to tee up again and this time he succeeded in crossing the lake but barely. For his fourth shot he had an uphill chip which landed close enough to the pin for him to putt for five. Meanwhile I successfully sank my putt for a second birdie.

'Fat lot of good a five is on a par three' Shay ground out through gritted teeth as we approached the third tee box.

'Well played Ella. It's your honour my dear. You have earned the right to tee off first. The time has come for the pupil to teach the teacher.'

I was pleased to see that Uncle Shay was trying very hard to focus his mind on the next hole and forget his disastrous first two holes. He waited while I teed off. Shay walked back to the men's tee box, teed up and sliced his ball into the bushes. What happened next will be forever seared on my consciousness. With a howl of rage Shay hurled his driver into the bushes after the ball, passing so close to my face I felt the whistle of the wind in its wake. Then upending his golf bag without concern for anyone or anything he swung club after club above his head and let them fly as far as he could pelt them right and left into the bushes and over the boundary into the bog. Then grabbing his empty bag he dragged it towards the lake and with all his strength heaved it into the water. Then stumbling forward he made his shambling way off the course without a backward glance or a word to me. Shay never took a golf club in his hand again.

After sharing these experiences Robert and I had to agree that as far as Shay's ill temper was concerned Jeremiah was at least accurate. Then I had to admit that a tendency to fly off the handle was in fact a family failing. I further confessed that I myself had had my moments. My beloved Dada when I turned to him for help had worked through some exercises with me when I was very young so that over time I had learned to control my temper. It had been many years since I had let it get the better of me but occasionally even yet I would find myself losing patience. As recently as a week ago when I had gone in especially to the hotel to book the boardroom I had had a most aggravating incident. Not having a lot of time to spare I had parked my car in a rather expensive city centre car park at an extortionate hourly rate. I approached the desk in the foyer behind a lady who was checking in for the night. Within seconds a long queue of good-humoured people had formed behind me. It was obvious from their attire that they were guests at a wedding and staying in the hotel overnight. The lone receptionist whose name tag identified her as Lynda dealt quickly and efficiently with the customer ahead of me and then rang a number and turning to me said that Sharon from bookings would be down in a minute. Then turning to the next people in line continued to check them in. The group consisting of mostly young families though somewhat noisy were patient and polite. I waited for five minutes and watched as four groups and two individuals were checked in. I was beginning to get bored and not a little impatient as another five minutes dragged by and still no sign of the elusive Sharon. Lynda was dealing with her fifteenth customer when a young man called Ralph appeared behind the desk. Ralph asked me if I was alright and I replied that I had been waiting rather a while for Sharon from bookings. Lynda explained that she had already rung Sharon but now she wasn't answering her phone. Ralph volunteered to go in search of Sharon. Lynda continued with her work and I continued to wait with increasing frustration at the delay. After another six minutes had elapsed Ralph returned with the news that he couldn't find Sharon who was no longer in her office. At this stage twenty three minutes had elapsed since I had first spoken to Lynda about booking the boardroom. Lynda apologised explaining that she couldn't take a booking as she was busy at check-in. Ralph shrugged his shoulders with classic indifference leaving me with no option but to walk away. By now I was seething. My journey had been a complete waste of time and the glorious apathy with which I had been treated was bad enough but the realisation that I had overshot my parking time slot by five minutes and would have to pay an extra hour's parking fee was truly maddening. But I knew how to control my temper and by the time I had walked back to the car park in the crisp evening air my equilibrium had been restored. Next day I could laugh it off especially as I had succeeded in making the booking by telephone in thirty seconds flat. Ruefully I admitted to myself that perhaps that's what I should have done in the first instance. I could empathise with Uncle Shay because I knew just how it felt.

When it came to Shay's work both Robert and I were equally impressed with his style but whereas Robert admired Shay's clear and unequivocal descriptions of his relatives, warts and all, I couldn't help but sympathise with the sensitivities of the older generation. Despite the generosity of Mom's statement earlier at the hotel I knew that she would prefer to let the dead rest in peace.

Later that evening all the Corleys and their significant others with the exception of Kitty, who hadn't been invited, were gathered at Michael and Betty's Foxrock home. We were chatting in the comfortably large sitting room and Betty was busy plying us with champagne and canapés. The conversation had turned to the happenings of the earlier meeting but by now everyone had recovered and we were teasing each other and laughing off our earlier discomfiture. Even Betty's good humour had been restored and she put everyone else at their ease by opening proceedings with the comment

'Welcome all and please get stuck in. I'd like you all to have been served at least before I get drunk and fall over and prove Jeremiah right'.

As we had all been worried that Betty would either be in a sulk or refuse to appear at all the tension was immediately dissipated by her self-deprecating comment. Michael was nicely relaxed and we were all enjoying a pleasant evening of quiet reminiscence. Hendy had been sitting quietly and smiling to himself throughout. He looked like someone who was hugging a very pleasant secret to himself. I pulled my chair close to Hendy and whispered "Go on Hendy, spill."

Clearing his throat Hendy stood up and announced "Today I went to see Edwin. As usual I did all the talking. On my last visit I had given him the proofed copy of Shay's book to read. Of course I was curious to know what he thought of it but knew I would have to wait for a letter to find out. So I began to tell him all about today's events. After a while I noticed that Edwin was listening intently and he seemed to be encouraging me to go on. I'd been talking non-stop for ages when I paused to get a drink. I sat down again to resume my story and wondered aloud 'where was I?'

"In the middle of Jeremiah's tirade" I heard. My heart nearly stopped. I turned to stare at my son. It could only have been Edwin who spoke. Edwin who had not spoken a word in years. Convinced I had dreamt the interjection I continued with the rest of my story. When I finished the silence remained unbroken but as I leant over to hug him Edwin whispered

"Thanks Dad I realised a long time ago that you didn't blame me for Mother's death but until today I couldn't forgive myself and so I couldn't speak. Reading Shay's story made me realise it is time for a new beginning." Hendy was thrilled to be able to share this wonderful news with the Corleys. The babble of congratulation and excitement eventually died down and the party continued with renewed vigour.

The exchanges were lively, the banter gentle and enjoyable and as is always the case when like-minded people get together in an atmosphere of trust the wine flowed, tongues loosened and story followed story as the party got into full swing. We were at the stage when everyone was happy that the night was developing into a platform for sharing music and song. Constance had just fallen into her usual role of acting informal mistress of ceremonies and was about to announce the running order of the first three performances when the doorbell rang. A startled silence descended on the room as Michael made his way to the front door. Even before he opened it everyone had a strong feeling who he'd find on the other side. In the hushed quiet of the sitting room we all heard the exchange

'Michael, before you shut the door in my face and believe me I wouldn't blame you if you did, I come in peace. Please may I come in? I know the others are all here and I'd really prefer to only have to say this once'.

Heaving a sigh Michael asked

'Where's the shadow? Don't tell me Jeremiah has let you out on your own? Wonders will never cease. I suppose you'd better come on in Kitty'.

When Kitty appeared in the doorway of the sitting room Betty went forward to help her out of her coat. There was a gasp from the assembled womenfolk when we saw Kitty's face. On her right cheek was a livid bruise and the skin around the eye was already beginning to blacken. She had obviously had a nosebleed and her efforts to hide the damage with make-up had failed miserably. Everyone gathered around her in sympathy and started to quiz her about what had happened. Kitty couldn't help preening at all the attention and gratefully sank into the chair which Robert had drawn forward for her. She bowed her head and took a few moments to compose herself. Then she described in detail what had transpired between herself and Jeremiah once everyone else had left the hotel earlier in the day. Even before the room had cleared he had launched into a tirade berating Kitty for not supporting him screaming at her and spraying her face with spittle. It was when she pleaded with him to keep his voice down that he had brushed her roughly aside bruising her cheek in the process. This was the final straw as far as she was concerned. They had been here on numerous occasions down the years. But on the last occasion he had hit her she had sworn it would never happen again. She had gathered the final shreds of her dignity and just walked away saying over her shoulder

'Jeremiah, you know this is the end. I'm giving you three days to remove yourself and all traces of you from our home. There is no earthly point in arguing with me, the law is on my side. Do not even think about thrashing the place. The cost of repairs will only come out of your pocket so don't waste your money on giving vent to your spleen'.

Michael put his arms around Kitty's shoulders to comfort her and then asked

'Did he just walk away then'?

'Of course not! You know Jeremiah. He followed me out pleading with me to forgive him and promising me he'd never lay a finger on me again. I ignored him and got into a waiting taxi. It was only then I realised I had nowhere to go. I felt that none of you would want to see me again today. I wish I knew where my daughter was and if she could ever forgive me for my neglect and abandonment of her.

I wouldn't blame her if she never wanted to set eyes on me or her father ever again. In the end having outstayed my welcome sipping coffee in the foyer of the Shelbourne hotel I gave in and got a taxi back to the Gresham hoping Jeremiah would already have checked out. To my great relief he wasn't there but there was no sign that he had returned to the room either. I'd had a bath and ordered scrambled eggs and bacon from room service when he came in. He was probably as surprised to see me as I was to see him. He'd had time to think about our situation and I could see that he was doing his best to appear reasonable. He said he'd only come to pack his overnight bag and be on his way. But finding me there had given him hope that he might be able to make me change my mind. He even got on his knees to beg me to give him another chance. When it became obvious that I was sticking to my position he became violent and that's when I left or tried to. I had almost reached the door but he beat me to it. Banging my face into the door jamb was the final straw. I know I should have done it years ago long before he ruined the life of our unfortunate daughter but there never seemed a good time.'

Constance wheeled herself closer and taking Kitty's trembling hands in her own capable ones she said

'Sh! Sh! Kitty a stór, sure there is never a good time but there is always a right time and now Thank God you've made your decision. Welcome back to the family. There's no one like your own people to love and care for you. You'll always be safe with the Corleys.

We were just about to start singing but as Mama used to say *Is túisce deoch ná scéal. A drink takes precedence over a story.*

Won't you have a cup of tea love'?

No sooner had she asked the question than Betty appeared with a tray bearing a china cup and saucer, a little pot of tea and a selection of canapés and snacks. She disappeared into her kitchen and this time reappeared with a liberally buttered scone and a soft and delicious queen cake on a plate.

'This is more like what you need Kitty, proper home baked food, one of Constance's unbeatable scones followed by one of May's inimitable queen cakes'.

It was this simple act of kindness that almost undid Kitty completely. The unsophisticated home baking took her straight back to the days of her childhood. After she had nibbled at the tasty cake and before she finished the cup of hot sweet tea Hendy was prevailed upon to fill her in on the good news regarding Edwin's long-awaited recovery. By now she was feeling a good deal better. Within a short time the party had recovered its momentum and Kitty was happy to observe her siblings enjoying themselves as she used to when they were all young and unscarred by the troubles of adulthood. Her siblings tried to surround her with love and comfort in as unobtrusive manner as they could. The party continued late into the night with lots of singing and music but most of all plenty of conversation and reminiscing. Bit by bit Kitty began to feel that she had a right to be there. She now realised that over the wasted years it was not so much that her family had turned their backs on her but rather that she had selfishly neglected them. Initially she was so under Jeremiah's spell that she had allowed his negative attitude towards her family to completely colour her views. Later even as she recognised just how prejudiced Jeremiah was she couldn't bring herself to leave him not only because she still loved him but because he so obviously depended upon her. And by then of course it was too late. She was expecting a child. With the sound of 'You've made your bed and now you must lie in it' reverberating in her inner ear she had faced the pregnancy and the subsequent miscarriage alone and unsupported. Not long afterwards she discovered that she was expecting again. She had taken to motherhood surprisingly well. With the birth of their daughter Roseanne the Meehans had settled into a family routine and Kitty had grown to accept that life with Jeremiah must be endured after all. Kitty had thought that her life was so unutterably miserable that it couldn't possibly get worse but Jeremiah was to prove her wrong. As Roseanne grew older he shifted the focus of all his venom and attention on her. Kitty did her best to protect her daughter from his badgering and verbal abuse but despite her best efforts she couldn't be with her twenty four hours a day, seven days a week. And then her beautiful intelligent and warm-hearted daughter had become pregnant at the age of seventeen. Jeremiah immediately threw her out and banished her forever from the house. Kitty was forbidden to make contact with her daughter. To her eternal shame even then she didn't have the courage to defy her husband. Now at last she was back in the bosom of her birth family but at what a price. She no longer had a husband for which part of her was relieved, but she had also lost her self-respect and her daughter. She hadn't laid eyes on her in nearly twenty years. She would go to her grave knowing that she had failed her. Her abandonment of Roseanne cut deep and she knew that she'd never be able to forgive herself for her false pride and her cowardice. Now she regretted the wasted years and the damage done to her lovely daughter. She hoped that someday they would be reconciled.

31

Ella and Greg

On the morning of November 15 of 2013 I woke early. In fact I hadn't slept very well. It was excitement rather than anxiety that had caused my disturbed slumbers. Today was the day at last when Shay Corley's book "Kilroe to Kilburn" was being launched. I sprang into action. Even though I had everything in order for the launch there were still some last minute details to be attended to. I had booked the same hotel where almost a year before the Corleys had gathered and I had finally got the go ahead to proceed with publication. I had already the large function room booked and had ordered wine and nibbles to be served as I was expecting not just the extended family but a large number of friends as well as representatives of the publishing house, booksellers and even members of the Press. All I really needed to do was get myself ready and look over the notes for my speech. I had made appointments for the morning with the hotel's hairdresser and beautician. The same family group would re assemble with the exception of Jeremiah Meehan. It was doubtful if his baleful presence would be missed by anyone. In any case I was secure in the knowledge that he wouldn't disturb proceedings today because I knew he was currently detained at Her Majesty's pleasure in Wormwood Scrubs. I hoped nobody would even mention his name as I really didn't want to have to explain how I knew of his whereabouts. Neither did poor Kitty need to know that her former partner had been arrested and jailed for brawling. In the eleven months since his departure things had improved beyond measure for Kitty. She had settled back into the farmhouse and discovered that she was well capable of running the business side of farming. With a little help from her neighbours and advice when needed from her brothers-in-law Brendan and Hendy she was coping very well. In her wildest dreams she couldn't have imagined last January that she would be looking forward to Christmas and the increasing possibility of a reunion with her daughter. She could barely dare to hope that she might even meet her granddaughter for the first time. Early in the spring she had tried to establish contact with Roseanne but to no avail. But then I had managed to find out where Roseanne had got to all those years ago. I had put mother and daughter in touch with each other. Since early summer they had been corresponding. At first their letters were cool and formal but as time went on they had slowly begun to re-establish a certain amount of trust. Bit by bit Roseanne was revealing more and more about the missing years. She never once asked about her dad so Kitty didn't mention him in her early letters. Eventually she told a half-truth by letting slip that she was now managing the farm as Jeremiah was no longer a part of her life. Kitty was reluctant to push her luck by suggesting that perhaps they might someday meet. With each exchange she prayed that Roseanne would forgive her and might even propose a meeting. But to date that hadn't happened. In Kitty's latest letter by way of filling Roseanne in on family news she had told her all about the publication of and upcoming launch of her Uncle Shay's book. To her surprise she found that in her reply Roseanne seemed to know all about it and expressed her pleasure that Ella's project had finally come to fruition. Roseanne had signed off by saying she was looking forward to reading the book and wishing her mother a peaceful Christmas and all the best for the future. Kitty was convinced that there was a degree of warmth in this letter which was absent in the previous correspondence. It gladdened her heart and helped to lighten her spirits as she got ready to drive to Dublin for the book launch.

At 1.30 I was coiffed, composed and relatively comfortably waiting in the foyer to greet the first of my guests. The book displays were attractive and a long green baize covered table was in readiness for me to sign copies of the books as editor when the speeches were over. Seated behind the table were James Whitford from the prestigious Whitford chain of booksellers and Lucy Holohan who had undertaken to assist with the selling and look after the cash box. True to form May and Constance were the first to arrive with Kitty and Nora hot on their heels. Michael and Betty came next and so they formed a welcoming party for the younger generation. Brenny, Tess and Jody had travelled together from Kiltyroe bringing Johnno with them. At the last minute Greg with young John in his arms quietly appeared at the door in silent support. Just before I stood up to make my speech I spotted Father Dan Conneran slipping in at the back. He was accompanied by Hendy and a younger woman. I found myself smiling as I enjoyed the prospect of revealing the huge surprise I had for Aunt Kitty which I had been hugging to myself for the past few weeks. But now I had to get on with the business in hand. I opened by describing the events which led to my interest in Uncle Shay's writings before going on to briefly outline for the assembled crowd my reasons for wanting to publish the memoir. In particular I drew attention to Shay's use of language, his masterful characterisation and his uncanny ability to engage an audience whole-heartedly in the story he was telling. I explained how I had undertaken the process of editing and re- ordering the sequence of the anecdotes and adding detail from my interviews with Shay's surviving siblings and his friends and neighbours. Then I introduced Maria Mountford representing the publishing house who was the guest speaker at the event. Maria was an inspirational speaker who entertained the audience with amusing tales while giving a wonderful insight into all the different stages of the publication process. She praised me for my insightful editing and skill in bringing Shay's memories to the finished product we had today. To highlight what she had been saying she quoted from the original and then she requested me to read aloud some marked passages from the published version. She thanked me for my work and the entire Corley family for their co-operation and welcoming assistance. She ended by saying

"Now Ladies and Gentlemen this is a book launch fortuitously a few weeks prior to Christmas. Please form an orderly queue and beat the Christmas rush by buying your copies of this beautiful nostalgic memoir. All members of the family will of course want a copy and I'm sure Ella will be happy to sign them for you. But every home should have one so you'll need at least one extra copy for your favourite person at Christmas."

While the crowd began to disperse most of them to get in line and the rest to form excitedly chattering groups I quickly grabbed Lucy and Aunt Kitty and we made our way towards the three late-comers at the back of the room. The granddaughter Kitty had never met was now twenty seven years of age. And the secret I was bursting to reveal was that Kitty's granddaughter was none other than my best friend Lucy Holohan who had already met most of the Corleys though of course she was totally ignorant of any family connection. The mystery woman who had arrived with Father Dan and Hendy was Lucy's mother Rose Holohan aka Roseanne Meehan. Then I had to return to the table where I found that the ever alert Constance had taken over Lucy's duties.

With Maria's words of encouragement how could anyone resist buying the book? Three exhausting hours later after two extra boxes of the book had been couriered over from the warehouse I signed the last of the 586 copies of "From Kilroe to Kilburn" sold that afternoon. I stretched my sore fingers and yawned. Then I threw myself into Greg's waiting arms and happy that I had let Shay's secrets die with him I headed for home.

Lightning Source UK Ltd.
Milton Keynes UK
UKOW02f1024200315

248208UK00002B/2/P